Choke Up

NEW ORLEANS MAGICIANS
Book 1

C.M. Kane

COPYRIGHT

∼

Editing & book design by Maggie Kern @ Ms.K Edits

Cover art by Dar Albert at Wicket Art Designs

Photographer: Tonya Clark Photography

Model: J Tackitt

BOOK ONE

Dedication

For AJ, Clint, Jimmy, and Luis. Thanks for making my first trip to New Orleans, one I will never forget.

Prologue

Nick...

"The fuck you are," Dad said, glaring at me as I stood in the kitchen. "Your mama's already lost one son to the Corps. I'll be damned if she loses another."

"Dad," I said.

"Nope," he said. "And if I find out you did it behind my back, I'll beat your ass so bad you won't be able to keep your commitment. You feel me?"

He was right, and I knew it, but it felt like something I kinda had to do. I mean, Paw was a Marine, Dad was a Marine, Uncle Brian was a Marine, and Lucas, my older brother, had been one. We were a Marine Corps family. It's what we did.

"You best get those fucking fliers out of this house before your mama sees it or it'll send her to her death," he said.

I nodded, knowing exactly what he meant. When we got the news that Lucas had been killed in action, she damn near died right then and there. It was the fucking worst time in my life, and it was just my brother. She lost her son. Something I wouldn't be able to understand until I became a father, and even then, I didn't think I would ever get it.

"Okay," I said, moving to toss the papers into the trash.

"Out," Dad shouted.

I shook my head and stuffed them into my backpack, figuring I'd take them with me to school, and put them in the recycling box in the office.

"Don't you fucking say a word about this to her," he said. "You play baseball. That's gonna be your ticket out of this life. It's not something you'll die doing, and that's what's really important. Your mama needs to know you're gonna be around a good long while. You feel me?"

"I feel you," I said, then walked away.

I was a pussy anyway, and would probably fail right the fuck out of the Marine Corps. No, it was Lucas who was the one destined to do that. Me, I just played a fucking game.

Chapter One

Ten years later...

N**ick...**
"Hunter," Coach called as I came into the dugout from batting practice.

"Yeah?" I asked.

Sundays were my favorite days at the stadium. Since we were in San Diego, with the Navy base so close, we always wore our uniforms with the camouflage to honor the service members who came to the games. It was a tiny thing, but I felt really good about doing it. The stands would be filled in certain sections with military members, in their uniforms, there to cheer us on. It was the least we could do to honor them.

"Come on," he said, walking down the tunnel toward the clubhouse.

It was an odd thing to have the coach lead you from the field, and I had a sinking feeling in my stomach the closer we got to the locker room. There were still a handful of guys heading out for batting practice, what with it still being a few hours before the start of the game.

"Sorry," he said when we got to his office. "You've gotta grab your gear and head to the visitor's dugout."

"Traded?" I asked, beyond surprised.

"Afraid so," he said. "No hard feelings or anything. It wasn't my decision."

"Damn," I said. "When did this go down?"

"Just now," he said, and the door opened.

The general manager walked in, trying not to look happy, but I could tell he got someone good.

"Hey," he said, closing the door behind him. "I wish it hadn't gone down like this, but that's baseball. At least you don't have to go far, just across the diamond."

I knew he was lying about not wanting it to go down the way it had. I was nearing the end of my contract, so I knew I had the potential to be traded. It just sucked that it had been right before a game. No way to figure your shit out before moving on to the next team. The only good thing was, I was being traded to the Magicians, which meant I wouldn't miss a game. Problem was, they were flying out that night, and I didn't have a bag packed.

"Please tell me you got someone good," I said, not really caring.

"Some good options for the rebuilding of the team," the GM said.

The team had been rebuilding for three years, so my guess was they got a better shortstop at a cheaper price, and I was just the fat they were cutting out of the diet.

"I got time to say goodbye to the guys?" I asked.

"About five minutes," the GM said, then turned and walked back out.

"Seriously?" I asked the coach when he was gone.

"Sorry, man," he said. "I know it sucks, but like he said, that's baseball."

I got up, opened the door, and walked to my locker. When I first was drafted by the Flyers, it was the best thing I'd had since the College World Series we'd won playing with San Diego State. Playing in the place I'd made my home was exactly what I was looking for. Now, though, I was gonna have to move to the other side of the country, where it was hotter and muggier than home, and it wouldn't feel right.

At least it wasn't in the middle of the game that they made the trade. That would have sucked ass. I'd seen it happen one time, and the guy ended up sitting for the rest of the game, because of the stupid rules on roster slots and shit. Now, though, the Magicians had the option of having me start, which I wasn't sure I was happy about, but playing every day was what I wanted, and it might happen.

Hanging my head, I pulled out my bag and stripped, so I could change and move across the stadium. I'd already decided I was gonna take at least one jersey with me. If they didn't like it, they could fuck right off.

"Hey, Hunter," Jackson said as I was shoving shit into my bag. "What's going on?"

"Got traded," I said, not bothering to keep the anger out of my voice.

"Damn," he said.

"Yeah," I said. "So, maybe I'll be out at short today against you guys."

"To the Magicians?"

"Yup," I replied. "Nothing like fucking me up right in my own home ballpark."

"That fucking sucks," he said. "I mean, you're good, and I don't wanna play against you."

"Same, brother," I said. "Same."

"Well, you come back, you let me know, and we'll go out for drinks or something," he said.

"I'd like that," I replied. "My number ain't gonna change, so you got it."

"Sure thing," he said, slapping me on the back.

Other players must've heard about the trade, because more and more came up to me to give me a hug or a handshake, all saying they were gonna miss me. Truth was, most of them would probably be going to other teams, too, if the higher ups kept selling everyone off. My biggest question was what the fans would do when I came out onto the field in the enemy's jersey.

The walk with my gear through the bowels of the stadium felt much longer than it actually was, but when I stepped into the clubhouse, the place was hopping. It took longer than it should have for someone to realize I was there. At first, they weren't too happy, but then the manager came out of his office and shook my hand.

"Welcome to the Magicians," he said.

"Thanks," I said. "Where do you want me?"

He looked out into the area and saw an empty locker in the corner and pointed me in that direction. Walking over, I felt every eye on me. It was like I was the new kid in school, moving in the middle of the year, and it fucking sucked. Some of the guys I knew, but most were simply players on the other team, and not anyone I'd really had much interaction with.

"Hey," the guy beside me said, and I turned to look at him.

"JP," I said, recognizing him.

"Welcome to the magic show," he said, then all the guys around started laughing and coming up to welcome me to the team.

Apparently, this was their way of indoctrinating new players, which was kinda fucked up, but at least it only lasted a few minutes.

"You GONNA MOVE?" JP asked as we sat on the runway waiting for takeoff.

"Nah," I said. "My mama's here, and I don't think she'd wanna move again. We did that growing up, so when my dad retired, she wanted to pick the place, and San Diego was it."

"What about your dad?" he asked.

"He died three years ago," I said.

"Oh, damn," he said. "I'm sorry. I didn't know."

"Yeah, it sucks," I said. "But my mama is a fucking rock star. She didn't even bat an eye. I mean, yeah, she cried and shit, but then she just soldiered on. Tough as fucking nails."

"Sounds like it," he said. "I think you'll love the city, though. I mean, it has absolutely everything anyone could want. Trust me, you'll end up moving, eventually."

"I mean," I said with a shrug. "My contract is up at the end of the year, so I may end up going somewhere else."

"You should stick with the club," he said. "It's a great group of guys. We have a lot of fun, and we're doing really well this season. You came in right at the right time, I'm telling you."

"We'll see," I said as the plane began to move, readying to take off, and take me across the country to my new home team.

With the amount of traveling I'd done in my life, even before I became a professional ball player, I knew the ins and outs of flying, and I'd learned all the tricks to getting good sleep on a plane, as well as which seats were best. I packed snacks, had a pillow specifically for flying, and was an old pro, as my mom called it. Most of the guys also did the same, having their shit together well enough that it was a simple thing for a whole team, trainers, coaches, and everyone else associated, along with the television and radio crew, to get on the plane, stow our shit, be ready, and off without much delay. It was when we had to fly commercial that issues usually came up. We were all well aware of how to travel.

Just over three hours later, we landed in New Orleans. I knew that teams had apartments available for players who were just coming in, either by a call up or from a trade, so I assumed the same would be true for me. I didn't want to try to buy anything, at least not until things settled down and I knew what the plan was. It was the middle of July, just after the All-Star Game, and heading into the last half of the season. I would only be here for three months before the off season, so settling down right away was just not logical.

"Hunter," Coach said, as I stepped off the plane. "You got some-where to stay?"

"Was hoping to use one of the team's apartments," I said.

"Figured as much," he said. "Here's the number to get them there. Should probably have gotten that to you right after the game, but it kind of slipped my mind."

"I get it," I said. "Not like you weren't busy doing something else."

"True," he said.

The game had been wild. Between the walks, the home runs, and everything else that happened, it was a miracle we got out of the stadium and to the airport before our charter left without us. Not that it would, but still, it was not usually after eight when the plane was ready to take off. Add to that the fact that New Orleans was a couple hours ahead of San Diego time zone, made it so we didn't get there until well after midnight.

"Probably will stay in a hotel tonight," I said. "I've gotta get up early enough to have someone go to my condo back home to send me some clothes for the home stand."

"Oh yeah," he said. "I completely forgot about that. You got enough to get through the next couple of days?"

"Yeah," I said. "And if I need to, I'm sure I can find something online to order. I'll call in the morning to figure out housing."

"If you need anything, give me a call," he said. "I put my cell number on the back of the card, just in case you need it."

"Thanks," I said. "I also have JP's number and can hit him up if something comes up."

"Good," he said. "You good to get to a hotel?"

"I can figure it out," I said. "Not exactly that complicated."

"I guess so," he said. "See you at the field at noon tomorrow?"

"I can make that happen," I said. "Thanks for the info."

"You're family now," he said. "And not the kind of family we don't want to invite over. No, you're the kind that we look forward to having as company."

"Thanks, man," I said.

"Go on now," he said, and I did just that.

The terminal our charter landed us at was separate from the rest of the airport, which was nice. Some cities had a whole different airport where the planes landed, so the fact that this one was at the actual airport was a dream. Meant getting a ride share and hotel close by was not at all difficult.

I did just what I'd planned and looked for a hotel that was close by. Once I'd booked a room, I ordered a car, and waited for it to pick me up. As late as it was, you would think the city would have died down, especially since it was a Sunday night. Not this city, though. It apparently wanted to rival New York for that "up all night" vibe. Not that it was a bad thing, just very different from San Diego. And it was still warm. Not as hot as it likely was during the day, but definitely warmer than I'd have liked in the middle of the night.

"You Nick?" a man asked as he stepped out of the car.

"Yeah," I said, confirming the car was the one I'd ordered.

"I can get your bag," he said, popping the trunk.

"Thanks, man," I said, wheeling it over to him.

He quickly stuck it in the trunk, then went back around to the front of the car while I climbed into the back seat.

"Just get in?" he asked as he eased out onto the roadway.

"Yeah," I said. "Can't wait to get to the hotel, and get settled, too."

I didn't really like talking in taxis or the like, but I would never say that outright to the driver. My parents taught me to be polite, and so I was. Simple chit chat wasn't a big deal, and I could handle that for the couple of miles it was to my hotel.

We arrived quickly, and he pulled up into the breezeway, putting the car in park before turning it off. I got out the back as he popped the trunk.

"Enjoy the city," he said, handing me my suitcase.

"Thanks," I replied. "Have a nice night."

He got in his car and drove away as I walked through the automatic doors to the lobby of the hotel. Hopefully, tonight would be the only one I needed to stay, but I'd have to play it by ear, which I was more than willing to do.

Chapter Two

Charlotte...

"You all done?" Gretchen asked.

"Yeah," I said, pulling my gloves off and dropping them in the bin.

"Big plans this weekend?"

"Maybe," I said, being as noncommittal as I could. No need for her to know what I got into during my off hours. "Gotta get home first, though, and wash the old off me."

"I feel that," she said, dropping her gloves into the bin where I'd dropped mine.

"How about you?" I asked, hoping that the change in subject would make her ask fewer questions.

"Well," she said, and her face colored.

"No," I said.

"Yeah," she replied.

"When?"

"This morning," she said. "I mean, I have to go get the confirmation from the doctor, but yeah. I'm gonna be a mom."

"Oh, sweety," I said, giving her a hug. "I'm so happy for you. I know you've been wanting this for so long."

"I have," she said.

"So," I said. "When do you think you're due?"

"Oh, I have no idea," she said, wiping an errant tear that slipped down her cheek.

"Sweety," I said, pulling her into another hug.

She and her husband had been trying for over a year to get pregnant. They had a couple of false positives, then she lost a baby right around March. That she was pregnant about five months later seemed a bit fast, but then again, I didn't really know much about that. No, my life was my work.

"I'm sorry," she said, pulling away and rubbing her hand over her eyes. "I'm kind of a hot mess express right now."

"I think that comes with the territory," I said. "Emotions run wild, especially in the beginning, from what I understand."

"Oh no," she said, her eyes sad.

"No," I replied. "It's not a bad thing. I've pretty much come to terms with the fact that a baby and me just aren't in the cards, and I'm okay with that. I've got nieces and nephews, so I get all the good bits, and can hand them back to their mom when they start to act up."

"I just kinda feel bad," she said.

"Don't," I replied. "It's totally fine. I'm really happy for you."

"Thanks," she said. "I kinda can't wait to tell Doug, you know? He's gonna freak out and wanna tell the world. I will, hopefully, contain him, and remind him that we need to wait until we're out of the danger zone."

"Well, your secret's safe with me," I said. "When you announce it here, I'll act all kinds of surprised. I'm just so happy for you."

"You don't need to act surprised," she insisted.

"Nah," I replied. "It's your big news, and all attention should be on you, and not on me not reacting. Besides, some might think I'm upset, and we don't need that."

"I appreciate that," she said.

"Hey," I said. "Are you okay to be using the chemicals we use in here? Have you talked to your doctor about them?"

"Oh yeah," she said. "That was one of the first things we asked way back when we first started trying. It's all been deemed safe to use, and if anything new comes in, I have quick access to find out from my doctor's office."

"Good," I said. "I would hate for something to happen, and have it be because we didn't know what we were doing."

"For sure," she said.

"Well," I said as we walked to the door. "I've gotta get home and cleaned up before the rest of my weekend gets away from me."

"I'm just happy that I could tell someone," she said. "You don't know how much you helped."

"Glad to be of service," I said.

The walk from the workroom at the far end of the museum wasn't long, but in the dark building, it could sometimes feel a bit ominous. It was already closed to the public for the night, but no alarms were set until they were sure everyone had vacated the building. We walked in companionable silence through the exhibit spaces until we reached the lobby, where we used our badges to let us out of the building, making sure we each swiped to keep the ledger correct. They were pretty picky about us not swiping in or out and just following someone through, so we'd gotten into the habit of one of us swiping, then stepping out while the other did as well.

It was muggy, but that wasn't anything new. New Orleans was always muggy in the summer. We were about halfway through the hottest month, but there was no guarantee August would bring any kind of relief. Instead, we had to wait until September, or even later, for the temperature to cool down enough that a jacket was needed. Some years it never got cold enough to need more than just a light sweater.

"Have a nice weekend," I said to Gretchen as we got to the parking lot.

"I'm sure it's gonna be amazing," she said, smiling brighter than I'd seen in a long time. "Thanks again."

With that, she slid into her little blue sedan, shut the door, and drove off. I walked just a little further down the parking lot to my car, one I'd had for years and absolutely loved. It had been my dream car since I was a kid, and my parents found one from some collector the year I turned sixteen. Anyone who looked at me would never guess that I'd drive a vintage 1966 Mustang convertible in candy apple red, but here I was. Of course, most folks wouldn't guess I liked to dominate men, either, but that was a secret I kept much closer to the chest.

I unlocked the door to the car, and let the heat escape before I climbed in, rolling down the window before shutting the door. The towel I kept in the car came off the steering wheel, and I set it on the seat before unlatching the top on both sides. I started the car up, felt that rumble from the engine Daddy had helped me put in it vibrate up through my body. Daddy didn't know why I wanted the more powerful engine, but that was fine.

Pressing the button to get the top to drop, I waited until it was down and into its slot before I slid the shifter into drive. Daddy had made sure that the model he bought for me had an automatic engine. Not that I couldn't drive a stick, but he didn't want me to have to worry about it. There would be enough issues with finding parts for the car since it was considered a classic and was old enough that nothing was readily available.

I sometimes wondered whether there was some sort of misogynistic reason for him demanding I didn't drive a stick, like he thought his little girl couldn't handle the complications of driving while also having to shift. Whatever the reason, it was nice to have one less worry when I drove my baby. She was more than just a beautiful car, too. She was a status symbol at the clubs I frequented, and even though I didn't always drive her, when I did, it gave me more clout.

Tonight would be one of those nights when I would go home, shower and clean myself up, wash the day away, and mentally prepare myself to play. Once that mental preparation was done, I would dress for the night. I knew some of the scenes I'd be in, but was always willing to participate in others, if it felt right. I'd said no more often than I'd said yes lately, and I really wondered whether the club had run its course. Whether new blood was needed to make things exciting again. I guess I would just wait and see. It was the summer months, and there had always been a lull during the summer months, but this year seemed worse than years in the past.

Pulling my stockings on, I clipped them onto the garter that was already around my waist. They weren't exactly fishnet, but looked enough like the finer type with holes that didn't really show much but held up better than the cheaper versions available. The lace along the top was lined with a nice satin that kept the itching to a minimum. My style was specific, and everything I wore, no matter when I went, had most of the members eagerly anticipating my choice for the night. After the stockings were in place, I picked up my panties to pull them up and over the stockings and garter. It was amazing to me how many women showed up in stockings and garters who put them on in the wrong order, having to undo the garter to get their panties off. This way, they could be removed without disturbing the aesthetic of garter and stocking, and also without taking anything away from the scene that was being portrayed. There was an art to seduction, and the better you were, the more fun you had.

Since I was driving my baby, I was dressing in red, so the hooks on the garter, as well as all the embellishments, matched the car. I picked up my corset, loosening the lacing on the back so I could get into it. It was my favorite one with its deep red satin covering the stays, and I'd learned early on when I started wearing corsets how to do them myself, and which ones would work that way. This partic-ular style worked perfectly, as I could hook the front with its silver eyes, then hook the lacing onto the doorknob of my bedroom and use my body weight to tighten it up. It had taken years of practice, but I had perfected it.

The black tulle that covered the bodice, along with the intricate embroidery, with stones woven in along the top and bottom, just accentuated my hourglass features even more. I had a decent sized chest, not too big, but definitely big enough, and my hips were what my mama called child-bearing, meaning they were wide enough to let a kid slide through the pelvis. It was almost grotesque that the term was used on me when I was a teenager, but that's what I'd been told since I hit puberty and started filling out. It was one of the reasons I held off on having kids, and why I wasn't at all upset that I wouldn't be putting my body through that test.

After I'd gotten all the undergarments on and felt like I was fully into the mindset I needed for a night at the club, I picked up my little black dress that I wore to cover up enough that I wasn't in danger of being seen as indecent. No need to push my luck with the authorities. It was short enough that it covered my ass, but was still easy to see the cheeks, depending on how I stood. It slipped over my head and down my body, covering all my assets enough to be able to walk to and from buildings and my car.

The next project would be my makeup. I wanted to look sexy enough that I was wanted, but not to look like I didn't know what I was doing when it came to painting my face. The concealer was light enough to accentuate and highlight my high cheekbones, and the foundation was an exact match to my natural tone, blending in a manner to not show a line where the makeup ended and my skin began. Smokey eyes followed, with deep blues that brought out the natural color in my irises lined with the winged accent to either side, and false lashes to finish them out.

My blush was a deep rose, almost a red color, but not quite. It added just the right amount of color to my cheeks without making it overbearing. My lipstick was the last thing I added, and it was a perfect match to my car, and something that set me apart from others who were part of the club. Everything matched, from the car to the lips to the clothes. It was an ensemble that drew the eye of even the most reserved members of the club.

It was supposed to be anonymous, but you could only hide so much, and I honestly was to a point that I didn't care. I had enough money that I could retire, and play for the rest of my life, and still be just fine. If anyone wanted to out me to my employer, it would simply mean that they were revealing their own penchant for the less socially acceptable forms of entertainment.

Now that everything was on me, and my makeup was done, I slid my feet into my red heels, buckling the straps around my ankle. They had chunky heels, because I would never feel comfortable in skinny heels. You couldn't run in them, and though I'd never had to run away from someone, I knew some women who had to escape a room, and heels could slow you down if you didn't know how to wear them.

The final piece was my mask. The one I usually wore was black steel that had been shaped to fit my face. It was lace but hid enough that if someone didn't actually know me, they wouldn't recognize me outside the club. It was something the club had initiated long before I became a member to keep things a little more mysterious.

Mine had a nice satin strap that I could pull back under my hair to tie at the back of my head. The top of my hair was pulled up onto the top of my head, the lower portion down underneath. Once the mask was tied, I pulled the pins from the top, and let the locks fall over the strap to curl down and around my shoulders. It wasn't long, but long enough that I had to separate it into the two portions to get the tie to fit right around my head.

After I let my hair down, I went to my large mirror, turning fully around to check every angle I could to make sure nothing was out of place, and everything was covered enough to be decent by regular citizen standards. Fluffing my hair and tugging the hem of my skirt, I finally felt like I was ready to go. Grabbing my small handbag that I could hang over my shoulder without causing issues with the line of my outfit, I headed out the door and climbed into my baby, starting her up and feeling that rumble up under me, just getting my engine in gear for the night I had ahead of me. It promised to be a good one.

Chapter Three

Nick...

"So," I said. "What are the rules?"

"They'll be in the email," Maggie said. "Along with the invitation. Do you have a mask?"

Maggie had brought me into the club I frequented in San Diego many years ago, and she was the only one I trusted to give me advice on finding one here in New Orleans.

"I don't," I said. "I didn't get a chance to pack anything before I left."

"You'll have to go find one," she said. "They won't let you in without one. Oh, and you'll have to drive. You can't take a ride share or taxi, but they have a valet, so it's not like you'll just have to find parking somewhere. They have a small place for cars to park, but those are reserved for special guests."

"Guess I'll have to find a place for a mask," I replied. "And I rented a car until I can figure things out. I might have to ask you to pack some things to ship to me, if you wouldn't mind."

"Happy to help," she said. "Make sure you RSVP and give them a half hour window of when you'll be there. They're pretty strict on only letting folks in during their allotted time slot."

"Sounds like our club could take some lessons from this one," I said with a laugh.

"Oh, this is the best club in the country," she replied. "They have the most beautiful people, and everyone is safe there. Even though most folks who go there know who everyone is, none of them say a word, because it would out them as well. It's a really nice club with lots to offer. I'm sure you'll have a good time."

"I can't thank you enough for helping me," I said.

"I'll make sure you repay the favor," she replied.

The call disconnected, which was how she preferred things to end. Just shut down and walk away. She wasn't the sentimental type, which was something I could appreciate from her more than she would ever know. I didn't mind some emotions, but largely they ended up fucking everything up instead of fixing it. Aftercare aside, she was fine to fuck and walk away. No muss, no fuss, just fuck and fuck off.

My new goal for the day was to find a mask I could use at the club, something that hid my identity, but was comfortable. I didn't want a full-on face mask, just something that would obscure my face enough that my beard, short as it was, would cover the rest. I always wore long sleeves to hide my tattoos, but since I wasn't actually playing, it wouldn't matter much. I pulled out my phone to check the area, looking for a shop that would have something I could get relatively quickly. It didn't surprise me that many of the options were in the French Quarter of the city, which made sense since it was the hopping place.

Walking down Decatur Street, with the river on my left, I saw several shops selling all sorts of items that most tourists would enjoy, but none of them had a mask that I felt was worthy of the occasion. I continued on down, walking around cathedrals and shops until I found a shop that had been near the top of the list when I'd done a search. Stepping in, I could tell they had a much higher quality of product than some of the more novelty shops offered.

"Welcome in," a young woman said from behind the counter. "Let me know if you need any help or have any questions."

"Thanks," I said, glad she wasn't forcing herself on me.

The area was busy, but not overly so, and this shop only had a couple of folks inside, so I wasn't too worried about being recognized or anything. I mean, it wasn't exactly a known commodity, but for sure, once I started playing in the city, it might make it more of an issue. For now, I was happy to be just any other guy.

Perusing the walls where they had pegs on that held several more traditional masks, ones with feathers, leather ones and all sorts of animal styles. Nothing was jumping out to me, though, so I figured I'd keep moving on. Until something made me look behind the counter and that's where I saw it. Silver, a deep v in the middle of the forehead with arching over the brows. Nice nose piece that didn't go down too far, the cheeks going down further and out, but with a sort of leaf type feel. It was absolutely perfect.

"You like that one?" the young woman behind the counter asked.

"I do," I said. "Can I try it?"

"Oh, for sure," she said, turning and pulling the clothes pin from the peg before taking the mask off. "Here you go," she said, handing the mask to me.

It had some weight to it. Not so much that it would be uncomfortable to wear for long stretches, but it showed that it had quality behind it. I put it onto my face, feeling if it would fit well or not, and it was as if it were made for me. The nose piece was just long enough to go down to, but not over the tip of my nose. The sides flared out and around my cheeks, but didn't press too much, and that it had strings to use to tie it to me meant it wouldn't end up loosening like the elastic ones did.

"What do you think?" she asked.

"Do you have a mirror?" I asked.

"Right there," she said, pointing behind me.

I walked up to it, pulled my hat off, and held it up to my face. Yeah, this was definitely what I was looking for. Right fit, right feel, just everything I needed.

"I'll take it," I said, turning back to the counter.

The girl was young, but definitely old enough to consent, and I wondered whether she was connected to anyone. Then I realized I was getting that pervy thing going, so wisely kept my mouth shut.

"Anything else you need?" she asked.

I thought about saying, "you," but didn't. "That'll do it," was what I ended up with.

She scanned it into her kiosk and gave me the total. I slipped my card into the reader and waited for it to process.

"Receipt?" she asked.

"No thanks," I said.

"You need a bag?" she asked.

"If you have one," I said.

She wrapped the mask in some tissue paper, then slid it into a small, black paper bag. The kind with the paper handles that twisted at the top for strength.

"Come back any time," she said, smiling and blushing.

I wondered whether my thoughts were telegraphing. It wouldn't be the first time what was on my mind showed on my face. I thought I'd figured that shit out, but apparently not.

"Just might do that," I said, taking the bag from her.

Before I turned to walk out, I winked at her, and the bright pink that rushed to her cheeks was definitely worth it. Turning, I walked out the door and back into the summer sun. It was definitely hot in this city, and the humidity coming from being so close to the river didn't help. Instead of just grabbing a ride share back to the hotel, I decided to look around the Quarter a little more, see exactly what was what when it came to my new home away from home.

~

"You got plans?" JP asked as we were heading out to our cars.

"Yeah," I said without elaborating.

"Wanna share?"

"Not really," I said. "I like to keep my work and private lives separate if I can help it."

"Yeah," he said. "I noticed that about you. Well, have a good night."

"That's the plan," I said.

I climbed into my rental car and started it up. My mask was in the small bag in the passenger seat next to me. When I got to the location, which I'd cued up on my phone, I'd pull it out and put it on. I did try it on again before coming into the stadium. I wanted to be able to put it on quickly when I got there.

The stadium sat on the remnants of damage caused by Hurricane Katrina in 2005, right beside Lake Pontchartrain. Major League Baseball was set to grant two expansion teams that year, and after the hurricane and its aftermath, they felt almost obligated to give one to New Orleans. What the city had done, though, was build it as a testament to their resiliency.

It was completely self-sustaining, with power and water being supplied by the wind and water around it, and they had a compost rate that was among the highest in the whole league. Not to mention, the handful of storms that came in after it was built showed exactly why it was built the way it was. Absolutely nothing was damaged in it, except the field, which had to be refurbished every year anyway. Honestly, it was more than state of the art, it was futuristic, and now that I'd experienced it as part of the home team, I understood why they were so proud.

I'd traveled to New Orleans with the team as a visitor, but we never really got the chance to check out the town during our trips. No, most of the time was spent either at the stadium or at the hotel. We were working, after all, and not on vacation. Now, though, I had the opportunity to actually see the city, experience everything it had to offer, and in the few short days I'd been here, I had to admit that it was definitely a cool place.

The drive took less time than I thought, and when I arrived, it was too early for me to go into the club. They seemed to have things running like a tight ship, timed entrances, limits on guests, everything was lined up as to allow for the most efficient flow. I wondered if it would be worth the hassle it was to get into the place, but from what Maggie said, I wouldn't be disappointed.

Instead of taking up a spot in front of the home, which was fucking huge, I drove down the block a way and pulled into an open space. The whole neighborhood was incredible, with homes that seemed to be much older than those in San Diego. Not that there weren't older homes there, but these had that old world, classic design, type feel. Like they'd been born right out of the soil and rose up to become what they were. The trees in the area were towering, old, and magnificent. It looked exactly like it should for this higher income bracket area.

I shut the car off and pulled up my email to make sure I had everything I needed to get into the club. The instructions were there, just as Maggie had said, and I read them carefully.

from:TheLavenderLounge
to:Nick Hunter
subject: The Lavender Lounge Rules

Welcome Guest:
Please read all instructions prior to arriving on site. If you do not follow the rules listed within this email, you will be turned away and will face a one-month penalty for disobedience. If you are turned away a second time, your admittance into the club will be terminated and you will be put on a list of banned participants.
No recording equipment is allowed in the building. If you are found to be in possession of such a device, it will be confis-

cated, rendered completely unusable, and destroyed by the host. Additionally, you will be put on a ban list that will include all affiliated clubs. We will all know who you are, and you will not be invited to play at all, ever again, in the future.

First-time guests will be provided with a special piece of jewelry to wear during your night at our club. If you remove this item, you will be escorted from the property and receive a permanent ban. This is a one and done result of not following this specific rule, and there are no exceptions or second chances on this rule.

Participation is denied for first-time guests, but you are encouraged to watch and enjoy the scenes as they unfold. If you are interested in participating at the next open event, please notify the host when you leave, including your preferred scene and partner. This is not a guarantee that the requested partner will agree, this is only a request.

Your enjoyment is our pleasure, but punishment will be doled out in appropriate measures for insurrections against the rules set forth.

Sincerely,
The Lavender Lounge

The list of refreshments included mostly beverages, but you had to stay hydrated while you played or you'd end up a hot mess, and not the kind of hot mess you wanted. I planned on getting mostly the non-alcoholic type of drinks. I didn't like to drink when I played, and mostly stuck to water, but a little flavor when I watched was nice.

There was an alarm set on my phone to go off with enough time to get me to the house for the valet parking situation they had going, and when it went off, I started the rental and drove back around the block to pull up front. When I pulled up, I noticed a very nice, vintage Mustang convertible parked right in front of the home. I wondered who it belonged to but didn't have time to ponder it more. A young man in a mask came to my car.

"Your name, sir?" he asked.

"Nick Hunter," I replied.

He pulled out a small piece of paper and ran down what I assumed was a list of names for guests. When he came to mine, he smiled, and then opened the car door.

"Welcome to the Lavender Lounge," he said, holding his hand out.

I placed a hundred-dollar bill into his palm, what the required donation was, and handed him my key.

"Up those steps," he said. "Mr. Stone will get you checked in. I'll wait until you are admitted before moving the car."

"Thank you," I said, and headed up the steps.

"Welcome," another man, who I assumed was the Mr. Stone the parking attendant mentioned said. "Your name and ID."

I handed my ID to him. He put it under one of those lights like they use at the check point in the airports, ensuring it was valid.

"I see this is your first time," he said, and I nodded. "You have the option of a ring or a necklace. Which do you prefer?"

"The ring is fine," I said, not really into necklaces.

"Size?"

"Oh," I replied. "I'm not really sure."

"Your hand, please," he said, and I held it out to him.

He slid a sizing ring onto my finger, then set it below and pulled out a ring that had a collection of amethyst stones around it, wrapped in silver. It was absolutely beautiful, but a little bit too much for my taste. Nevertheless, I let him slide it onto my finger.

"This is yours for the evening," he said. "I assume you have your deposit and payment for refreshments. I'll take that now."

He held out his hand, and I placed several large bills into it. He counted them, then slid them into a slot in the podium he was standing at.

"You may enter the home and check any rooms that have open

doors," he continued. "If the door is closed, it is a private scene, and you may not enter. Since this is your first time, you are on a look but don't touch visit. If you find someone you are interested in having as a scene partner, please ask for a name. Have you chosen your club name? Or do you want me to assign you one for tonight, and you can decide on a permanent one for the future?"

"Didn't realize I needed one," I said.

"That's understandable," he replied. "Do you have something in mind?"

"Not really," I said.

"Fine," he said, looking me over from head to foot. "I think we'll go with Saturn for this evening. I will make a note of it in our records for the night. Do you have any questions?"

"Nothing I can think of," I said.

"Fine," he replied. "If you aren't sure about something, please look for someone wearing a lavender pin like this on their lapel. Those are hosts who can answer questions for you."

"Thanks," I said.

"Enjoy your evening," he replied, then opened the door to the house, and I walked inside.

Chapter Four

Charlotte...

It was still relatively early, but I'd already done one scene and was relaxing before my next one. My partner for the first scene was a shy guy, but did well as he played the top to my bottom. He was trying to build up the courage to top his favorite within the club, but still felt like he had some work to do. I was happy to help him learn the tricks that would work on his preferred partner when he got the nerve to ask for a scene with her.

I'd become somewhat of a tutor in the club, someone willing to help new players learn how to top properly, within the rules laid out upon membership, and to learn how to listen to their submissive, hear what they were saying, even if they weren't actually talking, and being a top who was desired. It was pretty remarkable to think about where I'd come from, and where I was at this point.

When my first boyfriend offered to tie me up during sex, I had no idea it would lead to the wonderful world I'd found my freedom in. The high society I was born into would never think to allow this kind of expression, especially if it was with strangers. No, they would likely clutch their pearls at the mere thought of someone tying them down, spanking them, or demanding an orgasm out of them. They didn't know what they were missing, though.

The second partner who I requested was a woman who had plenty of experience as a bottom but hadn't quite been brave enough to top. I knew she could do it, she just had to gain the confidence, so I had chosen her to work with me this evening. We were in a room with a closed door so she could feel safe in learning how to be the dominant in the situation instead of being the submissive as she had in the past.

"Think about what you want out of this," I said. "This is all about you learning what you want, and how to get it. I believe in you."

"You're too kind," she said. "I just can't believe you'd be willing to work with me."

"Starlight, you're wonderful," I said, using her club name. "I've watched some scenes you've done as the submissive, so when you wanted to learn topping, I was very willing to help you out."

"Charlie," she said, using my club name. "I never thought you'd choose me."

"Why not?"

"Because of who you are," she said, as if that explained everything.

"I'm just like you," I said. "The only difference is I've been here longer. You're just starting out, but you're making wonderful strides in your play. Now, what would you like me to do for you?"

We'd made some negotiations through the messaging service the club had set up, but there were always things you wanted to discuss in person. There were some nuances that could be missed in a text-based conversation. Even a phone call wasn't quite enough, so I always wanted to have at least a few minutes prior to the time the scene actually happened.

My phrase was the clue to Starlight that she was now in charge, and that whatever she said, I would do, so long as it didn't go against either my preset limits or club rules. We'd already gathered the tools she would need for this particular scene. She'd selected a spanking bench as well as brought in some rope to tie me to it. There was a collection of toys on the bed as well that she could use for penetration.

I was looking forward to what she would do during this session, because, while we'd discussed what were absolutely off the table, I had given her plenty of leeway in what she wanted to experience in dominating me. The thing I was most looking forward to, and hoped she'd use, was the strap-on with two dildos on it for double penetration. There was just something about being filled in both holes that flipped my switch, and I wanted her to experience giving me that pleasure.

Her ultimate goal, as she'd told me in our negotiations, was to be able to understand how a top thought, and how it felt to be the one in control. She loved bottoming but wanted to understand everything within the lifestyle. Her style of play was very much centered on penetration in every opening available but didn't involve play with her breasts or nipples. She said they were off limits when she was a bottom, which I could totally respect.

"Kneel at the end of the bench," she said.

"Yes, Mistress," I said, quickly moving to the position.

We'd chosen the term Mistress so that she could feel in control, but not so much so that it was overbearing for her. She didn't want to use Master, as that felt too close to what she called her favorite top, and none of the other terms we'd discussed worked for her, either. I was fine with whatever she wanted to use, as I wasn't too particular with what I called my tops. There were very few terms I refused to use, so was able to work with her to find one that she felt comfortable with.

"Lean over the bench, your arms down the legs at the front," she said.

Doing as she said, she made quick work with the rope, a soft bamboo material, that she used to bind both my legs and arms to the bench. I was still wearing my corset and panties, having not taken them off for the last scene, as there was no penetration for that particular one. It surprised me that she hadn't had me take the panties off, since we were going to have penetration for this scene.

"Oh, no," she said, and I heard the quiver in her voice.

"What can I do to help, Mistress?" I asked.

"I forgot to take the panties off," she said, and she was starting to fall into the submissive position again.

"Would you like to untie my legs and remove them?" I suggested, knowing she would have thought of it eventually, but also knowing she was still very new to being in charge.

"Oh, yes," she said, and the confidence came back to her voice.

I felt her soft hands as she slid them along my legs to get to the knots, untying me.

"Lean forward," she said. "I need you to straighten your legs so I can get these off."

"Yes, Mistress," I said, doing as she said.

It was a bit uncomfortable, and when we finished, I'd be sure to talk her through the thought process prior to getting her submissive into a position that had to be rectified in this way. Her hands were a bit shaky as she slid them into the hem of my panties, but then she pulled them down, and I heard her sigh as she saw that I was anxious for her to work on me.

"Knees down," she said once my panties were off. "You should have mentioned that before you knelt. You'll have to be punished for that."

There was a slight giggle in her voice, just barely there, but I could hear it.

"Of course I will, Mistress," I said, trying hard to keep the amusement from my voice.

This was all a game, and one that we'd both played many times, but it was also a learning time for her, and I wanted to ensure that she knew everything she had to know before we finished our time together. Turning my head, I looked over my shoulder to see what she would choose.

"Eyes front," she said, catching me looking.

I whipped my head back to face the tapestry that was on the wall in front of me.

"That will require another punishment," she said.

"Yes, Mistress," I said.

"Now what shall I use to punish you?" she pondered.

"You are in charge," I said. "I will accept whatever punishment you deem fit for my transgressions, Mistress. I trust you."

That last bit was something I wanted her to hear, so she knew that she was very much in charge, but that the rules we'd laid out were still there. I truly did trust her. She'd been a sub several times and knew what it meant to trust the person who was topping you. That was one of the nice things about teaching submissives, bottoms, and those who took on that role regularly. It was that they could be in charge, could do what they liked to have done to them to another, and it would all be just fine.

I heard movement, the sound of fabric and other things, as well as the clink of metals against each other, as she prepared for my punishment. It was excruciating to wait for it, which she likely also knew. The waiting was sometimes more exciting than the punishment itself. I absolutely loved the anticipation, not knowing exactly what my partner would choose.

Thwack!

She struck me hard across my ass, with what I assumed was the crop we'd chosen. It was a sharp pain, but the sting was concentrated on one of my cheeks, instead of across the whole of my ass. It also missed my pussy, which I was sad about. This would be another thing to discuss after we'd finished.

"You didn't cry out," she said, and the sadness was there, like she didn't know how to correct that behavior.

"No, Mistress," I said. "I assumed you wanted me to take the punishment without complaint."

The last I added so she would know that she needed to instruct her bottom on what was expected of them in each section of their time together.

"You will cry out each time I hit you," she said, her voice becoming more steel as she moved through the scene with me.

"Yes, Mistress," I said.

Thwack!

"Ow," I cried, but she hadn't hit me very hard, so it didn't really hurt.

"That was not a cry," she said. "I need to reposition you so you can feel the pain I am giving you."

"As you wish, Mistress," I said.

Her soft hands again went to my legs as she untied the binding, then moved to my arms to do the same. I stayed where I was, waiting for instruction, but she didn't give any.

"Mistress?" I asked.

"Charlie," she said, and I could hear the tremble in her voice.

"Do you want a pause?" I asked and saw her come into the peripheral of my vision to sit on the floor next to me, tears running down her face. "Oh, sweety," I said, sliding off the bench and pulling her into my arms.

"I don't know what to do," she cried. "This is too hard. I'm never gonna be able to do this."

"That's not true," I said, stroking her dark hair along her back. "You just need more practice. Let's talk it out and see where you can improve. Then we can get back into it. Okay?"

She nodded against my shoulder and I let her get herself together before pulling away.

"What do you want to see come from this scene?" I asked her.

"I want to be able to spank you," she said. "But I also want to make sure I hit everything. You know, *everything*."

"You mean you want to hit my pussy when you spank me?" I asked, trying to assure her that words were safe with me.

"Yeah," she said. "I know I like it, and you didn't say that was off the table, so I thought I'd see what it felt like on the other side."

"That's totally fine," I said. "If I didn't want that, I would have told you, so you were right to assume it was an option. Now, why do you feel like that didn't happen when you spanked me?"

"Part of it is because you weren't set up in a way to take the hit there," she said. "And I didn't pick a good tool."

"Those are good observations," I said. "So, now that you know what the problem is, look around and see if you can figure out a way to change things so you get your desired result."

It was as if I could hear the wheels turning in her head as she looked around the room. If I were in charge, I would take the leg spacer into consideration, as well as possibly using the bed and the cushion that was triangular, to lift my hips enough that it would open me up completely to her view and ability to punish.

"I have an idea," she said, standing up.

I stayed where I was, seated on the ground, as I watched her move some of the toys off the bed and onto a table that was next to it. Almost everything went there, except the three paddles she had, the leg spacer, and the cushion. She also went to the side of the bed and pulled out the restraint that was fastened to the base at the middle. I felt like I knew where she was going, but I was going to let her tell me what she wanted instead of just doing what I thought was right.

"Come here," she said, and the steel was back in her voice, a light in her eyes, and a smirk on her lips.

"Yes, Mistress," I said, rising and going to the foot of the bed where she was now standing.

"Widen your legs," she said, pulling the spacer off the bed. "Wider," she pressed, then slid the instrument between my knees.

She undid the Velcro cuffs and wrapped them around my upper calf, first one, then the other, forcing me to keep my legs a little more than shoulder width apart. Normally, these would be hooked to the ankles, but this way forced me to be even more open, and I'd seen her wear the device the same way, so assumed it was how she understood for it to be used.

"Good," she said. "Now, umm..."

She hummed a bit, like she was working through her head what she needed to do next, which was a good sign. That meant she had learned from her earlier mistake and made an adaptation for moving forward. She would be a wonderful top if she let herself go to that type of play.

"Lay down with your legs on the floor and your chest against the bed," she said. "I need to see if I need the pillow."

"Yes, Mistress," I replied, doing what was asked of me quickly.

The bed was low enough that I couldn't really get flat on it, and knew I'd need the pillow to cushion my hips.

"Get up," she said, and I was pleased to hear the firmness in her voice again.

She moved the pillow so that it was at the edge of the bed with the larger end of if closest to me.

"Down," she said, and I leaned forward, the angle much better for my hips and body. "Good," she said. "Give me this hand," she said, pulling one of my hands toward the edge of the bed where she cuffed it nicely. When she got to the other side, she said, "This one, now," and proceeded to do the same. "Now I have you where I want you. You are going to cry out each time I strike you. Do you understand?"

"Yes, Mistress," I said, letting myself go into that space of relax that was my own, where the world outside ceased to exist, and all that mattered was the person I was with and myself and the experience we were sharing.

Thwack!

I hadn't even heard her move when she stung my pussy with the crop.

"Ow," I cried.

"Louder," she said. "And I want you to count."

Thwack!

"One," I cried out, delighting in the sensation she was giving me.

"That was number two," she said sternly. "Now we have to start over."

33

"Yes, Mistress," I said, but barely got it out before she struck me again. "One," I cried.

"That's a good girl," she said, and struck me again.

This went on until I'd reached ten.

"Now," she said, and I heard her set the crop down. "You've been such a good girl; I want to do something you'll enjoy more."

I could feel her running her hand along my back and down to the rounded globes of my ass, squeezing them just a little as she looked at me from behind. The way she had me tied to the bed, with my arms stretched wide to be held in the cuffs on either side of the bed, made me have to keep my head down on the bed, even though it was turned to the side. With my ass in the air, though, and the cushion under my hips, it meant that I couldn't see her when she was behind me.

"What shall we do next?" she asked.

"Whatever you wish, Mistress," I said.

I knew what I wanted, but I wasn't about to ask for it. No, this was about her learning to listen to her bottom and do what they wanted, while simultaneously enjoying what you were doing. I'd topped a handful of times, but much preferred being a bottom, so this role of teaching those who tended to be more submissive how to take charge was one I relished.

"Your pussy is so pink," she said, and I could tell she had lowered herself to the floor behind me. "It would be a shame to not taste it."

Without more than that, I felt her tongue slide from my clit all the way to my asshole, which made my legs shudder and made me thankful that I was tied where I was.

"So pretty and delicious," she said, swiping her tongue again along my slit from front to back. "But I can't just lick it, now, can I?"

Her finger slid into my pussy, so delicate and tentative, sliding in and out in a slow pace.

"You like that?" she asked.

"Yes, Mistress," I said.

"But you want more, don't you," she said.

It wasn't a question, but I felt the need to answer.

"Yes, Mistress," I said. "I want much more but will accept whatever you are willing to give to me."

"Yes, you will only get what I am willing to give you," she said. "But tell me what you want. Tell me exactly what you want me to do to you. Then I'll decide if you're worthy of getting it."

"Fill me," I said.

"Fill you, what?" she asked.

"Please, Mistress," I said, trying hard to add a pleading sound to my voice. "Please fill me completely."

"You mean your pussy?" she asked, shoving another finger inside me.

"Yes, Mistress," I said.

"How about your asshole?" she asked, sliding her thumb up and over the opening, pressing the pad of it against that place, but not pressing it in.

"Yes, Mistress," I said, and this time I didn't have to try to put a pleading in my voice. "Please fill my pussy and my asshole."

"Maybe I'll wait," she said, pulling her hand away from my body.

I whined just a little bit and didn't even realize any noise came out until I felt the sting of the wider paddle slap across my cheeks.

"Ow," I cried out.

"You will count," she said, striking me again with equal force.

"Two," I said.

"No," she said, smacking me a third time. "You have to start over. This will be strike one," she said, then I felt the sting across my cheeks again.

"One," I cried out, loving the quick sting she gave me.

"Good girl," she said, sliding her hand along my ass. "It's so pretty when it's pink like this. I might do this some more before we get to the additional games I have in mind."

Again, the sting of the paddle, and I cried out, "Two," knowing where we were in the cycle.

She hit me until we reached ten, then kissed each cheek gently, her lips soft on that sensitive skin she'd raised.

"You were so good," she said. "I think you deserve a reward."

Sliding one of the dildos into my pussy in one swift motion, I moaned with the way it filled me. She'd already worked me up with the foreplay we'd done, so there was no pain when it went in. Add to that the fact that she'd chosen the smallest one, which I could tell by feel, and it was just a nice sensation.

"Thank you, Mistress," I said and moaned when she slid it out and slammed it back in, my cunt throbbing around the foreign object.

"I want you to get worked up well," she said. "But you are not allowed to release until I tell you to. Do you understand?"

"Yes, Mistress," I said, though the way she was working me, I could tell it was going to be a struggle.

She stopped her movement, and I wasn't sure exactly what she was doing, but then she pulled the dildo completely out of me.

"Mistress?" I asked, still unable to see her from where she was behind me.

Then I felt her tongue again on my pussy, and I moaned with the sensation. She sucked on me, pulling me into her mouth. It was warm and wet and did all the right things to me. I shifted my hips, trying to press further back onto her mouth, but she let me go and slapped my ass.

"Don't move," she said.

"Yes, Mistress," I said and clenched my ass a bit at her reprimand.

I could hear her moving, then heard metal and leather working together. I was sure she was putting on the strap-on so she could fuck me properly. Just the thought of it made my pussy clench in anticipation, knowing she was getting ready to use her body and the toys we'd picked out to bring me to a climax.

"I don't want you to make a sound right now," she said. "No asking anything, no acknowledging what I'm doing, no moaning or whining or anything. The only noise you're allowed to make is if something hurts. If that happens, I want you to snap your fingers."

I waited, knowing she was testing me like she'd been tested in a similar situation. I could feel her body behind me, the heat coming from it, but what I didn't anticipate was that she would slide her hands down my legs and use the restraints on the base of the bed at the foot to strap me to the posts on either side. I was already spread open with the spacer, but the way she hooked me in, it was like she wanted me completely immobilized, unable to move at all. She even moved up to the edge of the bed to pull the straps tighter.

The sight of her strapped and ready just made me want her more. I felt the pull on the other side of the bed as she tightened the restraints to get me completely helpless and at her mercy and, my lord, did it just make me ache for her all the more.

"Now," she said, running a hand along my ass. "Let's get you all lubed up and ready to take these cocks into you."

I felt the cool gel of lube as she dripped it at the top of my ass. It slid down the crack, using gravity to get it into the right place so she could enter my asshole without tearing me. Then, she slid one of the cocks that was strapped to her up and down the break, sliding it from my clit all the way up to my asshole.

"I need you to relax," she said, and I followed her instructions, letting my body just experience what was going on.

Pressing the head of it in just a bit, I pushed out some, just to open up for her to enter me, and it was an experience I loved every time I got to do it. She backed away a bit, then pressed in again, and I could feel the other false phallic rubbing against my clit just a little bit.

"This isn't working," she said, and was in that place where she was lost in being in control.

Shifting my hips the little bit that I could, I tilted up and the dildo she wasn't pressing into my ass slid just right against my pussy and I clenched, pulling in the one that was at my ass.

"Oh," she said, noticing that it went in just that little bit.

She moved her hips just a bit, but I held onto the penetrating object, keeping it in me as well as I could. I could feel her hands as she reached down to grab the second one and slipped it into me after sliding it up and down along my pussy, and then I had that full feeling I loved.

I must have let out a moan of some sort because she slapped my ass.

"Silence," she said, and I bit my lip enough to keep from making any more noise.

She began moving again, and I kept that tight hold of my lower lip, biting it each time I wanted to make a noise. It took her a bit to get into a rhythm, but finally, she was thrusting in and out of me in slow, sensual movements. My pussy quivered around the false dick inside me, pulling it into me as she moved away, and my God, she actually got it. She understood the movements that worked and was really good at the movements.

"You like that, don't you?" she asked.

I wanted to answer but was sure it would result in another smack on my ass. The smack came, and she said, "Answer me."

"Yes, Mistress," I nearly shouted.

"Good girl," she said. "You're allowed to make noise, now, but only moans and sounds of pleasure. The only words you are allowed to say are in response to direct questions from me. Do you understand?"

She'd kept the movement up, sliding in and out of both my pussy and my ass, and it was a sensation that gave me that full feeling even more than normal, and I loved it. Double penetration was one of my favorite things, but we'd chosen larger strap-on sizes for this particular scene. She wanted to see if it was possible, because all of hers had been the much smaller sizes.

When she stopped moving, I was confused, so tried to look at her, but was so tight against the bed that I couldn't see what she was doing. She pulled out of me and I whimpered, wondering what was wrong, then I heard the sound of a footstool being moved along the floor. I also heard things shifting on the table that she'd set the toys on.

"I want to watch your face," she said, and I could now see her above my ass more, peering up and over my body. "I also want to have a little penetration of my own, so you're gonna have to give me a minute before I go back in."

"Yes, Mistress," I said, and couldn't keep the disappointment out of my voice that she might be awhile before resuming.

Instead of giving in to my whine, though, she smacked my clit with the crop we'd used earlier, and that sting sent shockwaves through me and I yelped.

"Count," she said and smacked me again.

"One," I said.

"Good girl," she said and struck me again, but this time she'd dropped behind me and licked me right after, and oh, did that just send me off. She must have felt my arousal increasing because she stopped and said, "Do *not* orgasm."

"Yes, Mistress," I said, clenching my cunt tight to keep it from having the reaction it wanted.

I wondered how she was going to handle being penetrated while penetrating me at the same time, and wanted to ask her about it, but then I heard the door open. My eyes went toward it, and I saw Apollo enter the room. He'd been my top for many years, and always knew how to get me to that peak and keep me there for what seemed like days.

"Starlight," he said, looking at her and dismissing me without even a glance.

"Apollo," she replied. "I was hoping you would help me with this."

We'd negotiated a possible third, and decided that if she wanted help, she could call him in, but he was the only one allowed to enter the room. That was one of the nice things about the club; if the door was shut, the room was occupied, or being prepared, and you were not to enter without an invitation from the guests who were using it.

"I see you have our toy tied up nicely," he said, the deep rumble of his voice vibrating across my skin as if he'd touched it. "How would you like me to help you?"

I couldn't see either of them now, as they were both standing behind me. The suspense was nearly enough to kill me, but I waited, hoping I'd soon be allowed to let go and float on that everlasting cloud for a moment.

Thwack!

That sting came back, and I said, "Two," following the directions she'd given me before.

But it wasn't followed by her tongue. Instead, I felt his thick fingers against me, a couple sliding into my pussy while his thumb slid easily into my ass, and I moaned deeply.

"Oh, she is very ready," he said, and I could hear the smile in his voice.

There were whispers while he pumped his fingers in and out of my pussy, pressing his thumb to the base of his hand in my ass, and sort of wiggling it up and down. Then they were gone, and I whined at the loss, only to be stung again with the crop on my pussy.

"Three," I cried, but there was pleasure in my tone.

That was the thing most people didn't understand. How closely pain and pleasure were to one another. Pain heightened the senses, making the pleasure larger than it would be without the stimulation of the pain.

Again, I felt the ooze of lubricant as it slid down my crack to my asshole, and then she was pressing into me again, giving that full feeling one more time.

"Good girl," she said, and I could see her over my back.

With her on the footstool, the angle was different, and I hadn't realized that just that shift of a couple of inches would do so much for me. I looked back and could see her over my shoulder just enough to know that she was definitely up on the block. Then she leaned forward, having pushed fully into me, and her warm body on my back was a nice distraction.

"Are you ready?" Apollo asked her.

"Yes," she said, and then I could see him behind her.

"Fast or slow?" he asked, and I watched as she smiled and looked over her shoulder.

"Fast, and only in my pussy," she said.

Then I felt the force of him slamming into her, which pushed her further into me, and... Oh. My. God. I exploded, I couldn't help myself, I was just sent all the way over the top and down the waterfall to crash on the rocks below. I vaguely heard her orgasm right after me, but all I could really tell was that it was a fast blow and we were both off to heights that were unbelievably wonderful.

As I came back to myself, I felt her pull out of me, and my body quivered with the aftershocks of the magnificent orgasm she gave me. I could hear them both talking, mostly Apollo, but her as well.

"You were a naughty girl," she said.

"My apologies, Mistress," I said. "You were just too wonderful, and I couldn't help myself."

"You know you will require punishment," she said, but her heart wasn't in it, and I could tell.

"Would you like me to punish her?" Apollo asked.

"Please," she replied.

I felt the straps on my ankles loosen, then the bracer was removed from my legs. He moved to the side of the bed I was facing, and I saw his sun inspired mask bright on his dark skin, his smile white against it.

"I am going to enjoy this," he said, and I couldn't help but shiver.

Chapter Five

Nick...

The scent of sex, and the sounds of pleasure, echoed through the space. I passed a few doors that were closed, so I kept on going until I made my way to what likely was a living room when this house was occupied by a family.

"Welcome," a woman said as she passed me going down the hallway I'd just come from.

While she wasn't necessarily my type, I could see that she was likely pleasurable to spend time with. Her corset was tight, pushing her tits up to nearly spilling out the top. The thong she wore on the bottom accentuated her ass as she went by, and the heels she had on made it shake with just the right amount of sass that I wanted to smack it.

"Hello," another woman said as she came up to me. "My name's Tiffany, like the jewelry. What's yours?"

"They told me I could go by Saturn," I said.

"Ah," she said. "You spread your seed."

I hadn't correlated the name to the god, but I suppose I should have.

"Not if I can help it," I said with a laugh. "Only to willing partners, and only with conditions in place for any seedling that might result from it."

"Well," she said, rubbing against my cock with her hand. "If you ever need to plant some seeds and watch them grow, I'm your girl."

With that, she walked past me, but not before she tugged on my cock through my pants. This was definitely a different kind of club than what I'd been to back home. On one end of the couch, I saw a man sitting with his pants down to his ankles, his cock disappearing in and out of the mouth of a woman with a cat mask on. She had her hair up in twin pigtails at the top of her head, and he was using them to pull her up off him before, yanking down and grinding himself into her. Every time she came up for air, she inhaled deeply, just enough to get a breath in before being shoved back down.

Behind her was another man on his knees, his condom covered cock sliding in and out of her pussy. In her ass was a plug with a tail on it, and he was using the tail to tip it up and down. He'd pull it out just a little bit, then shove it back in, then repeat the process in time with his thrusts.

At the other end of the couch, a man was bent over the arm, a woman in front of him with her ass in the air, his face buried in it as she sucked a man in front of her. Behind him, another man was fucking the guy bent over hard and fast, holding his hips, and moving the couch with each thrust.

"You wanna play?" a woman asked as she slid her hand around from behind me.

I held out my hand, showing her the ring I'd been given.

"Oh, sorry," she said, pulling her hands from my body.

"Don't be," I said. "It's not my rule you're breaking."

"I don't want to be banned," she said. "I have entirely too much fun here. Maybe you wanna watch?"

"I love to watch," I said. "What do you have in mind?"

"What's your pleasure?" she asked, her eyes lighting up.

43

"I am fine with whatever you desire," I said. "Just lead the way, and I'll follow you."

"Ooh," she said. "I like the way you think."

She crooked her finger at me, then turned and walked away. I waited a beat, wanting to see her ass, because I was, after all, an ass man, and damn, she did not disappoint. The panties she wore were low slung and made of lace that did nothing to hide her assets. The top she was wearing was little more than a bikini top with postage stamps to cover her nipples and nothing else.

"Apollo," she said. "Will you play with me in front of our new guest?"

"Sorry, Angel," he said. "I've been called into a private session. Maybe when I'm done, if you haven't found anyone, let me know and I'll try to be back."

She pouted, and it made me want to fuck her mouth, but I wouldn't get the chance tonight. Maybe the next time I came to the club I could. We continued into the kitchen of the building, and there were many folks negotiating what they wanted, or fucking right there on the counter, and it was wild to think all this fucking was going on.

"D'Artagnan," she said. "I need a partner to entertain our new guest."

"Oh, Angel," he said, a smile crossing his lips. "I would love to play with you. And such a handsome audience we'll have, too. Do you have a preference on location?"

She turned to me, and I just shrugged.

"Let's go to the den," she said. "He seems like someone who knows his way around an office. Maybe I'll play a secretary and you can be my boss. Then, our new guest can simply watch us work. You know, as one does."

"And you can take my dick-tation," he said, emphasizing the dick part of the word.

"I love it when you dick me," she said, her smile growing. "Do you want him to dick me?"

"That sounds like a wonderful idea," I said.

"What's your name?" D'Artagnan asked.

"I'm Saturn," I said. "Not by my choice, just what I was assigned."

"Don't let Tiffany hear that," he said.

"Little too late for that," I said with a laugh.

We walked back down the hallway I'd come in from and there was a door open that hadn't been before. It was, in fact, an office set up. But this office had much more than just a desk and some chairs. This was decked out with all sorts of apparatus that could be used during play, and I looked forward to what these two, who were obviously exhibitionists, would entertain me with.

"You good if we leave the door open?" she asked.

"The more the merrier," I said. "Where would you like me to sit?"

"Behind the desk," he said. "This way, I can fuck her right in front of you and she can watch you get off from it."

"Not sure I'm allowed..."

"You just can't touch us," she said. "And we can't touch you. But you are more than welcome to help yourself, if you're so inclined. I like to watch, too."

She gave me a wink that said she would very much like to watch me masturbate in front of her.

"We'll see how the show goes," I said, not wanting to commit to anything, especially as this was my first night here.

I walked around the large desk to see a woman's foot peeking out from underneath it.

"Hey there, doll," I said. "You doing okay?"

Her eyes were red, muddy streaks running down her cheeks from her mascara, and it looked like she had a split lip. I crouched down so I was on eye level with her and she scooted further under the desk, more in the shadows than she was before.

"Hey, sweetheart," I said, reaching my hand into the space. "I won't hurt you, but I'm gonna need to know how to help."

She was shaking her head so fast I was worried she'd hit it on the edge of the desk. Angel must have heard what I was saying, because she came around the desk as well, but from the other direction.

"Oh, no," she said. "Paris, who did this?"

I slid back, not wanting to cause her any more discomfort than she was already experiencing.

"Fuck," D'Artagnan said. "I'll be right back."

He went out the door and toward the front door, where I assumed he would get a bouncer of some sort to come in and take care of the situation we'd found. I moved to the door to keep anyone else who wanted to come in out until we figured out what was going on. Across the hall I could hear the sound of a couple of women having orgasms nearly simultaneously, the first one was a high keening sound, then dropping low to where I couldn't hear it any longer. The other one was a piercing squeal that went quickly away.

"Where is she?" a man asked as he came to the door.

I stepped back and aimed my arm toward the desk where Angel was crouched behind it. He strode over, clearly pissed off at what was likely a rape that was not consented to. His manner indicated that he was not only the one in charge, but the one who would take the hit if something like this got out.

"Paris, sweety," he said as he crouched near the desk.

I heard her sob, then he was pulling her out and into his lap. I couldn't see everything because they were still behind the desk, but I heard his hushed low tones as he spoke to her.

"You wanna go?" D'Artagnan asked.

"Nah," I said. "I kinda wanna see how this goes. It'll tell me more about the club than anything else."

"Where is she?" a man shouted as he came down the hall at a run. "Paris!" he shouted.

"Hang on," I said, putting an arm out to stop him.

"He's her partner," D'Artagnan said. "Let him in."

"River," I heard the woman cry, and he was past me, and nearly sliding around the desk.

The bouncer who had come in earlier turned the woman over to him, then came to me, with Angel following him.

"What did you see?" he asked.

"Nothing," I said. "We walked in and I went around the desk and saw her leg kind of sticking out. When I ducked down, I could see she was hurt. That's pretty much it."

"You see anyone come out of here?" he asked.

"No," I said. "But in my defense, I was a little distracted."

"Completely fine," he said.

By this point, word must have run through the house, because a crowd had begun to gather. The door on the other side of the hall opened, and Apollo came out, shutting the door behind him.

"What's up?" he asked.

"It's Paris," D'Artagnan said.

"Fuck," he said.

"Yeah," Angel said, going to hug him.

"I gotta let Charlie know," he said, turning back into the room he'd come out of.

"I thought..."

"Charlie is her mentor," Angel said. "She's been working with her for a while to make sure she knows how to refuse things. This is gonna set Paris back, and I don't know if she'll recover. God, this is just fucked up on all sorts of levels. Like, many women here are willing to do con-non-con, so why did someone have to take something that wasn't offered?"

"Some people don't know how to accept no," I said. "It's an unfortunate reality of the human race."

"Paris," a woman cried as she came out of the room across the hall.

"Charlie," I heard from behind me, and a goddess brushed past me, shoving me out of the way as she rushed to her friend.

The name Charlie didn't fit her at all. No, Aphrodite would have been more appropriate. She seemed to be the goddess of all things passion related. I didn't miss the opportunity to see her ass as she walked by, even if it wasn't exactly the right time to be doing that.

I hadn't really been paying too much attention to everything going on, just trying to figure out where I should be and what I should be doing. Should I leave? Stay? I didn't know, so I kind of just stood at the edge of the room waiting to see what would happen.

"You," the bouncer said as he walked up to me. "Come with me."

"Yes, sir," I said and followed him out of the room.

He walked with purpose, separating the people who were standing in the hallway. The tone in the building had paled harshly, with most folks covering themselves and looking around with worry etched in their expressions.

"Lucy?" one woman asked the man who was leading me.

"Not now," he said, not even slowing his stride.

We went through the living room and kitchen before coming to a small space near the back of the home. It was full of computer screens that showed the common areas, which I thought was odd, what with the rules about no recording equipment in the building. Whatever, I wasn't in any of the images that would cause me harm. I hadn't done anything. He saw me looking at the monitors and flipped a switch that shut them all down.

"They don't record," he said. "I'm a voyeur, but the rules are clear. No recording, so I don't, which is fucking awful now, because I could have caught someone in the act, and had clear evidence to give to the cops. Of course, if we gave over videos of the assault, we'd be required to give over everything we had, which then would shut us down so fucking fast our heads would spin."

"So, what do you need from me?" I asked, sitting in the chair he'd indicated.

"Since I'm security, I can ask lots of questions," he said. "I know you're new, but that's why I asked you to come with me. Others might try to protect someone, but you have no loyalty, so hopefully that'll make you honest."

"Wouldn't matter if I'd been here years," I said. "No one should be raped, and there are plenty of willing partners around to get your rocks off that it shouldn't happen."

"You'd be surprised," he said.

"Nah," I replied. "In my line of work, it happens entirely too often. I don't stand for it, and no real man should, either."

"You and I agree on that," he said. "So, what did you see? Who did you see? What information can you give me?"

"Few problems with this," I said. "Everyone wears masks, so identifying someone is going to be rough. Plus, the door was closed when I got here, and open when we went back there so I could watch them. I didn't hear anything that sounded like distress or, rules or no, I'd have gone into that room."

"That's good to know," he said.

"So," I continued. "When we went in, it looked like the room was empty. They asked me to take the chair behind the desk. I saw her leg sort of sticking out from under it and I crouched down to see if I could help her, or if she was just hiding or resting or something. Her face told me everything I needed to know. I barely caught a glimpse of it, but her lip is split. She's been crying, too, cause her eye makeup is a mess."

"Yeah," he said, pen to paper making notes. "I noticed those things, too."

"Do we know who she was supposed to be with?" I asked. "Because the guy at the front when I got here said that people could request partners, so I thought it might be something that was set up before that got out of hand."

"I've already asked Mr. Stone to give me a list of pairings that were set up ahead of time," he said. "Unfortunately, if someone is interested in doing something without prior commitment, we may not know about it. It is always recommended to make note of who is with you so that we will know who to deal with if something like this comes up. Unfortunately, Paris is one of our more timid members, and she has a hard time saying no. We're working on it, and she usually has a chaperone, but they must have been distracted or otherwise engaged when this started. We'll ask them, but I think the predator watched for this opportunity."

"I hope she's willing to say who it was," I said. "Because those are the reasons that clubs like this get a bad reputation. Not that the club in and of itself doesn't get it simply because of the nature of membership and activities, but that bad apple tends to spoil the whole bunch."

"You are correct," he said. "We are the most open secret in the city. Everyone knows we exist, and everyone knows what happens here, but no one knows anyone who is a member, and members don't acknowledge they know another member when out in the real world."

"That's actually a really good thing to know," I said. "My line of work tends to be more front facing, so running into another member at my office, so to speak, would, and likely could, destroy any reputation I have."

"Thus the masks," he said. "It's not exactly fool proof, because most folks can figure out who's who. It just makes most members feel a little less exposed."

"Now that you're mentioning it," I said. "Paris wasn't wearing a mask."

He paused for a moment, then said, "You're right. I'll have to ask about that once we get her calmed down."

"Do you need anything else from me?" I asked.

"Do we have your contact information?" he asked.

"I mean, the guy at the front looked at my ID," I said. "And I assume you have my email address since I got the email with all the instructions."

"Why don't you give me the email address, your first name, and your phone number," he said, sliding a pad of paper over to me with a pen. "That way I'll have it if it gets lost somewhere in the shuffle."

"Sure," I said, writing the information he'd asked for down on the pad.

"Who invited you?" he asked.

"It was actually a friend of a friend," I said. "My friend from San Diego asked one of her friends to extend an invitation. I have Maggie's information for you to check with her, but she did not tell me the name of her contact within the club."

"Please add her information to that note," he said, and I did as he asked. "Thanks. We'll reach out to see who she contacted about extending the invitation. Do you live local?"

"I actually just moved to town earlier this week," I said. "It was a transfer in jobs that brought me here. I am currently living out of a hotel for now, and depending on how things go, I may decide to purchase a home sometime this winter."

"Well, we'd love to have you stay," he said. "You seem like the kind of gentleman that would bring some class to this club."

"Thank you very much," I said. "I just have to wait and see what the future holds for my current job. The contract is up this fall, so things may shift, and I may be sent somewhere else entirely."

"If you ever need anything," he said, pulling out a card from the desk drawer. "You just ring me up and I'll be happy to help you find a new home for your more creative endeavors."

"I really appreciate it," I said. "Should I wait around? Or am I free to go?"

"I have your contact information," he said. "You are free to go if you'd like."

"That may not be a bad idea," I said. "I just don't want anyone to think that the new guy did it, just because I'm the new guy."

"There were several new guests this evening," he said. "It could be any number of them, or someone who has been here years. We will find the culprit, rest assured. We have connections that are helpful in that manner."

"Good to know," I said, not wanting to know the details. The less you knew, sometimes the better.

"Have a pleasant evening," he said, standing up from behind the desk.

"Thank you," I replied. "And if I can be of any further assistance, please reach out to me."

"We definitely will," he said, and escorted me out of his office.

I headed back toward the main house through the kitchen, which had been pretty much emptied. The living room had a handful of people sitting around, and the mood was somber. I headed toward the front door and noticed that it had also been cleared out, with all the doors on either side of the hall open. When I walked to the door of the office, I saw that there was just one woman in there, the one that had come across the hall. Charlie.

Chapter Six

Charlotte...

"I am going to enjoy this," he said.

There was a commotion outside the door, but I was completely oblivious to what they were saying. I was in my own little bubble of post-orgasm space and didn't want to think of anything.

"Shit," Apollo said, and headed out the door.

I simply stayed where I was. I could have unhooked my other arm, but I was comfortable, and didn't want to go anywhere.

"Fuck," he said when he came back in, and I could tell something was wrong. "Let me unhook you. It's Paris."

"Shit," I said, pushing myself up.

"Hang on," Starlight said, coming to the far side of the bed to undo the cuff on my other arm.

I slid off the end of the bed and headed out the door at a near run.

"Paris," I called, and heard her faint cry from across the hall in the den.

I ran across and shoved a guy who was standing in my way and went to her where she was cradled into River's arms.

"Baby, talk to me," I said, crouching down next to the couple.

"I didn't want to," she said through sobs. "I told them no, told them to stop, but they just wouldn't."

"I know, baby," I said, brushing her hair back from her bruising face. "You did nothing wrong."

"They wouldn't stop," she said, breaking down even further.

She had a split lip. Her eye was bruising and would likely swell shut, if my guess was right, and she had marks on her throat and shoulders. Whoever did this to her knew what he was doing. He probably started with her saying yes, and when he pushed, she tried to make it stop, but he silenced her, probably with something around her neck. It had happened before at the club, but not in a long time. I was sure that Lucifer would get to the bottom of it, because he was that thorough. He knew everyone who was in the club tonight, so he would figure out who did this, and then would use his connections to the club we didn't talk about. How he knew them was beyond me, but it didn't matter. He got results, and these things only happened once.

"Do you know his name?" I asked her, but she shook her head. "Okay," I said. "That's okay, we'll figure it out. What kind of mask was he wearing?"

"I don't know," she said, her tears running down her face in dark tracks through the mascara that was already smeared there.

"Can I take her home?" River asked.

"She should be checked out," I said. "If she wants to press charges..."

"No," she shouted. "I'm not doing that. I don't care."

"Baby," I said, my voice low and level. "If you don't, he's gonna think he can get away with this."

"I won't do it," she said. "I don't want my family to know about this. They can't know about it."

"Okay," I said. "That's okay. But maybe Lucifer can find out who it is. Are you okay with that?"

"He'll protect me, right?"

"He will do his best," I said.

"Okay," she said. "But I don't want anyone to see me. How can I get out of here without everyone looking at me?"

I turned to look at the door, and Apollo was standing there, effectively being a door between us, and the rest of the house.

"Apollo," I called, and he turned his head over his shoulder to look at me. "Can you find me something to put on her? We're gonna get her out of here."

He turned back to the hall but didn't move.

"Apollo," I called.

"On it," he said over his shoulder, and I saw there was someone on the other side of him that he must have asked to get something.

I didn't question it further and turned back to Paris. She'd buried her face in River's shoulder. I took a look at what else might have happened to her, and saw that her wrists were also red, which meant he had held those tight, too. It just pissed me off that people took things that were freely offered by others. There were a ton of members who were willing to do con-non-con, so why did he take it from Paris when she didn't want it? I swore if I ever found out who it was, and it was within my power, I'd see them pay for what was done to her.

"Here," Angel said as she slipped past Apollo. "I got this from one of the other girls. It's plenty big enough to cover her completely, just in case she wants that. It's even got a hood to hide under."

"Perfect," I said. "Thanks."

"How is she?" she asked quietly.

"She's a mess," I said. "I just hope she'll go to the hospital. I don't want her to end up pregnant, or with an STD."

"Oh, God," she said. "I didn't even think about that."

"I'll make sure she has plenty of help in that regard," I said. "She won't have to worry about anything."

"We're gonna go," River said as he hugged Paris to his side.

"Here," Angel said, holding out the cloak.

River took it, but Paris wouldn't let him pull away enough to put it on her.

"Here," I said, taking the cloak, and wrapping it around her shoulders.

I was gentle when I set it on her shoulders, but she still flinched. River pulled the edges of the collar around her, and I lifted the hood up and over her head, hoping it would give her enough protection to get out of here without having to answer questions.

"Thank you," she whispered from under the hood.

"Baby, you are more than welcome," I said. "I just wish I could make it not have happened."

"I know," she said.

"You need anything, you call me," I said. "Day or night, you call. Don't feel bad. Don't think it's too late or too stupid or anything, you hear me?"

She nodded her head, but I was pretty sure she wouldn't.

"River," I said and waited until he looked at me. "Stay with her tonight. If you can get her to the hospital, do it. We need evidence if she decides she wants to press charges."

"I'm not," she said, and the look she gave me from the shadows told me she was going to stay strong in that decision.

"If you do," I said, then held up a finger. "You want to have the option. I won't push, but I don't want you to give it up without at least thinking forward."

"Thank you," she said. "I trust Lucy to figure out the answer."

"Get checked," I said. "Even if it's with your regular doctor. And pick up a morning-after pill."

"They didn't come in me," she said.

"If he raped you, it could still cause a pregnancy," I said. "Trust me, get the pill and get tested. Please do that for me."

"Okay," she said with a deep sigh.

I looked at River and he gave me a nod, so I knew he'd make sure she got tested and would get the pill for her. I had to trust him to take care of her.

"Call me," I said and she nodded.

They walked over to the door where Apollo was still standing guard. River put his hand on the larger man's shoulder, and Apollo turned to look at him.

"You want an escort?" he asked.

"No," River said. "We're just going out the front."

"They brought your car around already," Apollo said. "Anyone gives you shit, you tell me and I'll make sure they never give anyone shit again."

River nodded, and Apollo stepped into the hall, which had emptied a bit, and stood back to let them go to the front of the house, and down the steps to their car. I looked around the room, trying to see if I could find anything that might be worth holding onto in case she changed her mind. We may not get the DNA from a rape kit, but if I could figure out who had raped her, I would. God, I fucking hated this part of the club life.

It wasn't that I didn't trust Lucifer, just that I sometimes wanted to see justice come from the authorities. There were just too many high-profile people who were part of this club, and that meant that secrets were far more important than justice, which just pissed me off all the more. Maybe it would be better to walk away from the club and find something else to entertain me. But I fucking loved this place. Whatever happened with Paris might let me know where I should go from here.

"Hey," a man said, and I looked up from where I was standing next to the desk.

"Yeah?" I asked.

"You need any help?" he asked.

"Why?"

"Because you jumped in to help her," he said. "That's an admirable trait."

"You could go get me my clothes," I said, pointing out the door.

"Sure," he said, turning around, then turning back. "What am I looking for?"

"There are some panties on the floor," I said. "And then there's a black dress in there as well. Grab them both for me, would ya?"

"Sure," he said, walking out and across the hall.

At least he wasn't just in here to look at my naked ass. I hadn't thought about anything other than getting to my girl, and making sure she was safe. I didn't know where Apollo had gone, though. I thought he was gonna stay here, but he must have had somewhere else to go.

"Here you go," he said as he walked across the room to me. He was holding my panties in one hand, and the dress in the other. "Want me to close the door and wait outside?"

I laughed, because he'd already seen my ass, so it's not like he wasn't gonna see something new.

"No," I said. "Just turn around."

Why I said that, I had no idea, but it felt right. Like I was trying to test him or something. He did as I asked and turned his back to me. I slid the panties up over my legs, and onto my ass before pulling the dress over my head to cover me the rest of the way.

"Okay," I said, and he turned back around.

"Anything else?" he asked, and it just seemed like there was something more he was looking for.

I didn't recognize him, but that didn't mean it was his first time at the club. Was he the one who'd raped Paris? Was that why he was here checking on the room? Maybe he was trying to find something he left behind. But he looked somewhat like I'd seen him before, but I couldn't place it.

"I found her," he said, and that made me do a double take. "I came in with Angel and D'Artagnan. I didn't do this, wouldn't do this, and would love to have just a few minutes alone with whoever did, if you get my drift."

He didn't sound like he was from here, so I had to ask.

"Where are you from?"

"San Diego," he said.

"First time here?"

"Yeah," he said. "I'm new to town. Was referred by someone from a club back home. I appreciate the privacy and anonymity they offer."

"It's an important piece of what makes our club different," I said. "So, talk to me. Tell me what you saw."

Chapter Seven

Nick...

"So, talk to me," she said. "Tell me what you saw."

"Not really anything," I said.

How I was standing here talking to this woman without simply asking her to let me fuck her was mind blowing. It was all I could do to keep my eyes on hers, and not leer at her like a fucking teenager. It was absolutely not the time or the place, but it did cross my mind.

"Anything might help," she said.

"We came in and thought the room was empty," I said. "I already told this to the security guy. Why are you asking?"

"Because I feel responsible," she said, and looked like she meant it. "If I'd taught her better, or given her more time, or spent time with her tonight..."

"You didn't do this," I said, cutting her off. "Whoever did this is the responsible one."

"But I should have..."

"You can should yourself to death," I said. "It won't change the fact that it happened, won't stop it from having happened. What you can do, though, is make sure she's okay. Make sure she seeks counseling for this, and if you need someone to pay for it, let me know. This may break her, but it might just make her stronger, too."

"Why do you care?" she asked, and I could tell she was completely baffled by my reaction.

"Why wouldn't I?" I asked.

"You don't know her," she said. "Hell, you probably don't know anyone here."

"That's kinda the point, isn't it?" I asked. "I mean, it's why we all wear masks, and use names that aren't ours. This way we can play like we like, so long as we don't hurt someone else, and enjoy an evening out without repercussions."

"Until this happens," she said sarcastically.

"It doesn't seem like it happens often here," I said. "In fact, I don't think I've been to a club that is as well run as this one. The rules you have in place, the way you screen members, and visitors like me, and that you have protections in place, is probably why this is hitting you so hard. Not that it isn't a fucked-up situation in the least, but still."

She looked like she was taking what I said to heart, and actually thinking about it. I hoped she would tell me that this hadn't happened before, or at least that it was so rare that she didn't remember when it happened last.

"Tell you what?" I asked. "I'll give you my real name, my real phone number, and my real address. I'll tell you what I do for a living, and where I'm currently staying. You can do any kind of background check you want to on me, and I'll come up clean. I guarantee it wasn't me."

"I believe you," she said. "I don't know why, but I do."

"Thank you," I said. "So, what can I do to help?"

"I don't know," she said, looking around the room. "Do you see anything that's out of place? Anything that strikes you as odd or anything?"

"That's a loaded question, darling," I said.

"Charlie," she replied.

"Like I said, Charlie," I replied. "This is not a normal office, so pretty much everything looks out of place if we're going by normal standards."

"Okay," she said. "Do you see anything that looks like it was used for this?"

I looked around the room, but everything could have been used. There were toys of every shape and size lying around the room. It was a fuck room, and it looked like it had been used all night. There was shit everywhere, and condoms in the trash can, so there was no telling whether the guy used one or not. I didn't see any clothing anywhere, so if he ripped something off her, he took it with him, but that was assuming she didn't keep it with her.

"I can't see anything definitive," I said. "But I'm far from an expert in this type of thing. Will they call the cops?"

"Not hardly," she said, laughing. "We don't call the cops to this place unless someone dies. Even then, we figure out what happened before we call."

"Yeah, I can see that," I said.

"So," she said. "I guess you'll be going."

"I suppose," I said. "How about you?"

"Yeah," she said. "There isn't anything else I can do here."

"Can I walk you out?"

"Why?"

"Being polite," I said. "Besides, I don't want you to be alone. You look like this hit you pretty hard."

"No shit," she said. "My mentee just got raped, and I was across the fucking hall. How do you think I should feel?"

"Sorry," I said, holding my hands up. "I was just trying to help."

"Well don't," she said. "You can fuck off."

She was fucking sexy when she was pissed, even if all I could see was her lips, and that sexy as fuck lipstick that matched the classic Mustang out front.

"I'll leave you be then," I said. "But feel free to call me."

I walked over to the desk and pulled out a pen, writing my name and phone number onto a piece of paper that was on top, then folded it in half, and handed it to her. "Any time," I said, then walked out.

What I wanted to do was bend her over the desk and fuck her, but it wasn't either the time or the place. What I would do, though, is request a session with the spicy Charlie of the red Mustang. Maybe we could make use of the back seat. I mean, the top went down, so it wouldn't be impossible.

I walked out the front of the house, and Mr. Stone met me.

"Your car is here," he said, handing me my key. "Most everyone else is gone. Sorry it turned out to be a shitty night."

"Not your fault," I said. "But I'd like to come back. I'd also like to spend some time with Charlie. Can that be arranged?"

"I'll make a note," he said.

"See ya," I said, then went down the stairs, and got into my car.

Chapter Eight

Charlotte...

"Dammit," I shouted, looking around the room.

"Hey," Lucifer said as he stood in the door.

"You find anything?" I asked, praying he did.

"Sorry," he said, shaking his head. "I have the list of everyone that was here. I'll check them all out and see what I can find. Someone had to have seen something."

"I know," I replied. "I'm just pissed that I was so close but couldn't help her."

"You didn't know," he said, pulling me to him.

Lucifer had been at the club for years and was one of the reasons I felt safe here. He was always watching, always keeping an eye on everything that was going on. Everyone knew there were cameras everywhere, but very few of us knew who was watching. I just wondered who would know how to avoid them. That's the only explanation as to what happened. Someone figured out how to get around the cameras to keep him from seeing what was going on. There were tricks to keep the cameras from viewing something if you were in a private session. Closing the door was one of them, but that didn't always turn the cameras off. No, that required the participants to request it, or for there to be a glitch. If that were the case, though, Lucy would have known.

"Were there any requests for privacy?" I asked as I drew away from him.

"Just the room you were in," he said.

"Then why didn't you see it?" I asked.

"I don't know," he said. "I must have been otherwise occupied. It's my fault."

"No," I said, realizing he was doing exactly what I'd been doing. "It's the fault of the asshole who raped her. I just feel like this might end the club as we know it."

"It'll definitely shift things," he said. "You should go home. We're not gonna find any answers here. I'll make some calls and see what I can find out about everyone. I'm also gonna be calling a couple of the other clubs to see if they've had the same thing happen there."

"You think he's done it before?"

"He avoided my gaze," he said. "Nothing avoids that. That tells me he's a pro, and has figured out how to make himself invisible, and what he does, invisible, too. I've got some things to check in here, and I don't want you seeing what I do. Are you cool with leaving this up to me?"

"I don't really have a choice," I said. "But I trust you."

"Thank you," he said.

Trust was something that was earned in this lifestyle. You didn't jump into bed with just anyone, and while Lucy and I hadn't actually had any sort of interaction in that regard, he was still around, and I knew him well enough that he would do whatever it took to get to the bottom of what happened. He thought of all of us as his kids, his fucked-up, perverted kids, but still, we were his, and he felt responsible for making sure we were safe.

"Good night," I said.

"Sleep well," he replied.

"You and I both know that's not gonna happen," I said, but he still smiled at me, then shut the door as soon as I was out.

I walked to the front, after checking the room I'd been in that night, and seeing that nothing was left behind. When I walked out, Mr. Stone was still there, and I was confused.

"Aren't you going home?" I asked.

"Not until the last guest leaves," he said. "Tonight's my night for closing up, and I know there are still a few folks inside."

"Okay," I said. "Well, goodnight."

"Charlie," he said, and I turned around. "I had a request for you."

"Who?" I asked, thrown off by it.

"New guy named..." he paused and looked at his screen on the kiosk. "Saturn."

"Don't know him," I said. "And I'm not really interested in meeting with someone new, especially after tonight."

"He was actually very helpful tonight," he said.

"How do you mean?" I asked.

"Lucifer told me that he was the one who found Paris," he said.

"Wait, what?" I asked. "You mean the guy in the black suit with the purple tie? Leaf style mask?"

"That's him," he said. "I have all of his contact information here if you're interested in vetting him before answering. I know it's not protocol, but for you, I'm willing to break rules. Especially after tonight."

"Let me think about it," I said. "I'm not saying no, but I'm not willing to say yes. At least, not yet. I want to see what Lucy finds out before I am willing to meet with someone new."

"I'll let him know it's under consideration," he said.

"No," I said. "Hold off on contacting him for now. If he asks about it, tell him that all sessions with new members are on hold until the issues from tonight are figured out. Tell him that until this is cleared up, the club may be on hold."

"That's not what Lucy said," he replied.

"You know that and I know that," I said. "But he's new and

doesn't know how we operate. Once Lucy finds the one responsible, and deals with them accordingly, no matter who it is, then we can go back to business as usual. For now, he just needs to know that he's on hold for anything. But only if he asks. Don't reach out first. I want to see if I can get some answers before we go there."

"I'll let Lucifer know," he said. "Now, you should head home."

"Good night," I said, then walked down the steps to my car.

Because I was such a valuable member of the club and had such a long list of partners and mentees, I was one of the few allowed to park at the curb, and not be subjected to the rule of valet parking. It was cool outside, but not cold, but I was glad I had my blanket in the car. It wasn't like it was that far to my home, but I didn't want to have to deal with the cold seat. I unlocked the door, then reached in, and pulled the blanket across to cover the driver's seat before climbing in.

When she started up, I felt that nice rumble under me and closed my eyes to just experience it for a moment before putting the car in gear to drive myself home. Fortunately, since it was so late, the streets weren't that full, and it was an uneventful drive, and I pulled into my garage after pressing the opener. Turning the car off, I pressed the button to close the door, then climbed out of the car.

Keying my way into my house from the garage, I flipped on the light in my kitchen, and locked the door behind me. Walking across the space, I got to the other end and turned the light off before flipping the switch for the stairs and made my way up. I had remodeled the home from its original shortly after I purchased it, ensuring that I could turn lights on and off from either side of the room. Growing up, it was always hard to move throughout the house without having the opportunity to do that.

When I got to the top of the stairs, I turned down the hallway to my room, shutting the light off after turning mine on. I loved the quiet that I'd ensured would be my home. I made sure that they installed extra sound barriers when they redid the exterior walls. I told them I worked from home sometimes, and needed to make sure I could do that without having outside noises to mess that up. The contractors tried to talk me into just one room, but I insisted they do the entire house that way. It cost a fucking fortune, but it was definitely worth it.

No one needed to know that the work I did at home had nothing to do with my job and was more related to the things I did after working hours. My basement was completely decked out as a dungeon that I could use if the club wasn't open, or if someone wanted to have more personalized attention. It's where I had been working with Paris and her partner, River, for the last several months. I wondered whether it was my fault that she began to feel more comfortable in her own skin, and that made her a little bolder in her choices.

Either way, I knew it was the fault of the man who did it, and not anyone else. I just couldn't help but feel like my teaching may have put her in harm's way, and I'd forever be upset at that thought. Would she heal? Physically, yeah. Mentally though was another subject. River knew he could bring her here to work with her if she felt up to it, but I didn't know if that would ever happen. Instead of wondering, though, I sent a message to him reminding him of my open door for them to explore. I couldn't make it happen, but I could offer.

I pulled my dress over my head, and dropped it into the hamper, then undid my corset before setting it to the side. It had to be cleaned much more delicately, so I couldn't just toss it into the washer. I pulled the panties off, and dropped them in the hamper, kicked off my shoes, and then peeled out of my stockings, throwing everything where it belonged for the next day's clean up. Then, naked, I walked to the bathroom to clean myself of the night.

Normally I would climb into the tub with a bath bomb, or something to relax and ease my muscles from the exertion I'd used, but I couldn't do that. Not tonight. No, tonight was a quick shower to clean the smells from my body. Maybe tomorrow I'd deserve a bath, but tonight I still needed to be punished for letting my friend get hurt. I didn't question my thought process, just went along with it and stepped into the shower, turning it on as hot as I could stand before ducking under the spray.

On any other night, I would enjoy the feel of the heat seeping into my body, and perhaps pleasure myself just a little bit more, but tonight was about cleaning up and going to bed.

Chapter Nine

Nick...

Walking into my hotel room, I was pissed. Not only had my night been fucked up, but I didn't get a chance to get more information about taking Charlie, or at least negotiating that. I was hot because it was still hot outside, and I was uncomfortable with all the clothes I still had on. Add to that the fact that I hadn't gotten to watch anything more than the simple orgy happening in the living room, and that the girl I found had been raped, seriously gave me a buzz kill. All I wanted was to find out if the club was right for me, and possibly find a partner or two to have a little fun with.

Now, though, I was in a hotel that was most decidedly boring, and I hadn't gotten my dick wet, or even had the chance to take care of it while enjoying a show. The only thing I could think of the whole drive home was Charlie, running across the hall in that corset that pushed her tits up and nearly over, and her bare-naked ass with those fucking stockings that went all the way up, accentuating how long her legs were.

Her lips were still red with the lipstick that matched the

Mustang, and all I could imagine was them wrapped around my cock. The blonde curls at her pussy matched her hair, so I knew she was a natural blonde, which just flipped my switch, too. Fuck, all I wanted was her. Watching others was all well and good, but finding someone who hit every one of my fucking kinks just did something to me, and I missed it all because of some asshole who wanted to take what wasn't being offered.

I dropped my jacket on the bed, damn near tore my tie as I pulled it loose and off and did lose a couple of buttons when I yanked my shirt off. Then it was my belt from the slacks and shoving those down to pull them off after kicking my shoes off. I stomped to the bathroom and turned the shower on, climbing in to do some daydreaming and taking care of my own needs.

Yes, Sir, I imagined her saying as I pushed her down onto the bottom of the tub on her knees. *Please, Sir,* I could hear her say in my imagination as she looked at my cock, then I had to use more imagination, because my hand was a very poor substitute for a mouth, and I knew it wasn't her, which just made it worse.

Try as I might, it just didn't work, so I simply thought about what she'd looked like, standing there in her stockings and corset, bare bottom and pussy, not giving one single fuck as to who might see her. She was a goddess, and so much in control. I wanted to see how far I could bend her to my will. Those thoughts were what sent me over the edge, shooting my load against the shower wall while the water ran over my back.

Once I was spent, I cleaned up, took the showerhead and turned it toward the wall to get my come off, then got out and dried off. Walking back to the bed, I thought about the night, and how Charlie had said something would be done about it, and they'd figure out who it was, and I wondered about that. I mean, yeah, there were cameras all over, and yeah, the head guy, Lucifer, watched. But he said they didn't record, and that he hadn't seen anything, so I wasn't sure exactly how they were gonna do that. Not my problem, but it just meant that I'd have to wait a little longer before I could have my prize, because she was a prize, and I was determined to have her. At least for a little while.

Instead of going right to sleep like I should have, I opened my laptop, and sent an email to Maggie to see if she knew of another club here. I wasn't gonna go this weekend, but maybe the next time we were in town I would. We were scheduled to head up to New York after Sunday's game, then over to the West Coast for a set in Seattle, then down to Sacramento, before hitting Houston on the way back to New Orleans. It was a brutal road trip, but then we'd be here for a long home stand.

That was the way baseball went, though. Travel was part of the deal, so if I didn't want to travel as much, I'd have gotten a boring desk job. If I had, though, I likely wouldn't have seen Charlie, and that was something I didn't want to give up. Even if I couldn't have her for a while, I still had the opportunity to see her, even from afar. Maybe they'd get me connected to her somehow, and I'd get a taste of that beautiful woman. Fuck, even thinking about her was making me hard again.

My computer pinged with a notification, so I looked at my email and saw that it was from the club. I opened it up and went to the encrypted site they sent me to, logging in with the QR code and my biometric access on my phone.

Saturn:
We trust your evening with us was enjoyable, even with the disturbance. Your request to meet with Charlie has been denied. We trust you understand.

Sincerely,
The Lavender Lounge

"Fuck," I said, not at all happy that she denied me.

I guess I'd just have to figure out a way to get her to change her mind. One thing I knew, though, was she would be punished for her refusal. Of that I was sure.

"WHAT'S UP YOUR ASS?" JP asked.

"Shitty night," I replied.

I'd just walked into the locker room, and was obviously not in a good mood, but I didn't think it showed that much.

"Take it out on the Anglers," he said.

"Plan to," I replied.

"Good," he said, then went back to pulling on his warmup gear.

I did the same, undressing and pulling on my pre-game gear before heading out to do a little batting practice. Nothing fixed my pissed off mood more than smashing balls with a bat. There was a certain set of balls I wouldn't mind smashing, but I doubted I'd even know who they belonged to. Either way, I would just have to take my revenge out here.

It had taken the whole week to get myself used to going to the home team clubhouse, rather than the visitors, which was where I'd always gone. They'd set me up next to JP, since we knew each other from the time he was with San Diego, so at least there was that. I hadn't really talked much to the rest of the team, but that was just the nature of the game. Eventually I'd get to know a few more along the way.

"Hey, Nick," one of the players said, and I turned to look at him.

"What's up?" I asked.

"Just wanted to welcome you to the team," Alejandro said. "Thought we might want to talk about turning two. Maybe do a little practice?"

"Sure," I said.

He was the second baseman to my short stop, so we had to have good communication, especially on those quick turns when the ball was flying and such. There was an art to the double play that a lot of people who had never played didn't understand. We headed out toward second base, behind the screen they had up during BP to keep us from getting hit when we weren't paying attention and began to talk.

"How do you like the ball fed to you?" he asked, and I looked at him.

"I'm usually the one feeding," I replied. "But yeah, I guess low and underhand if possible."

The discussion continued, each of us learning how to work together, taking our time to try out several options. During a game, you never knew how the ball would come, but it was always good to be ready for anything. We'd done fine in the couple of games we'd had, but having this time to actually work things through was very nice. I loved being in control, but knowing that I could work well with my new teammate really helped me feel like I was gonna be fine. The infield coach came out to us about half an hour after we'd begun to see how we were doing.

"You get it figured out?" he asked.

"I think so," I said. "Alej is good, which I knew, but he has this insider knowledge that some don't see. His ideas are great, and I think we'll work well together."

"Hell yeah, we will," my new teammate said.

"Good to hear," he said. "Care to do some practice?"

"I mean, we have been," I said. "You got something you want us to do?"

"Come on," he said, nodding his head toward the outfield.

He had a bat and a bucket of balls, so I figured he'd have some drills to run for us. It was still too early for any fans to be in the stands, so that was nice. We could do our work without an audience. They'd be in soon enough, but for now it was just the rest of the team. By the time we got to the outfield fence, he'd explained his plan on how he was gonna work us.

"You guys ready?" he asked, and we both nodded. "First one to Alej," he said, batting a ball out to my teammate.

Alejandro scooped it from the turf, turned, and threw it to me, where I swiped it as if I were tagging a runner on a base.

"Perfect," Coach said. "Now you."

He then took the bat and hit a ball to me, and I did the same, scooping it up and tossing it to the second baseman who did the same sweeping motion to indicate tagging a runner who was sliding. We ran these drills for a few minutes, then he had us stop.

"Now," he said. "I want you guys to do the foot tag on the base and throw to first instead of just tagging a runner."

"Sure thing," Alej said, and took the first ball that was batted.

I caught the throw, then made like I was avoiding the runner, and throwing to first. Didn't actually toss the ball, just made the throwing motion.

"I wanna see your throw," the coach said. He looked at the fence and then said, "There. Right in the center of that 'O' on the fence. That's your target. That's the first baseman's glove. I want you to hit it every time."

"Got it," I said, then tossed the ball I had to him.

"Okay, let's go," he said, and tapped the ball down to Alej again.

My first throw was dead on, right in the middle of the letter he indicated. He nodded his approval, then hit the ball to me. This would be a bit trickier since Alej would have to make a turn to make the throw. I fed it to him nice and even, right at his mitt, and he turned and threw to our target, hitting it dead center as well.

"Nice," I said.

"Thanks," he replied.

We did that for a bit more, each time either hitting the center of our target, or just slightly off it, where the first baseman would easily be able to adjust.

"Now," he said. "I need you guys to work on your throws from the back side. You first, Hunter."

He hit the ball to my right, where I had to nearly dive to get it, but I snagged it, did a turn, and hit the wall. Only problem? I hit it about three feet above where the mitt we were supposed to aim for was, which would mean it either went past my guy, or he'd have to jump to catch it and miss the tag.

"Fuck," I said.

"Just do it again," Coach replied, and hit another one in the same place.

This time I got it and turned to make the throw, but it bounced in. Not ideal, but better than above the head.

"Again," he said, and bounced a ball at me.

Snagging this one, I turned and threw right in the middle.

"Fucking, finally," I said.

"Nice one," Alej said.

"Thanks," I replied.

"Your turn," Coach said, then hit a ball to the right of Alej.

He reached out and snagged it on a bounce, turned, and threw a strike right in the center of the letter.

"Nice," I said, dragging the word out.

Coach worked us for quite a while before calling it good and sending us back to the infield to grab some actual batting before we went to the locker room to get ready for the game. By the time we got up to the cage, the crowd had started coming in. One of the best things about batting practice was trying to hit bombs over the fence. The balls were lobbed in at just the right height for us to do it, and it was almost more of an adrenaline rush than hitting a home run in a game. Almost.

By the time we got back in the locker room, I was definitely ready to start the game. We all dressed and headed out to the field once the opposing team had completed their batting practice. I headed out to the field to start my stretching and other warmup exercises, knowing the game was gonna start soon. The stadium was fairly full, which is what I expected on a Saturday night, so having that energy coming in was a blessing.

Sunday would be the real test for me. Back in San Diego, Sundays were filled with a sense of pride, having the stands full of service members from all the branches in attendance. It was like I could feel my brother with me on those days. Every day, I'd write his name on some tape and stick it inside my hat, just so I could feel like he was a part of this insane life I'd ended up with. I often thought about what would have happened if he hadn't died. Would I still be a professional baseball player? Or would I have followed in his foot-steps and joined the Corps? I guess that was a question I'd never get an answer to.

"Where you at?" JP asked as I was stretching.

"Home," I said.

"This is home, now," he said.

"Yeah," I agreed. "I guess."

Chapter Ten

C harlotte...

"Hey, are you okay?" Gretchen asked.

"Huh?" I asked, turning to look at her.

"You seem like you're a million miles away is all," she said.

"Oh," I said, looking down at what I was doing. "Sorry, had a busy weekend. Still feeling the aftereffects of it."

"You need to go home?"

"Nah," I said. "I just need to refocus. Maybe some fresh air will do me good."

"Sure," she said.

I stripped off my gloves and tossed them into the bin. I'd been working on a piece that was supposed to be part of an upcoming exhibition, but it had been sent to us in terrible condition. We'd all been working hard to get it ready for its release in just over a week, and I wondered whether it would be done in time.

"Need anything while I'm out and breathing?" I asked.

"No," she said, her head ducked down to work on her own piece.

We couldn't have anything in the room where we worked on the art, which made absolute sense, so I hadn't had anything to drink in about three hours. Walking out of my space, I headed to our lockers to grab my wallet and phone, before walking down the hall to take the elevator up to the first floor to go to the café. I'd taken my smock off and hung it by the door before walking out, so I was in just my jeans and a button-down blouse.

As I stepped off the elevator, I had to do a double take. Standing in front of me, waiting to step in, was Paris. I knew it was her, because of her eyes. The split lip and black and blue marks on her face helped me piece it together as well.

"Hi," I said as I passed her.

She did a double take as well, but then stepped in with the rest of the crowd before the doors closed. I stood there, wondering whether I should follow her, or ignore her as she had done to me. I didn't want to out her or the lifestyle choices she made, but I wanted to check on her, and see if she was doing okay. I watched the lights on the elevator until they stopped on the third floor. I pressed the up button and waited for it to come back down. I had to check on her, to know that she was all right. When the doors opened, she stepped out.

"Come with me," I said, taking her elbow and walking with her toward the café, and restrooms near the back of the museum.

She followed without question, and as we stepped into the café, I knew it wouldn't work to talk there, so I turned us around, and moved to the courtyard that was much less busy. There were a handful of tables scattered around, and that it was summer and warm, many of them were occupied. I took us to one along the far wall where we were away from anyone that might overhear.

"How are you?" I asked, and she kind of just shrugged.

I gave her a pointed look, and she finally spoke, but her voice was harsh and gravelly.

"I'm fine," she said.

"Did you get checked?"

"I'm not doing that," she replied with force.

"Please tell me you took a pill," I said, hoping she'd at least done that much for me, but she shook her head. "Will you get tested?"

"I will," she said.

"Why that, and not the pill?"

"I told you," she said. "They didn't..." She looked around the area, and seeing no one was looking at us, lowered her voice and continued. "They didn't finish in me, so there's no need. Besides, I'm on birth control, so it's not like it would happen."

"Paris," I scolded. "That's not a guarantee. If he was inside you, the little asshole could have left his sperm in there. Not all birth control is perfect, either. You could end up pregnant."

"I don't care," she said, and there was a determination in her voice I hadn't heard before. "I'm not going back there, so no one will know."

"What about River?" I asked.

"We're through," she said, and I could see a tear slide down her cheek.

"Will you check in with me?" I asked. "I won't ask you more than if you're okay. I care about you. I want you to be happy. Even if it means you don't come back to the club. I still want you to check in with me. Will you do that?"

She hesitated, and I was sure she was gonna refuse, but then she nodded.

"You need anything," I said. "Anything at all, you call me. I won't tell a soul what you need, or even that I've talked to you. Trust me that I'll keep your secrets safe."

"I know," she said, because I'd proven that in the past.

"I mean it," I said. "I will help you however I can. All you have to do is reach out. Okay?"

"Okay," she said.

"Rachel," someone called, and Paris turned her head.

"Shit," she said under her breath.

"I'm just helping you find something," I replied, holding a brochure I always had copies of with me out on the table. "So that's where the Louisiana art is located," I said as the person came to our table.

"Thanks," Paris, or rather Rachel, said. "Can I take this with me?"

"Sure," I replied, handing her the brochure. "If you have any more questions, please let me know."

"Thanks," she said again.

I hoped she would accept my offer of help. It was like something inside me knew she was gonna end up in a bad place, and I didn't want that for her. Hell, I didn't want that for anyone, but she was so young, so naïve, and so trusting. It broke my heart at what happened, and I wished I could undo it, but that just wasn't gonna happen. All I could do was offer help, and hope she'd take it.

Pressing my fingertips into my eyes, I took a deep, cleansing breath, and let it out slowly. Getting up, I went back to the elevators, and down to my workstation.

"That was fast," Gretchen said.

"Yeah," I replied. "I'm not feeling the best, so I'm gonna go home. You good with that?"

"Sure," she said. "I'll let Frank know if he asks."

"I'm gonna shoot him a text," I replied.

Picking up my stuff from my locker I felt my phone vibrate, so I looked at it, and it was a message within the club system. Instead of answering it, I stuffed it into my purse, then headed out to my car to head home. I'd driven my ordinary, boring, very not flashy car today, just not feeling the need for driving Ruby, so I didn't have to wait for a top to go down before getting on the road.

Traffic was light, and the drive home was uneventful. I'd sent a text right before I left, and Frank had responded right away, telling me I was good to go on leaving early. I knew it would be fine, but it was always good to make sure your boss knew what was up. Not that I needed to work, but I liked it, and wanted to keep doing what I was doing.

The door to my garage opened, and I drove inside, clicking the button to close it behind me, after shutting off the car. I climbed out and headed inside, unsure why I was feeling out of sorts, but figured it was just the fact of seeing Paris again and all the emotions that brought up. I just wished I'd be able to find out who did it, so they could be punished, and not in the fun way, either. I had to trust Lucifer to do that for us, but it was so hard to relinquish that control. Even when I was being a submissive, I always had control. At least I liked to think I did. It was something that was a fact within the world I was a part of and was where I'd felt at home for about half my life.

At sixteen, my boyfriend and I decided that it was a good idea to lose our v-cards to each other. The problem was, he was having a hard time lasting, and nothing he did would even come close to giving me anything that felt good. He tried everything to get me worked up, but it was kind of just silly to me, and I kept ending up giggling, which just made it worse. We decided to give up that weekend and planned to try again later. My parents had planned my debutante that year, and it was killing me waiting for it. It was why Robert and I had tried to get this little thing out of the way before then.

Growing up in the upper class, going to all the right schools, all the right parties, with all the right people, made me feel like my life was destined to be boring. When Jack showed up at a party I was at, everything changed, and I've never looked back. He was the friend of the older brother of one of my friends and had come by the party to hang out with him. The minute I saw him, I was lost. Tall, strong, obviously from the wrong side of the tracks, and oozing sex appeal. He knew exactly what he was doing, too, because he played cool, like he didn't even notice me, when I knew he did.

Just thinking about him, even twenty years later, made me squeeze my thighs together, and clench my ass cheeks. He must have known we were all underage, because he never even spoke to me. I'm sure I looked desperate, and it must have come off me in waves, because he did everything he could to avoid me at that party. I'd asked Kelsey about him, but she thought he was a jerk, so she was of no help.

Try as I might, I didn't get a chance to lose my virginity before the ball, and it was not lost on me that it truly was a coming out party, as if my parents were finally offering me to the world as a virgin sacrifice. It took two years before Jack would even look at me when I was looking at him. We saw each other all the time, what with him being friends with the older brother of my best friend at the time, and every time he looked at me, I melted.

Finally, after what felt like forever, he said hello, and that was the end of me. He teased me, told me I was too young, that I wasn't experienced enough, that it would never work between us. Everything he said, though, just made me want him more. About a week before graduation, he met me in City Park. He'd been very secretive about what we were going to do but had given me instructions on what I was to wear, and what I was specifically not supposed to wear.

I'd told my parents that I was going out with some friends to get some pictures for the senior presentation, which was why I had to wear my uniform. The fact that I didn't have panties on, and that I had other things in my bag besides my camera, were none of their business. He'd told me to meet him by the singing oak. It was far enough away from most of the active areas of the park, but not so secluded that I'd feel afraid.

When I got there, he was leaning against the tree, looking like all of my fantasies wrapped up in a nice leather jacket. I stumbled as I got close, not really able to contain my excitement. He was all I thought about, all I dreamed about, and my entire fantasy, all standing there just waiting.

"Hey, babe," he'd said.

"Um, hi," I'd muttered, feeling the blush rush all the way up to my hairline.

After an awkward conversation, he'd told me that while we did what we did, he would call me Charlie. It was the first time anyone ever thought of changing my name or giving me a nickname. He'd told me that if he used that name, it meant that he was in control, that whatever he said would be a demand, not a request, and that we had to set up specific rules before he would even touch me.

Of-fucking-course I agreed, and readily at that. I was itching to touch him, or rather for him to touch me, and all the talking was driving me insane. That's when he told me to stand still, and when I didn't, he reached his hand around, and swatted my ass, hard. I yelped, did a little jump, but then just stared at him. He was looking back at me as if daring me to say anything.

It was the first time in my life that anyone had ever struck me. I wasn't spanked as a child, wasn't hit at all, and nothing like that happened within my life. Some of my friends had talked about it happening when they were younger, but it was an all-new experience for me. What was weird was that I liked it. Really liked it, in fact.

His next command was a bit more direct, in that he told me he would punish me if I didn't follow directions, but that we had to have some rules. He'd reached out and grabbed my hand, pulling me to him, and I went willingly, loving the fact that I was actually touching him. The hand that wasn't in mine reached up and tipped my chin up so that I was looking up into his dark eyes, so full of all sorts of emotions, most of them I wouldn't have a name for until I'd experienced many more things.

Leaning down, at an excruciating pace, he put his lips just a hair's breadth from mine, not touching me at all. I wanted to press up and close the distance but wasn't sure what he would do if I did. My eyes were locked on his, waiting patiently for him to do whatever it was he was going to do, which I desperately hoped would be to kiss me. Licking my lips, I pulled my lower lip into my mouth, biting it to keep it still. The hand under my chin reached up and pulled down, moving my lip from inside my mouth.

"Don't do that," he'd said.

I'd nodded, but he wouldn't accept that, and told me to use my words, so I'd said, "Okay."

"You will use the word Sir when you address me," he'd said.

"Okay," I'd responded, but then he looked at me, an eyebrow raised, and I added, "Sir," to the end.

"Good girl," he'd replied, and my heart had burst into butterflies that migrated to my stomach, and even lower.

He stepped away from me, then tugged me to his side, and slung his arm around my waist. I followed suit, doing the same. He guided us along the walkway, my backpack slung over my opposite shoulder. The walk was nice, but it really wasn't enough, and I began to feel frustrated at the lack of anything intimate, including a simple kiss.

Walking along the paths in the park, we finally ended up at its edge, crossing to the other side of the street before going over the bridge across the canal at the edge of the park. I'd asked where we were going, only to receive a swat on my ass. It took me a bit by surprise, but I wanted this. No, I needed this.

When we got to one of the many cemeteries in the city, I wasn't sure what to make of it. I mean, it was closed by the time we got there, because they closed so early. It wasn't like we were there at midnight, but more like late evening. While the sun hadn't set, it was dipping toward the horizon, and evening was definitely setting in. I wasn't the least bit superstitious, but it sort of felt like it would be a bit sacrilegious to go in there when we weren't going to visit the dead. I hesitated when he pulled me up against the fence, which earned me another swat on my ass.

"It's fine," he'd told me. "My family is in here, so if anyone asks, I can tell them the truth, we were visiting them."

I didn't move, so he looked at me, and I could feel the disappointment coming off him in waves. The last thing I wanted to do was disappoint him, so I went with him up to the fence. I wasn't sure how he was gonna get us in, but I'd come this far, so I figured I might as well keep going. It was for sure that if I didn't go along with him, he wouldn't do anything with me, and I'd miss out on experiencing sex for the first time with him, which was really what I wanted.

He'd tossed his leather jacket over the top of the fence, used the bottom railing to get him leverage enough to get him over the top. Using the edge of one of the crypts as a balancing agent, he reached down an arm, and offered it to me. It only took a moment for me to reach up to grab it, pulling myself up the same way he had, with the railing. Once I was up to the top, he helped me steady myself with the crypt before dropping down behind the fence.

When he looked up at me, he smiled, and I realized he could see up my skirt, and with me not wearing any panties, could see absolutely all of me. I flamed with embarrassment and moved to get down, but he pressed his hand against my leg, holding me up in the air above him. He'd said he wanted to enjoy the view for just a moment before he let me down. I stood there, embarrassed to my core, for an eternity until he finally let me get down, helping me so I didn't impale myself on the top of the fence.

His praise and telling me what a good girl I was just fueled the fire burning in me, and racing to my pussy, causing it to weep. I was embarrassed by the feeling of wetness there but would soon learn to love that feeling.

Tugging me along the walkway through the crypts, rising high on either side of us, as we moved toward the middle of the sacred space. Cutting along a pathway, we went closer to the center of the tombs, always moving closer to the back. Eventually, he pulled me between a couple of the larger stone structures, and into a sort of courtyard that was nearly surrounded by them, hiding the space from anyone who wasn't standing in there with us, which meant we were utterly alone.

There was still enough sunlight that it wasn't creepy, but we were standing in the middle of a field of dead people. Not under our feet, but all around us, and it wasn't lost on me that Jack may not be who I thought he was. Me and my fucking need to be so damn independent, adding to the desire to have my virginity removed, put me in a position of danger, and that fear was pressing against my chest, causing me to start breathing quick, nearly panting.

"You want to stop," he'd said, then pinned me with a look that said to listen carefully. "You say Santa."

I laughed, but quickly sobered up when he didn't join in.

"I'm serious," he'd said. "If you can't speak," he added, and I sucked in a breath. "You snap those pretty little fingers of yours."

I nodded, but he didn't move, once again giving me a look that said to answer him with my words.

"Yes, Sir," I said, desperately hoping it was the right answer.

Jack pulled me to him, kissing me hard, one hand at the back of my head, the other at the small of my back. It was punishing, and I couldn't get enough. His tongue pressed against my lips as his hand pulled my hair, causing me to open my mouth, which he savagely devoured, thrusting his tongue in and out, tangling with my tongue as I navigated this new experience. Somehow, he'd backed me up against one of the solid structures we were surrounded by, and pressed his knee between my thighs, raising it enough for it to press against my pussy, the rough material of his jeans doing strange things to me.

The hand that had been at my back slid down and pulled my skirt up further, as he leaned in against me, then delved between my legs, sliding along that most intimate part of me in quick motion. My arms had come up to go around his neck, holding him to me, as I angled my hips to get more pressure where I thought I wanted it. His hand stopped and pressed my hips against the wall, his mouth pulling off mine.

"Stay put," he'd said, and the look he gave me melted me even more. "You do what I say, otherwise you are still. Do you understand me, Charlie?"

"Yes, Sir," I'd said, my body freezing where he'd put me.

"Good girl," he'd said, then stepped back a bit.

My arms went to my side as he stood away from me, looking me up and down, taking in what I was wearing, and how my body was positively buzzing with anticipation. Stepping closer, he reached up and began to unbutton my top, taking each button at an excruciatingly slow pace, his eyes never leaving mine as he watched my expression at his movements. I licked my lips, and pulled the bottom one into my mouth, biting down on it when he stopped, reached up, and pulled my chin down, making the lip pop out.

"I said don't do that," he'd said.

"Sorry, Sir," I'd replied.

God, he was so focused on me, it was wonderful. His hands went back to unbuttoning my shirt until he reached the waistband of my plaid skirt. He'd told me not to wear a bra, along with the no-panties rule, so I was nearly naked as he pushed the blouse up onto my shoulders, exposing my chest. His lips turned up in a crooked smile, and he reached into his pocket, pulling out a chain with something at either end.

I'd never seen anything like it and was surprised as he slid one hand to the end, squeezing the clamp that was there. The black rubber was a sharp contrast to the shiny silver of the chain, and I was curious as to what he was going to do with them. His other hand came up to my throat, sliding along it to the back as he leaned in close.

"If it's too much," he'd said. "I want you to tell me. I don't want to hurt you, but I want to ensure you enjoy this. Okay?"

"Yes, Sir," I'd said, unsure what he was planning.

The hand at my neck slid to the front, then dipped down along my sternum until it reached my breasts, where it veered to my right one, and his palm skated across my nipple, eliciting a gasp from me. He kneaded the flesh there, squeezing it in his strong hand, causing me to feel that dampness increase between my thighs, which I squeezed together. Jack stopped what he was doing and slid his knee against my pussy lips again, effectively separating my thighs. The look he gave me was one that brooked no argument and demanded obedience.

When I'd stilled sufficiently for Jack, he resumed his attention to my breast, kneading it again, which caused my nipple to peak, pressing against his palm. His smile returned as his hand slid along the fleshy part of my breast until it met my nipple, pinching and rolling it between his thumb and forefinger, pulling it away from my body, causing me to gasp and lean my head back against the stone behind me.

He pinched the clamp in his other hand, and brought it up,

sliding it behind his fingers that had pulled my nipple out as far as was likely possible, letting it close slowly on that tender flesh. I sucked in a breath as it tightened, but it didn't get too tight, and he watched my face for a reaction that indicated pain.

"You good?"

"Yes, Sir," I'd said, sucking in a sharp breath as he let go of the end of my nipple.

The cool of the chain bouncing against my stomach was an odd sensation. He repeated the process, first kneading, then pulling, then squeezing and rolling, until he brought the other end of the chain up to clip the clamp on the other nipple, using the same care as I winced initially, then relaxed into the tightness of it on my tender skin. I'd desperately wanted to squeeze my thighs together but didn't dare move. Instead, I'd stood there, legs apart, arms to my side, my nipples clamped and open to the air, and Jack gazing at me from just out of reach.

Licking his lips, he stepped closer, gently kissing me, then letting his lips trail down my neck, between my breasts, skipping over the chain hanging between them, until he was on his knees in front of me. I had no idea what he was going to do but couldn't wait. His palms slid down the length of my skirt to my thighs before pushing the material up and tucking it into the waistband, exposing me to his view. The cool air that was finally settling over the city was blown in, causing me to give a little shiver as it caressed the wetness between my legs.

Pressing my knees apart a little bit more, I slid down the wall slightly, my hands against the stone to keep myself upright. His head dipped closer, another swipe of his tongue across his lips, before coming into contact with my pussy, the tongue slicking out to slide along the slit there. My eyes rolled back in my head at the sensation. I'd done some fondling of myself, but this was so much better. He sucked me into his mouth, pulling all my focus to a single point of contact, and it was absolutely glorious.

Thinking back on it, even this much later, still gave me a thrill.

Nothing had ever been as good as the first time, but he'd opened me up to so many things that I had to appreciate all he did. A hand on my hip, his fingers pressing against, and then into me, and the way he pulled on that chain clipped to my nipples, all worked together in a rhythm I'd been swaying to since that one moment.

It was swift and sudden, that first orgasm, and my knees nearly gave out, barely able to hold myself upright with the waves rushing through me. He'd kept a punishing pace, finger fucking me while sucking on my clit, and pulling on that damn chain, and I almost wanted it to stop. Almost.

When I felt like I was more or less back to myself, he stood up and kissed me. It was the first time I'd tasted sex of any kind, and it was my own flavor he was thrusting into my mouth. When he pulled back, he smiled as I licked my lips, taking every bit of that taste into my mouth.

"You're such a dirty little girl," he'd said, but the smile on his face told me that was a very good thing.

"Yes, Sir," I responded.

"Do you want me to fuck you?"

"Yes, Sir," I said, and could hear the desperation in those two words.

He chuckled, his hand running down my body to the chain that was attached to it. He pulled on it, pulling my nipples hard away from my chest, and I sucked in air at the sensation. My whole body was tuned up, and so sensitive that I was sure I'd been ready to combust on the spot.

"First," he said, letting the chain drop. "I think I need to fuck that naughty mouth of yours."

He put his hands on my shoulders, pressing me toward the ground. I went, finally landing on my knees in front of him. The crypt was at my back, but I was far enough away from it that it wasn't actually touching me.

"Undo my pants, Charlie," he'd said. "Very slowly."

He was close enough that I hadn't needed to extend my arms far, reaching up to work his belt from the loop it was held firm in. My eyeline had me looking right at his cock, and it was pressing against his jeans. The fact that it was so big, or at least what I'd considered big at the time, gave me a little fright, but I was in this for the whole experience, and I wouldn't shirk this responsibility he'd given me.

Pulling the tongue of the belt free, I pressed it back to get the metal bit out of the hole it was in, then slid the leather out of the metal ring. Once it was fully out, I grabbed the button at the top, pressing it through the hole to release it. I gazed up at him from below, and he was watching me intently, and all I'd wanted to do was please him in that moment. I grabbed the zipper in my fingers, holding his jeans at the waist, and pulled it down. I wanted to go fast, but remembered he'd told me to go slow, so I went as slow as I thought I could. When it reached the bottom, I stopped and looked up at him again, waiting for more instructions.

"Good girl," he'd said. "Now, reach inside and pull my dick out."

Sliding my hand into the fly of his jeans, I realized he wasn't wearing any underwear, which was very exciting for me. Everyone I knew wore underwear, so this was all new to me. It wasn't hard for me to find his dick, as it was right there just begging for attention. Pulling it free, I got my first look at it, and yeah, it was much bigger than Robert's had been. He shuddered a breath, then looked down at me again.

"Let go of me and open that pretty little mouth of yours, Charlie," he'd said, and I did as he told me to, releasing his cock and opening my mouth. "Wider," he instructed, and again, I followed directions.

His hand ran up and down the length of his dick, as I'd seen Robert do when we were trying to figure the whole sex thing out a couple years earlier, except Jack was taking it slow and going from the base all the way up to the tip. The hand he wasn't using on his dick went to the top of my head, holding me in place.

"I want you to take as much as you can, Charlie," he'd said. "Open that mouth and let me fuck it. You know what to do if you need to stop?"

I nodded, but he used the hand on my head to sort of make me pay attention.

"I need you to use your words, Charlie," he'd reiterated. "I can't know what you're thinking or feeling if you don't tell me. So, what do you do if you want me to stop?"

"I say Santa, Sir," I replied.

"And if you can't talk?"

"I snap my fingers," I said.

"Good girl," he said, stepping closer to me.

His cock was right there, right in front of my face. I'd seen dicks, had even sort of given Robert a blow job, but this was so much different. He was longer and thicker, and he was so much more in control that I was both terrified and excited. He sort of flicked his dick on my mouth, not putting it in, but sort of sliding it along my lips. Maybe he was testing the waters or something, seeing if I'd back down from it, but I was doing this.

"Mmm," he hummed, then slid it inside my mouth.

I could taste the precum on the tip as it slid over my tongue, then felt the steel wrapped in velvet as it went further. He didn't push it in too far before pulling it back, then pushed forward again, a little farther the next time. This repeated, slow and steady, but not too terrible. He had a hold of my head but had slid his hand from on top to the back. It only took a few strokes before he was pushing against the back of my throat. He didn't stay there, just hit it and pulled back.

After a few times, though, he held my head where it was, pressing against my throat, cutting off my air supply. I could feel my lungs start to burn a bit, but then he backed off. I rolled my eyes up to look at him, and he was watching me intently.

"You okay?" he asked but didn't pull his dick out. I nodded, but then he said, "One snap for yes, two for no."

I snapped once, so he pressed into me again, holding me where I was, as he again cut off my air supply, nearly causing me to gag. God, that would be awful to vomit on him. He pulled back again, then pressed forward. This dance went on and on, him shutting my throat down before allowing me to breathe again, and it was exciting. The whole time he was watching me, looking for signs that I was going to give up or something, but that wasn't going to happen.

After a while, both too long and not nearly long enough, he pulled out of me completely, letting his dick just sort of hang there in the night air.

"You're such a good girl," he said to me, pulling me up on to my feet. "So good that I'm going to reward you. Would you like that?"

"Yes, Sir," I said, even though I had no idea what he was going to do for that reward.

"Turn around, Charlie," he said.

I did as instructed, turning my face toward the crypts that had been at my back the entire time. I hadn't seen it before, but there was a little step at the bottom of one of the crypts next to where we had been standing. He shifted me toward that one, then pressed a hand between my shoulder blades, forcing me to bend over.

"Hold on to that, Charlie," he said. "Don't let go and don't stand up. Do you understand me?"

"Yes, Sir," I said, grabbing the stone slab under my hands.

I could see between my legs and watched as he squatted down, a smile playing across his lips. He slid his hands up my legs, under my skirt, and pushed it up and over my ass, leaving me exposed to the whole wide world there in that cemetery. His hands came down to the globes of my ass and he squeezed, holding them tight as he moved his head forward.

"I'm going to fuck you with my tongue," he said. "And you're going to come all over my face. Then I'm going to finger fuck you, and you're going to come again. After that, you're going to take my cock in that tight little pussy of yours and I'm going to pound into you until you come again. Are you okay with that, Charlie? Do you want me to make you come?"

"Yes, Sir," I said, the words coming out in a rush.

"That's a good girl," he said and proceeded to tilt his chin up and follow through on his threats.

His tongue was magic, sliding in and out of me, and it didn't take long until I made that tumble, nearly losing my grip on the stone, but remembering that he'd told me to hang on. He'd barely let me come back to myself, before first one finger, then another slid inside me, stroking in and out at a rapid pace, his thumb coming up to rub on my clit, running circles over the sensitive nub. I was so enveloped with the feel of it that I didn't even realize I was coming until my orgasm took me over. My hands moved forward, pulling my body slightly away from him, but he persisted, pumping in and out of me as my body fell apart and came back together again.

Just as I was feeling like I could breathe, he swatted my bare ass, and I yelped and looked back over my shoulder at him standing behind me.

"You moved," he said. "I told you to stay put, but you moved. I had to punish you, Charlie. I know it isn't always pleasant, but I had to. Do you understand why?"

"Yes, Sir," I said.

"Tell me," he demanded.

"I moved," I said. "You told me to stay still, but I moved. I'm sorry, Sir."

"Good girl," he said. "Now, are you ready for me to fuck you good and proper?"

"Yes, Sir," I said, and didn't even try to hide the desperation in my voice.

He nodded once, then I felt his dick against my body, sliding up and down the slit at my center, picking up the moisture that was there from my orgasms and his mouth, until it slipped inside me and I sighed. It was barely in there, just the tip, but it was inside me, and that was all that mattered.

"This is gonna hurt for a minute," he said.

Then slammed into me fully, and I felt a pop inside me, a shooting sense of pain, but it all went away as he reached around the front of me and pulled on that damn chain. He had his thumb hooked in it, and it was pulling toward him, the chain long enough that it reached the top of my pubic bone. His fingers went further down, circling my clit as he pulled on the chain, and slid in and out of me, and all the sensations exploded at one time, my eyes rolled back in my head, my hands gripped the stone beneath them, and I felt myself pushing back into him as he slammed into me over and over and over again.

Stars burst behind my eyelids, and a noise I'd never heard escaped my throat, as the rapture consumed me, and I died the little death that I'd only ever read about. The other ones Jack had bestowed upon me were wonderful, but they paled compared to this one, and I would treasure that moment forever.

Even now, in my mid-thirties, I wanted to experience that again, but I knew it would never compare. Same guy, same location, everything else the same, it would never be my first, and that made me a bit sad.

I remembered he was holding me in his lap when I came back together, and stroking my hair, kissing my temple and telling me what a good girl I was, but I didn't remember how we ended up like that.

"I'm so proud of you, Charlie," he'd said. "You did so good."

"Thank you, Sir," I'd said without even thinking about it.

I would always be grateful to Jack for teaching me all the things he did, but especially for giving me the most epic night I'd ever had. With the memories fresh in my mind, I found myself standing in my bathroom, looking in the mirror, but seeing the eighteen-year-old version of myself, instead of the thirty-six-year-old one. Double the age, but so much more experienced than just those years would indicate. I was very much a different person than I had been that night in the St. Louis cemetery where I lost my virginity, and I was not at all upset about that.

Chapter Eleven

Nick...

The games on Saturday and Sunday were played with me pissed at the entire world, but it helped me in the box, having gone seven for eight with three home runs, two doubles, and ten RBIs. I definitely used those emotions for my benefit. It was Monday, and we were riding the bus to the stadium in Seattle. Whoever said it rained all the time here was an idiot. Sure, there were times in the spring that we would get some rain, but they had a retractable roof, so they could just shut it if needed.

Every time I'd been up here, though, it had been nice, sunshine and a few scattered clouds at most. We'd arrived late, and I was not at all ready to head into the stadium, but here we were. While it was definitely late enough, being about noon when the bus headed out, I certainly didn't get enough sleep.

We'd get our work in before the game, hitting in the cages and fielding out between the lines, but I'd much rather have slept a little longer, to be honest. Especially since my dream consisted of me bending Charlie over that desk in the club and fucking her. It was like I was obsessed with her or something, which did give me pause to consider it, but I just chalked it up to not getting my dick wet in any real way other than the shower.

I wanted her, sure, but I supposed it would have been fine if it were someone else, too. I'd take Maggie if it came down to it, but my real desire had blond curls up top and down below, and I wanted to see whether I could make her scream my name. Not the fucked-up one they'd given me at the club, though. No, I wanted to hear her actually say my name when I fucked her. I wasn't Saturn or any other name they decided to give me, but I understood the need for that anonymity. Especially with the number of people who were high profile that I actually recognized there that night.

It was like a dirty little secret that everyone knew, but no one talked about. The number of scandals that would come if anyone in that club named names was galactic. Being new in town and having known that my tattoos would give me away, I'd covered my arms to ensure secrecy on that front, but that could change if I got into something specific.

I usually wore a sleeve similar to what some players wore during a game, the compression ones for injury, but I would just use one to cover my tattoos when I'd go into clubs, but I had simply worn my suit with a long-sleeved shirt that first night. It wasn't something I ever wanted to get caught at. Not that I was ashamed, more like it was too much of a headache to try to explain that what I did with other consenting adults was no one's business but ours. Unfortunately, most folks wanted all the juicy details because it was titillating for them.

I'd never seen any type of scandal from a club, per se, but there had been that one time a few years ago when a girl snuck into one of the Seattle player's hotel room. It was front page, and he had to deal with all that shit for weeks. Even after it came out that it was totally the girl just trying to make herself into some sort of groupie or whatever. That was something I never wanted to deal with, so I did my best to keep my identity a secret, and why I never told any of the guys on the team about my extracurricular activities.

"You're thinking pretty hard," JP said.

"Just tired," I replied. "Nowhere near enough sleep for this bullshit."

"Yeah," he said. "I feel that."

We'd gotten off the bus and were already almost to the locker room. They'd put me next to him in New Orleans, and it looked like that continued for visiting clubhouses as well. I didn't mind. He was a decent guy who didn't get all up in my business, which was how I liked it. I'd never gone to a club in an out-of-town city but was definitely tempted to see if I could find one here. While I'd done a fine job taking care of myself, it didn't even come close to what I wanted. But finding a club wasn't just a quick search on the internet. They tended to be a bit more private than that. Besides, trying to get there without a car really wasn't feasible.

Nope, I was just gonna have to ride it out until I got back to New Orleans, which, fuck, that was gonna be almost two weeks. Instead of whining about my missing out on play time, I decided to work hard and use that frustration on the field. It had worked well over the weekend, so hopefully it would here as well.

Then again, I could always find a bullpen bunny to at least fuck for the night. They were always hanging around the field, some of which were so obvious, it was silly. Nah, if I was gonna fuck one, I'd find one that didn't try as hard, but showed a clear interest. I mean, it's not like they were in short supply.

Walking out to the field, I was glad I'd grabbed my shades, cause the sun was out in force, and it was too fucking early to be that damn bright. Alej and I had worked well over the weekend, much better than the first couple of games, so I went out to second base to see if he wanted to work more.

"Yeah, sure," he said. "Here or at the wall?"

"I'd rather work with the bag," I replied.

"Sure thing," he said, picking up a ball from the bucket that was there.

We worked on our turns without throwing after the tag, but it seemed silly to do that, so I called over and asked Lowe to join us at his position on first to catch our throws. He agreed, saying he wanted to work on his stretches for catches that miss the mark. Between working on our turns, and then trying to help Lowe with his digs, it took a while, which was good, because it kept my mind off my dick, and how it wasn't getting the attention it should.

Once we felt we were in sync, and Lowe felt comfortable with how the ball was gonna bounce here, we headed up to the cage to do some batting practice. I'd hit here at Cascades ballpark before, and while it was a beautiful park, it was mostly helpful for pitchers, as I'd seen hard hit balls that would have been out in most parks end up in a defender's glove. Don't get me wrong, I love getting guys out, and seeing the outfielders doing it. I just hate seeing my ball get caught when it should be out.

When it was my turn in the box, I stepped around the cage and ground my left foot at the back of the box, then took a couple of practice swings before looking up to Ramirez, our hitting coach who was throwing practice for us, and waited for him to make the toss. First one came in high, so I let it go and waited for the next. This time, it was right in my wheelhouse, but I got up under it and popped it up to hit the top of the cage, nearly hitting me on the rebound. Waiting for the third throw, I thought about how much I wanted Charlie, and the ball ended up going well over the right field fence, and well up into the seats where fans were waiting for them. A couple home runs later and I was stepping out of the box for the next player to take their turn.

"You keep that up, you're gonna be the hero of every game," JP said.

"Yeah, well, I keep being pissed off, it'll keep up," I replied.

"Because of the trade?"

"Nah," I said. "Well, I mean, yeah. Would have been nice to have been informed that they were shopping me around instead of walking off the field to change clubhouses. Not exactly the best feeling in the world."

"Man, I'm sorry," he said. "Totally sucks to get shoved off like that, especially when you had no idea."

"Yeah," I replied. "It's not like it's my life or anything."

"Right?"

I headed into the locker room to get changed for the game since our time on the field was finished, and they were getting all the cages off, and fixing the lines and such. As I was getting into my gear for the game, I heard my phone chime, so I pulled it out and saw that I had gotten a message from the club app they'd had me download. It had all sorts of security features, which kept it from keeping any real information, and had walls up in all the ways that mattered when it came to the cybersecurity of it all, which was why I had even downloaded it to begin with.

Ducking my head down, I opened the message to see that I was again denied a session with Charlie, which just pissed me off one more time. What the fuck was her deal? Did she only do things with people she knew? Because, how the fuck are you supposed to get to know more people if you stay in the same circles? The irony of that statement, and that I'd just been bitching about being traded, was not lost on me, either. But I stood by my thought process of wanting to figure out how to get to her.

"Bad news?" JP asked as he stepped up to the locker next to me.

"Sorta," I said. "Something fell through that I wanted to do. Not the end of the world, just a delay in my gratification, so to speak."

"Ah, yeah, I get it," he said. "You need anything, just let me know."

"Will do," I said, but knew he wouldn't be able to get me what I actually wanted.

Instead of dwelling on the thing I couldn't have, I decided to work toward something I could. I went to another hidden app on my phone and requested someone to meet me at my hotel bar well after the game would be over. I was very specific about what I wanted and let them know that it would be prudent to treat the order properly. After that, I finished getting ready for the game, shoving my phone into the lock box in the locker.

~

"DAMN, MAN," Alej said after I threw the ball to first, completing the double play at the end of the eighth inning. "You're killing it."

"Just happy to be playing well," I said as we walked off the field.

I was set to go up second in the top of the ninth and would likely be facing their closer. We were tied at three, but they would likely bring him in to keep the score the way it was. It would either be him or Kors, and both of them were likely to hit over a hundred on the gun. Because I'd been in the National League, I hadn't faced either pitcher much, so had to watch Brewer when he was up to see what I was expecting, although I was sure I'd get a steady diet of fastballs.

They started showing a train on the big screen, rushing along the tracks, so we knew we would be facing Kors. Honestly, I liked that option better, because from what I'd seen of the guy they called the Guardian, Kors would be a much better bet to hit off. Either way, I was gonna take at least the first pitch unless it was dead center.

Pitchers were a weird breed, for sure, and every one of them, especially those at the back end of the bullpen, had this ego that was bigger than it had a right to be. Sure, they were good at their job, but they were not gods. I never understood the mentality, which was probably why I never did well pitching when I was younger. Hit, sure, pitch, nah, I'll pass.

"Let's do this," Brewer said as he tapped the handle of his bat to dislodge the weight he'd added to it to warm up.

Brewer was good, but being left-handed, he had to watch out for the sinking ball this guy threw. The tape I'd seen on him from earlier looked awful, but at least I had a chance to see how he pitched to my teammate before facing him.

The first pitch was low and inside, bouncing on the dirt, and causing Brewer to have to back out of the box to keep from getting hit. The umpire gave a new ball to the catcher and tossed the first one out of play. Next pitch was up and in, but not so far that it was a ball, so the count was even. Seemed like this guy liked to throw inside, and I wondered whether he'd throw the same to me or have it tail away from me instead. He left the next pitch out over the plate, and Brewer swung, hitting it high and far and we watched as it went over the fence, and into the pen in left field.

"Fuck, yeah," I cheered as he dropped his bat, and went around the bases. "That's what I'm talking about."

"Yeah," he said after he touched home plate, giving me a high five. "Hit another one," he said to me before heading back to the bench for his accolades.

I stood just outside the batter's box on the other side of the plate and waited for the catcher to come back from his little conversation with the pitcher. My guess was, that wasn't the pitch he'd called, and he wanted to make sure the pitch-com was working.

"Let's go," the umpire said, then started walking toward the mound.

The party broke up, and the catcher and umpire walked back to the plate, both taking their place behind it.

"He gonna throw the same thing?" I asked the catcher.

"Fuck you," he said, and I laughed.

Digging my foot at the back of the box, I tapped the plate, took a couple swings, then stepped fully into the box, tapping my left toe for balance as my bat was up on my shoulder. Then it was watch the pitcher, see if he tips the pitch, wait for the wind up and throw, then swing. He was taking his sweet fucking time, though, so I asked the ump for a time out, which he granted.

Stepping out of the box, I took a couple more practice swings, tugged my cap a bit, then stepped back into the box to wait. I was balanced, weight on my back foot, front foot keeping me set. The pitcher came set, did his leg kick, and threw the ball in, backing me off the plate and nearly sending me to my ass.

"What the fuck?" I asked, glaring at the pitcher.

"He's wound up," the catcher said.

"Doesn't give him the right to hit me," I argued, stepping back into the box.

"Let's play," the umpire said, pointing out to the pitcher.

Once again, I was waiting, watching, hoping he'd leave one hanging out over the plate enough for me to pull it down the left field line like I'd done before the game. He came set, did his wind up, and made the throw. It looked like a fucking beach ball coming at me, high, out over the plate just like I liked it, and I swung, belting it down the left field line, but it pulled foul.

"Fuck," I mumbled, knowing that might have been the only pitch I'd get to take out of the park.

Stepping into the box, I got back into my position, weight level, feet set just right, bat poised and ready to go, just waiting on the pitcher. My guess was he was gonna either come inside even further than the first pitch or throw it so far outside the catcher would miss it. It was one of those situations where you hoped it was over the plate but had to watch out for it to come inside.

He came set, went into his wind up, and holy fucking shit, he threw another one in the same damn place, and I held back just enough that I got it right on the sweet spot and barreled it up and over the fence out in left field. I dropped my bat and headed around the bases, giving a high five to our first base coach, going past the infield players and around to third to give that coach a high five as well. Crossing home plate, I smacked Alej's hand as he was heading to the plate, before heading into the dugout to get my own congratulations.

It was looking like a win tonight, which made the night nearly perfect. The only thing that would make it better would be the order I'd placed. If it met my expectations, the night would end the way I'd wanted it to last Friday. Thinking about it, and her, just made me want to do this more and more. It was pricey, but if I could make it work, get my mind on straight, then maybe I wouldn't want her as much by the time we got back to town. Maybe I could let the thought of having her go, at least for a little while.

Chapter Twelve

Charlotte...

The week was long and dreary, with nothing at all fun going on. I mean, work was fine, but it was mundane. I felt stuck, like I hadn't really been living, and was looking forward to the club time I had on my calendar. There were several requests for my services, and I selected the ones that I felt would pull me out of my head and into a place of pleasure without thought. I didn't want to teach, and I knew that some of the people who requested me were looking for that, but it was just outside my mental capabilities at the moment.

I was also worried about Paris, and wondering what was going on with her. She hadn't sent an email or text and hadn't called. Not that I had expected it but had hoped she'd at least keep me updated on what was going on with her. Maybe I'd see her or River at the club, and I could ask about it.

"You look deep in thought," Gretchen said as she pulled her gloves off.

I shook my head, not realizing that I'd been all up in my head for so long.

"Sorry," I said. "Did you need something?"

"No," she replied. "Was just wondering if you were gonna head out. It's almost seven."

"It is?" I asked. "Why are you still here?

"I stayed a bit late to finish that piece," she said, pointing to what she'd been working on. "It's almost done, and I thought I could knock it out tonight, but I'm beat."

"You need your rest," I said. "You're growing a whole person in there."

"Pretty amazing, right?" she asked.

"I think it's awesome," I replied. "Good for you for following your dreams and building your family."

"You should probably go, too," she said. "You look tired. Are you sick?"

"Not sick," I said. "Just kind of not quite on my game."

I'd pulled off my gloves, and dropped them into the bucket, walking with Gretchen to the room where all our personal belongings were kept.

"Any plans for the weekend?" she asked.

"Maybe," I replied. "Just trying to figure out exactly what I want to do. How about you? Big plans this weekend?"

"We're telling our folks about the baby tonight," she said.

"I thought you were waiting," I replied.

"We were," she said. "But we're too excited. They're coming over for dinner, both sets of parents, and we're gonna tell them afterward."

"So," I started, but didn't really want to ask the question.

"We thought about that," she said. "I know both of our parents have been anxiously waiting, and we don't want to make them wait any more."

"And if something happens?" I asked, knowing they'd dealt with it a few times already.

"I know," she said. "But they've been there for us every time, so it feels right to let them know now. We talked about it a bunch this week, and we're just too excited. We're telling them they can't tell anyone until we officially announce, but yeah, they're gonna know."

"Well," I said. "I'm happy you're happy. If you need anything, feel free to reach out."

"I will," she said.

We'd made our way out of the working area and were stepping up to the door to go out into the evening air.

"Good night, ladies," William, the night guard, said.

"Good night," I replied.

"Night," Gretchen said.

He let us out of the building, pulling the door shut behind him. We walked to our cars in silence, her likely thinking about the dinner she was heading home to, and me trying to decide whether I should go with my traditional outfit or try something new. I had several outfits I could choose from, but finding the right one for what was going down wasn't always easy.

"See you Monday," Gretchen said as she got to her car.

"Have a nice weekend," I replied, walking past hers and to my own.

As I started my car, I turned the air conditioning on, and waited for it to cool a bit before I closed my door. Once inside, I headed home, through the traffic in and around the museum. Pulling out onto the main road, I looked over toward the cemetery, still thinking about that first night with Jack. Tonight, I wanted to try to recreate what it felt like that first time, so I decided to go with the outfit I'd purchased that resembled my uniform from my school days. Maybe I'd be lucky and find someone that wanted to have an extra session so I could match my memory.

As I pulled into my driveway, the idea of recreating that night was pushing further and further into my mind, and it was nearly enough to push me over the edge. As the door closed on my garage, I stepped into my home, walking through the space with just the light coming in through the windows. Climbing the stairs, I was already removing my clothes, gearing my mind up for what I wanted to do before I even left the house. Yeah, tonight was gonna be a great night.

Kicking off my shoes, I slid my jeans down, my panties going with them, and stepped out of them, then dropped my bra that I had undone on top of the pile after my shirt landed there. I had a stash of toys in the bathroom, so I headed in there and turned on the shower. Opening the drawer with my toys, I looked to find ones I wanted, not quite sure which, but hoping something would pique my interest.

Unfortunately, not a single one of them seemed like something that would help me get over the top. I knew I wanted to use my nipple clamps, though, so went back to my bedroom and opened the drawer they were stored in, taking them with me to the bathroom. The steam was beginning to billow from the shower stall, so I stepped into the spray, setting the chain with the clips on the shelf I'd had built in.

Turning, I tipped my head back and let the water run through my hair, raising my hands to run my fingers through the strands of hair. I pumped some shampoo into my palm, lathering it up before beginning the wash process, pressing hard to massage my scalp as I brought the suds to their full power. Again, I tipped my head back to rinse the shampoo out. I used my facial wash to clean the day makeup off so I'd have a clean slate to start with when I did it for the evening I had planned.

Conditioner went into my hair next, making sure I had it thoroughly through my locks. I grabbed the shower puff from the hook where it hung and got it wet, then turned the bottle with the scented liquid soap over, squeezing a good portion onto the rough material before placing it back on the shelf. The rough material felt nice as I slid it along my body, getting the suds worked up so I'd get clean before I got dirty later.

Closing my eyes, I let it run along my body, feeling it as it slicked down my abdomen, then up and around my breasts, making sure to press the roughness against my nipples to bring them to their peaks, before reaching over and grabbing the chain to clip them. The pressure was too tight at first, so I cranked the screw to loosen them just enough that it wasn't quite as painful.

The coolness of the chain bouncing against my body brought back the memories of my first time again, just making me want to recreate it. I knew it wouldn't be the same, but I wanted to see if I could get that same feeling again. I let the puff slide down my stomach and between my legs, sliding along my cunt, loving the feeling the roughness of it gave me. My legs spread further apart as I scrubbed myself, making sure I was good and clean for the night I had planned.

As much as I wanted to make myself come, I knew that with the late departure from work, I had to hurry a bit, so only enjoyed it for a short time before finishing cleaning myself off and rinsing everything off me, then toweling off, leaving the clips clamped on my nipples. I padded into my bedroom, going to the closet to pull out the outfit I'd decided on. While it wasn't the same one I *actually* wore in high school, it was a good substitute. I set it on the bed, then went back to the bathroom to comb through my hair, and style it.

I was going to go full high school slut, so combed out my hair and pulled it up into pigtails. Usually I left it down, the curls fluffy around my face, but I wanted the experience I'd had so long ago, and while I hadn't worn my hair up that night, I had several times after that. Jack had used them as handles a couple of times, which was fun once I was trained enough to take him all the way to the back of my throat, which he was very patient while doing it.

While I might not get the exact feeling I had that night, I was sure to enjoy myself. The two sessions I'd set up specifically would definitely challenge me, and I needed it. I needed to get out of my head and forget about all the shit that was going on around me. Particularly where Paris was concerned. I would talk to River if I saw him but wouldn't go out of my way to look for him.

Once my hair was pulled up into the bands on either side of my crown, I went back to my room and slid the skirt up and over my body, settling it at my waist. I walked to the mirror, and turned this

109

way and that, just making sure it was decent enough while I was on the street. Not that anyone would say anything, but I didn't want neighbors to complain. They'd gotten used to us all being in their neighborhood, and once they'd realized we weren't gonna fuck with them, they let us be.

Pulling on my blouse, I buttoned it up just enough to keep my nipples covered, then walked back to the mirror. It was very snug, and the clamps were obvious, but I had absolutely zero fucks to give about that. Satisfied that I was dressed appropriately, I went to my jewelry box and pulled out the black velvet collar that Jack had given me. It had silver tips and clipped nicely around my neck, with enough give that it wasn't tight, the silver cross hanging from the hoop in the front settling just below the hollow of my throat.

Back to the bathroom, I applied some foundation, lined my eyes, added mascara, and slid the clear gloss over my lips. Sitting on the edge of my bed, I slid my feet into my heels, tying the straps along my calves so they'd stay in place. I'd picked my blue and gold mask to match the skirt, and slid that, and my small purse over my wrist, then turned out my lights, and headed back down the stairs. I was driving my regular car tonight, taking advantage of the valet service the club offered. I was simply there to enjoy myself, nothing more. I would do the couple of scenes I'd scheduled, then see where the night took me. Hopefully, with a very different outfit, I wouldn't be quite as recognizable and could bask in that anonymity I experienced when I first joined. I would have to wait and see, though.

Chapter Thirteen

Nick...

My phone chimed as I stepped into the bar. I pulled it out of my pocket, using my fingerprint to unlock the screen. The black bell at the top indicated it was for my order. I stepped back into the lobby, wanting to pull it open and see the picture they said they would send so I would recognize the woman who was coming to meet me.

"Forget something?" JP asked.

I pressed the button on the side of my phone, shutting the screen off.

"Was gonna grab a drink," I said, hoping he wouldn't invite himself to join me.

"I'd join you, but I'm beat," he said and I sighed inwardly. "Some of the other guys are probably gonna come down later, though, so if you wanna be by yourself, I suggest you find a corner booth to hide in."

"I'm just grabbing a drink," I said. "Probably be out of there before they even come down."

"Well," he said, then looked at me. "Watch out for bullpen

bunnies. They're rampant, especially up here. I don't know how they were in San Diego, but Seattle has rabid fans, and some are wild."

"I'm pretty much good on that," I said, trying to keep the smile off my face.

"Just thought I'd warn you," he replied. "Enjoy your night."

"I plan to," I said and watched him walk to the elevators.

Again, I unlocked my phone, then pulled up the notification, typing in the code for it. I clicked on the message, opening up the picture they'd sent me. The girl was fairly young, but it was likely most of them were. She was blonde, but it didn't look quite real, so my guess was that the rug wouldn't match the curtains.

It was also obvious that she had had a lot of work done. Whether that was something the service gave her, or she did it on her own, was neither here nor there. I'd asked for natural, but they may not have had someone to fit my specific request, so they'd found the closest they had. I guess it didn't really matter, so long as she shut the fuck up, and let me do what I needed.

Walking into the bar, I looked around and saw her sitting at the end, a martini glass sitting in front of her. The lips were close to the right color, but she was turned just enough that I couldn't really make out much of her other than the blonde hair, which definitely was dyed. I could see the roots coming through, which meant it had been a minute since she'd been to the salon. Whatever. I didn't plan on seeing her, but using her as the substitute she was.

I moved down the bar, and noticed a guy was sitting next to her, definitely trying to hit on her. She was playing it up, but as soon as she saw me, she shut him down.

"Sorry," she said, and her high-pitched voice immediately grated on me. "My date's here."

Not only was it high, but it was also nasally, which just made it worse. The kid, because I swore he looked no more than eighteen, stood up and looked at me. I saw a flicker of something that looked like he might want to object, but I sort of dismissed him with a look, before turning my attention to what I'd paid for.

"Hi," she said, and it made me second guess my decision.

"Let's go," I said.

"But I haven't finished my drink," she whined.

I dropped a twenty on the bar, making sure the bartender saw it and gave me a nod, then looked at her and said, "I'm leaving. If you want to earn your money, get your fucking ass up, and follow me."

Turning, I walked out of the bar. If she followed me, fine. If she wanted to fuck around, she was going to find out that working for the business she did, she was supposed to make sure that the customer was always right, and right now, she was failing miserably.

I punched the button for the elevator, nearly cracking the plastic that covered the actual button, and waited for it to come down to the lobby from the upper floor it was on. I felt, more than saw, that she came up beside me. She slipped her hand into mine, but I pulled mine away, and glared at her. This wasn't a date, and it sure as fuck wasn't anything other than a business transaction. If she thought she was gonna get a boyfriend this way, she had a whole lot of growing up to do, and I was not the one to teach her. At least not that particular lesson.

The chime indicated that the elevator had arrived, and I stepped slightly to the side, hoping against hope that none of my teammates would be on it. Fortunately, it was empty, and I stepped inside, pressing the button for my floor. She'd come in behind me, and wisely stood on the other side of the small space. It was clear she was still new in this line of work, and maybe, just maybe, she would figure out that some jobs were not nearly as fun in real life as they sounded in theory. I stepped out of the elevator once the doors opened and began to walk down the hall. I could hear her as she sort of clomped behind me. God, what the fuck was I thinking?

Swiping my keycard, I opened the door to my room, then stepped inside. I almost shut it without letting her in, but I'd already paid, so I might as well use her. The perfume she was wearing was too much, but I could handle it. I'd just have to shower afterward, which was the plan anyway. I almost wanted her to shower first, but didn't want this to take any longer than necessary.

"So, baby," she said sidling up to me. "What do you want me to do for you?"

"I want you to shut the fuck up," I said, and it came out harsher than I meant.

"Okay," she said, a worried look in her eyes, as she stepped back.

Yeah, she needed to learn that some Johns were assholes, myself included, and she better get used to it if she was gonna keep doing this.

"Take your coat off," I said, and she hesitated. "Now," I barked, and she let it slide off her shoulders to the floor.

She had worn a corset, but it was blue, not red, and she was wearing stockings, but didn't have a garter belt on. I mean, it was sort of what I ordered, but not completely.

"Take the panties off," I said, hoping that they'd at least made sure I had someone with blond downstairs.

As she slid them down, I realized she was completely bare. Some guys liked that, but I wanted a fucking woman, not a child. She'd stepped out of the panties, her heels catching a bit on them before she stood back up.

"Fuck," I said.

Whatever. I had to get this over with so I could wash her off me and think about the real thing. Maybe I should have ordered something completely opposite, so I didn't try to compare. She stood there, sort of trying to look sexy, but failing miserably.

"Go to the bed," I said, and she turned, and walked that way.

"You gonna..."

"Shut the fuck up," I said, and it came out harsher than I meant, but I couldn't stand the sound of her voice. "Sit on the end of the bed and open that mouth so I can fuck it."

She sat down and did as I told her, opening her mouth to allow me to stick my dick in it. I grabbed the box of condoms I had on the dresser that held the television, and opened it, pulling one out.

"You don't have to..."

"I will wear a fucking condom," I said. "Because I know that it isn't your fault, but someone may have left something behind from the last time someone fucked your mouth. I can't catch anything, so I protect myself."

"Okay," she said, almost sounding sad.

After I tore the package open, I unzipped my slacks and pulled my dick out, stroking it some to get it hard. God, the fact that I couldn't even get hard with her sitting there ready to service me, said all I needed to know. Instead of looking at her, I closed my eyes, thinking back to when Charlie was standing in that den, confident as fuck, not caring that she was standing there without panties on in front of someone she'd never met. Yeah, that made me get there.

Sliding the disk down my hardening dick, I stepped forward to the whore sitting on my bed, and shoved it into her mouth. Her head went back a bit, but I reached out and grabbed the back of it, holding her where I wanted her, pulled my hips back, and shoved my dick into her mouth again, feeling it hit the back of her throat, and her trying to swallow around the head. Fuck, I wasn't even all the way in.

She must not have had much experience, because she sort of pushed against my legs when I held myself there for a bit, watching her eyes roll up to me, the tears starting to fill them. That's what I wanted to see. I pulled back and let her catch her breath a bit, then shoved myself down her throat again, feeling the desperation in her swallowing, and her hands pushing against my thighs. Again, I pulled back and let her catch her breath, watching the saliva drip from my cock as she swallowed, and looked up at me.

Once again, I shoved myself down her throat, this time holding it, until her eyes were fluttering as she tried desperately to breathe around it. I didn't want her to pass out, but I wanted her close, and she became desperate, trying to scratch at me with her hands, but my pants were between her nails and my legs. I let up again and she gagged, coughing around my cock, tears running down her cheeks.

Yeah, this would teach her that this was not a line of work for the faint of heart.

I stepped back, and she looked up at me, the spit dripping down her chin, and onto her legs.

"Turn around," I said, and she looked at me confused. "Get up, turn around, and lean over the end of the bed. Do you understand?"

"Okay," she said, and I gripped her hair, pulling it back, so her neck was at an angle that was definitely not comfortable.

"I said, shut the fuck up," I growled at her.

Her eyes went wide, and the tears started even more. She nodded, as much as she could with me holding her tightly at the back of her head. I sort of shoved her head away from me and she looked at me for a moment, then did as I'd told her to do, standing up and turning around to lean over the bed.

With my right hand, I pressed her head further down so it was against the mattress, then used my foot to kick her feet apart a bit, just enough so that I could line up better. If she hadn't been wearing heels, it wouldn't have worked, so at least that's one thing they got right.

I spit on my hand, rubbing it on the head of my cock, wanting to make sure I wouldn't have to go slow. Parting her ass cheeks with my hands, I could see she was wet, but not enough for what I wanted to do, so it was good I had done what I did. I liked myself up, pressing the head of my cock into her pussy, took a breath, then shoved it all the way in. She made this little mewling noise, and I smacked her ass.

"Do not make a sound," I said, low and next to her ear, as I leaned over her.

She nodded her head, the tears welling up again. I stood back up, pulled my hips back, and slammed into her again. Her grunt wasn't too bad, so I let it go. Pulling back again, I slammed into her, picking up the pace with each thrust. There wasn't the telltale slap of skin on skin, what with me not really taking my clothes off or anything. I saw her move her arm, sliding it up and under her, which just pissed me off even more.

"Don't you fucking dare," I growled and she froze. "You do not get to get off from this. I'm paying, I'm getting relief, you are here to be used. Got it?"

She nodded her head, pulling her arm back from under her, placing it on the top of the blanket on the top of the bed. I resumed my punishing of her pussy, slamming myself into her harder and harder with each thrust. I felt that tingling that indicated I was close, so I closed my eyes, thinking of Charlie and how sweet this would have been if it had been her. Except, if it had, I'd have made sure she got off, made sure she called out my name as she came around my cock. Not this bitch, though. She was just a tool.

Finally, after I got out of my head, I came, filling the condom, until I was sure I was done. Holding the edge close to my body, I pulled out, and walked to the bathroom, pulling it off my dick, and dropping it into the trash can that was there.

"Get dressed and get out," I said from the bathroom.

"But..."

"Did I fucking stutter?"

I looked out the door, and saw her blanch when I said it, then got up, picked up her panties, and shoved them in the pocket of the coat she had, pulling it around her shoulders. I'd shoved myself back into my pants, and came out, opening the door. She leaned up, like she thought I'd kiss her, but must have realized that wasn't gonna happen, and just walked out. I closed the door, flipping the latch at the top, and walked back to the bed.

Taking my clothes off, I tossed them on the bed she hadn't been on, until I was completely naked, then walked back into the bathroom, turning the shower on as hot as I thought I could stand it, then stepped in, letting the spray take the smell of her off me. I grabbed the soap, wetting it before rubbing it over my dick. Even though it wasn't actually touched by her, it still felt appropriate to clean it. Maybe tonight I'd sleep and not dream of the woman I fantasized about. Or, maybe I'd get that notification that she'd said yes.

Chapter Fourteen

Charlotte…

"That's a good girl," Sebastian said.

I'd done the two scenes I'd signed up, but then had run into Sebastian. He'd heard my story, how I came to the club, and what I had wanted, and jumped at the chance to help me recreate it. We weren't in the cemetery; we were in a bedroom. It was different in many other ways as well, but he did his best.

He'd given me the orgasms and had fucked me just the same way that Jack had. First, finger fucking me with my nipples clamped, backed up against a wall. Then bent me over, tongue fucked me, finger fucked me, and then fucked me for real. It was absolutely glorious, and I was exhausted.

"Thank you, Sir," I said, just as I'd thanked Jack so long ago.

"You are more than welcome, Charlie," he said, and I sighed, leaning against him more.

A knock at the door signaled that our time was up.

"You good?" Sebastian asked.

"Yeah," I replied.

He kissed the top of my head, then helped me to my feet, pulling the skirt from its waistband, before opening the door. I'd given up the idea of modesty a long time ago, and had absolutely zero fucks to give when it came to my body, and who saw it. Sometimes I covered up, but most of the time I didn't.

"Hey, you," Apollo said when he saw me.

"Hi," I replied.

"Got time for another thing?"

"I'm heading out," I said. "Been a long night, and a long week."

"Maybe next time," he said.

"Maybe," I replied.

I tended not to make plans for the next weekend at the club itself. It had that pressure of making a decision without thinking it all the way through. I was a planner and wanted time to decide what I wanted to do before being forced into something. As I buttoned my shirt, we walked out of the bedroom, heading down the stairs to the main level.

"Charlie?" I heard and looked up to see River standing in front of me.

"What?" I asked, and it may have been harsher than I intended.

"I can't get a hold of her," he said. "She won't answer my calls or texts, and she's blocked me in the app."

"If you can't get to her through the app, she may have deleted it," I said. "Sometimes that happens. Have you asked Lucifer if she's done that?"

"No," he said. "Everyone is kind of ignoring me."

"I know," I said. "They're putting their anger over what happened in the wrong place."

"No they're not," he said, and it was harsh. "I let her down, didn't protect her. I let this happen."

"Did you rape her?" I asked, and he shook his head. "Then it wasn't your fault. It was the guy who did it. That's where the blame lies."

"I feel like it was my fault," he said. "Since I don't know who it is."

"I know," I said. "I can't make you feel okay about it, and you shouldn't. But you can't keep blaming yourself."

"She trusted me," he said.

"She trusted me, too," I replied. "I wasn't there for her, either. If we could go back, we'd be able to stop it, but we can't. Now, we just have to learn to deal with it. Not a good thing to have to do, but it is what it is."

"Will you help me talk to her?" he asked, and I could hear the desperation in his voice.

"That's not my job," I said. "If she wants to talk, she'll get in touch with you. If I hear from her, I can let her know you want to talk to her, but I can't guarantee that, even if I do hear from her, she will do it. It sucks, and I know that. I wish I had an answer, some way to help you deal with all of this, but I can't. Go to therapy. Talk to someone. Just not me."

I wanted to tell him I saw her, but didn't want to break her confidentiality. She needed a safe place to go with her problems, and I would make sure that I was that safe space for her, if she ever reached out.

Walking away from him as he stood there was hard, but I couldn't do anything to help him. The only thing I could do was be there for her, if she ever reached out. I walked to the back of the house where Lucifer's office was, knocking and waiting for him to open the door. While everyone knew he was in there, we also all knew that we didn't open closed doors. Knocking was enough of an intrusion, so I waited patiently until he finally opened the door.

"Hey," he said, then looked around and behind me before adding, "Come in."

Stepping into his office, I saw all the screens on the wall, watching everything that was happening in the house. I knew he watched, just didn't realize that it was this extensive.

"You want me to turn them off?" he asked as he closed the door behind me.

"No," I replied. "They're fine."

"I'm glad you came," he said, and I wondered if he was going to seek me out if I hadn't.

"Did you find anything?"

"I can't answer that," he said.

"But..." I let the word hang in the air, waiting for the rest of what he was going to say to come out.

"Let's just say that my friends are doing a little digging," he said. "We have everything we need to probably figure out who it was that did this."

"Have you reached out to her?"

"No," he said. "It's on my list to do this week. I didn't want to rush her, and I wasn't sure exactly what my friends might need."

"Okay," I said. "I did see her on Monday."

"How did she look?"

"Like she'd been worked over hard," I said. "I gave her my real contact info and told her to reach out if she needed anything. I know you won't give me anything, but if she asks you, feel free to give her my contact information as well. I'll help her any way I can, no questions asked."

"That's good to know," he said. "If she reaches out, I'll confirm the information she has, and let her know you're available."

"Don't let anyone know I saw her," I said. "I told her I would keep it secret, so even telling you is a breach of that promise."

"You didn't tell me shit," he said. "I'll just say that you told me you would help her if she contacted me. It isn't a lie, so I don't feel like it would indicate you told me you saw her."

"Do you know when you might know anything else?"

"My guys are looking," he said. "When I know something that I can tell you, I will. But you may not ever know anything more than that they were caught and dealt with. This club I work with tends to not really tell me much. They have their secrets just like we do."

"That was my guess," I said. "I just wanted to know what you might know. You know, if I hear from her or anything."

"I will when I can," he said.

I looked up at the monitors and wondered how many hours of sex this man had watched, and whether he had a favorite person, position, or room. I turned to see him watching me, and I got to wonder if he masturbated while watching.

"I've watched you," he said.

"That's not what I was thinking," I replied.

"Ask away," he said with a wave of his hand, opening the floor to me.

"You watch," I said, and he nodded. "Do you want to participate at all?"

"Sometimes," he said. "But not most nights."

"So," I began. "What do you do?"

"That's private," he said. "But I have my own release."

"Here?"

"Sometimes," he said.

"Ever want someone to be with you while you watch?"

I wasn't sure why I was asking. Maybe I felt a little sorry for him, because he didn't participate.

"Never," he said. "But I appreciate the offer."

"If you ever change your mind," I said, leaving the offer unsaid.

I got up and he did, too, opening the door for me so I could step out. River was there, waiting to either talk to me or Lucifer, I was sure.

"I don't know anything," Lucifer said. "And when I do, I will let you know."

"I can't stand this," River said, tears running down his cheeks. "How did I let this happen?"

"You didn't let it happen," I.

"I let it happen more than you," Lucifer said. "My job is to make sure the place is safe. I didn't do that. I'm the failure, not you."

"Neither of you are failures," I said. "The guy who did it just figured out a way to get it done under all of our noses."

"Agree to disagree, Charlie," Lucifer said.

I shook my head. Neither of them was at fault. Were they

contributing factors? Sure. But they didn't do it, and once Lucifer figured out who did, they would be dealt with, of that, I was sure.

"I gotta go," I said, giving River a hug. "If I hear from her, I'll let her know you want to talk to her."

With that, I turned and headed out of the back toward the front of the house. A few people tried to stop me, but I just put my hand up and kept walking. When I got to the front door, Mr. Stone was at his podium, and he turned to me.

"Need your car?"

"Please," I said.

He pressed a couple of buttons on his laptop that was there. Before too long, my car pulled up in front of the house, the valet stepping out of it, and holding the door for me.

"Thank you," I said as I slid into the car.

Once he'd closed the door, I let out a breath, not realizing how tired I really was. At least I didn't have too long before I got home, and driving there was something I likely could do in my sleep. Pulling into the garage, I wondered whether I'd ever know what happened to Paris. My phone chimed, but I honestly couldn't muster any strength to check what it was.

Chapter Fifteen

Nick...

"You're still pissed off," JP said.

"You're not wrong," I replied.

"Thought you might have found something to work out your anger on last night," he said.

"Didn't turn out to be that helpful," I said.

We all found those kinds of things to blow off steam, so to speak, so I was sure he knew I found someone to fuck. What he didn't know was that I was a fucking asshole and had simply hired some woman to be a piece of meat for me to work out my frustrations on. I wasn't exactly proud of what I'd done the night before, so I certainly wasn't gonna go advertising it.

"Well," he said. "Take that out on the Cascades, then. That's where you need to put that energy."

"That's the plan," I replied.

We'd played pretty well the day before, so hopefully that would continue. I hadn't kept up the pace from the weekend in the box, but I did fairly well with a couple of hits and a walk. The plan for this game was to keep it up, maybe think about the fake I'd hired, and how pissed I was at her not being Charlie. That may work, but it may fuck me up, too.

Either way, I knew I had to get my mind in the game, off the stands, and looking toward the rest of the trip. We were only on game two of ten for this road trip, and it was likely gonna be long. It was hot here, which was unusual in some ways, as usually we'd see cooler temps in the Pacific Northwest. I guess the notion that August was the hottest month was true, and we were right at the start of it.

I'd worked with Alej for some more fielding, hit several balls into the stands during batting practice, and was now getting dressed for the game. Hopefully, we'd see another win, and a guaranteed series win overall, but we still had to go out there and do it.

"Hunter," Coach shouted.

"Yeah?" I asked.

"Come here," he said, and I did just that, walking to his office.

"What's up?" I asked.

"Some paper is running a story about you," he said.

"About me, how?"

My spidey senses were tingling, and I wondered if the girl that had come to me the night before may have been a spy of some sort or had told all when she left.

"Sort of a welcome-to-the-city kind of piece," he said.

I wanted to sigh with relief. It wasn't about last night, and it wasn't about the week before at the club.

"I guess that's a good thing," I said.

"Oh yeah," he added. "Our press does love to highlight the sports stars in the city."

"That's good to know," I said. "Never a bad thing to get some good press."

"Keep your nose clean," he said. "Don't need you out there doing shit that'll tarnish your image, or the image of the team. We're trying to run a tight ship in here."

"I get that," I said. "I always try to be a good guy."

The lie fell off my lips easily, and I wondered if I sort of believed it. Honestly, if last night was any sign, I might have to swear off sex for a while, just to be sure I wasn't outed as the fucking pervert I was. If that girl talked to anyone, though, the company I used would be in a world of hurt. Their assured security and secrecy were top-notch, but if anything leaked out, they would likely go under in a heartbeat. While that would be their own fault, in that they hired someone who didn't know how to keep their fucking mouth shut, it would also mean that many of us would lose out on the anonymity of using the service to find what we needed, when we were on the road.

"Well," Coach said. "Get your ass out there and do the job you're paid to do."

"Yes, sir," I said, my upbringing coming out of my mouth easily.

I made my way to the field, after grabbing my gear from my locker. It was gonna either be a great day or the worst of my life, and that all depended on what went on that was out of my control. Either way, my job was to get my ass on the field, and play. Other than that, there wasn't a damn thing I could do. It sucked, but it was what it was. Maybe things would all work out in the end.

"HOLY SHIT," JP said as I came into the dugout. "That was fucking awesome."

"Feels good to hit it out," I said.

"I swear you hit that fucker a mile and a half," he said, clapping me on the back.

We'd been out hit and out played most of the game, and it was the top of the ninth, with the bases loaded, and we were down to our last strike. Somehow, their closer threw a fastball down the middle, just above the belt, and it just sort of sat there waiting for me to hit it, and boy did I. I felt the rebound in my bat after it connected to the ball, and watched as it sailed out over the right field wall. Their right fielder tried to do that thing where they climb the wall to take away the hit, but he just couldn't manage to get ten feet above the wall. There was no way that fucker was coming back.

It was a good feeling to finally have figured out the guy in the league who seemed to be unhittable. Every time this guy was brought out, especially in a save situation, he was lights out. Lowe was up after me, and he struck out, but we were ahead by two going into the bottom of the ninth, and it was a good feeling to know that I'd put us there.

Running out onto the field, we took our positions, Lowe throwing grounders at the rest of the infielders for the warmup while our own closer, Bautista, came in from the bullpen. Over the last few games, I'd watched him work, and had to admit that it was really easy to work behind him. He tended to be a ground-ball pitcher, keeping everything low in the zone, so we had to be on our toes, but that was easy when your head was in the game.

Alej took the throw from our catcher, Harrison, did the swipe across second, then tossed the ball to me. I threw it to Lowe, who threw it back to Bautista. He knelt behind the mound for his moment to prepare, then climbed the bump to get ready to throw. I'd given us a lead, but it was small, and with their power hitter, Huffman, coming up to bat, we had to be on our toes.

"Slider, away," came through the pitch-com in my ear, and I prepared for a ball that may be pulled down the left field line.

That is, if he could find it. Bautista was notorious for burying the ball right behind the right-handed hitter's back foot, not giving them anything to actually swing at, even though it looked like it would sit out over the plate.

Huffman swung over the first pitch, and the umpire called it a strike. Harrison tossed the ball back to Bautista, who took a pinch off the rosin bag to give him a better grip on the ball. Getting himself back to the rubber, he engaged it, then looked in for the sign. Honestly, it wasn't what he was doing, but it was the muscle memory we'd had since little league when pitches first began to be called by a catcher. The pitcher would look into the catcher, and the middle infielders would do the same. Now, though, we had the pitch called in our ears instead of having to watch the signs.

Next pitch was a fastball outside and up, and my guess was that Harrison was hoping the change in eye level was going to mess him up. I wasn't sure that was the best option, but it wasn't my call. Bautista rocked and threw, but the ball sailed way outside and ended up going all the way to the backstop, bouncing back to Harrison. The umpire threw the ball out of play and handed another one to the catcher to throw back out.

Harrison looked to the dugout to get the call, then relayed it through the electronic device to the middle of the field. Another fastball, but this one was supposed to be inside. Not so far that it'd hit him, but closer to where the first pitch landed. The rock and the throw, but it kind of hung out over the plate, and Huffman smashed it.

Up and up the ball went, high into the deepening night sky. I turned to watch as Crawford, our center fielder, ran toward the bullpen fence, keeping his eye on the ball and waving off Brewer in right. He reached the warning track and settled in to catch the ball easily. That was one. Just two more to go and we'd take this game and win the series.

Their designated hitter was up next, and he was a beast of a man. Huffman was big, but this guy was huge. Definitely not someone you wanted to get into a brawl with. From what I'd seen of him, though, indicated he was much more of a teddy bear than a grizzly one. Still, best not to tempt fate when it came to that.

Call was for a slider, and this time it would tail away from the left-handed batter. Pitch happened, and the batter swung, missing badly. Another was called, and I figured Bautista would throw it even further outside. My guess was right, and the batter swung again, spinning himself around in the batter's box without making any kind of contact with the ball. Next pitch was a cutter, which for Bautista, meant it would start just about letter high, and dive as it went across the plate. Sure enough, that's exactly what it did, and the guy swung and missed wildly, striking out.

"That's two," I said, putting my index and pinky fingers up as the ball was tossed around the infield.

Their next batter was the catcher, and he dug his toes into the back of the right-hand batter's box before stepping in. This guy had done well in the game, getting on base by a walk and two singles, including one that drove in the go ahead runs in the bottom of the seventh. He wasn't exactly a pull hitter, but did tend to hit it toward the left side of the field, so we shifted that direction, hoping to keep the ball on the infield to try to throw him out.

Bautista got the call for a fastball outside, and while I knew he could hit his spot, this seemed like a bad pitch to call. Wasn't my job to make that decision, though, so I did what I needed to in order to back up our pitcher. The rock and the throw, and the batter swung, catching the ball just right, sending it up and well out into the bullpens.

"Fuck," Bautista shouted as he watched it go over the fence.

Harrison took the new baseball from the umpire and walked it out to his pitcher, my guess to try to cool him down. We still had a one-run lead, so as long as we kept them in the ballpark and in front of us, we'd likely do just fine in keeping them from getting a run and winning the game. Of course, that meant that our pitcher had to keep his head in the game.

Once the home team had finished their celebration of the home run, we were ready to get back to it, and another of their outfielders was climbing into the box, and we were on for keeping them from getting around the bags. First pitch called was a cutter, which would hopefully either result in a bad swing and miss, or a ground ball we could handle to end the game. I was hoping for the latter so we could get out of here.

Bautista gave his rock, threw the ball, and the batter connected. But it was over the top of the ball, driving it down the third base line where JP scooped it up and tossed over to Lowe who dug it out off the bounce and was on the bag to get the force out, and that was the ball game.

We did our little celebration on the infield while the outfielders did their own, then it was high fives, or whatever other celebration the players had, before we all headed into the clubhouse to shower and climb onto the bus for the ride back to the hotel, which couldn't come soon enough. Unfortunately, because I hit the grand slam in the top of the ninth to put us ahead, the press team that followed us on the road waved me over to do the post-game interview.

"I'm Ashley," she said. "You good for an interview?"

"Sure," I said, standing next to her.

The light on the camera went on and she greeted the audience back in New Orleans.

"We're here with the hero of the night, Nick Hunter," she said. "First, welcome to the Magicians."

"Thanks," I said. "Happy to be here."

I wasn't, but there was no reason in letting the fans know I didn't want to play for their team.

"Walk me through that last at bat you had," she said.

"We knew he was hard to hit," I said. "Everyone in the league knows that. I was just looking for something I could put my bat on, put the ball in play. Fortunately, I was able to get ahold of it and sent it into the stands."

"Since you're new to the league," she said. "This was your first time facing Nakamura. How did you prepare for this?"

"I knew we were coming up here," I said. "I watched some film, but talked to my teammates who'd already faced him. There's nothing to prepare you for that first time seeing a pitcher. You've just got to trust your training, trust your gut, and be prepared for whatever comes your way."

"Sounds like good advice for most everything in life," she said.

"That it is," I replied.

"I'll let you go and celebrate with your teammates," she said to me, then turned to the camera and said, "Back to you guys in the booth."

The light on the camera went off, and she turned to me.

"Thanks," she said.

"Sure thing," I replied, then walked down the steps into the dugout to head down the tunnel to the clubhouse.

The rest of the time at the stadium was spent showering and gathering my shit to head back to the hotel. Once there, I got into the elevator, and rode it up with a couple of the other guys. As I walked down the hall to my hotel room, I wondered whether what the coach had said was true, that they were doing a story about me. Then I wondered whether anything had come out about the happenings at the club the week before.

I thought about doing a search when I got to my room, just to see whether there was anything I could find about it, but then thought that just might bring it on, so I opted to leave it alone, and deal with whatever happened when it actually happened. It wouldn't be the first time I ended up in a position of having to explain something that should really not be anyone else's business. Hopefully, no one would correlate the fact that I was new to the city, and that something terrible had happened there.

Chapter Sixteen

Charlotte...

"What are you talking about?" I asked.

"It's all over the news," Gretchen said. "Everywhere I look, there's something coming out about it. It's just awful."

The weekend had been quiet after I'd gotten home from the club on Friday night. I'd gone grocery shopping, done laundry, and all the other little things one puts off until their day off. What I hadn't done was look at the news or social media. It had been the absolutely perfect way to wind down from the week, especially after everything that had happened the weekend before. Now, though, it seemed everything was coming to a head, and word was getting out about the shit that did go down, and I wasn't sure what would happen.

"I didn't even know there was one of those things here," Gretchen continued, scrunching her nose up in disgust. "Like, what kind of person goes to a club just to have sex? Can't they just find a girlfriend or boyfriend and do it like normal people."

She was coming dangerously close to insulting me and my way of life, but she had no idea I was part of it, so I couldn't blame her.

"I'm of the mindset of, 'live and let live,'" I said. "What someone chooses to do with another consenting adult is none of my business."

"I get that," she said. "I just think that these kinds of places are asking for stuff like this to happen. How could it not when you've got all these worked up people?"

"Pretty sure that happens outside of places like that," I said. "I mean, college is one of the most dangerous places for women, so why aren't you rallying against colleges?"

"It's not the same," she argued.

"But it is," I replied. "Think about when you were in college. Were there frat parties? And if there were, was there sex at those parties? When I was in college, that was normal. If I went to a frat party and got drunk, I probably would have been raped. My choice was to either go and not drink, which was not something that could be guaranteed, go with someone who was my party buddy, and we watched out for each other, or go, and know that I might end up in someone's bed, whether I wanted to or not."

"Okay," she said. "I guess I see your point. I just think that a club that is purely for sex, like this one they're talking about, is just a place for degenerates and horrible people to go and get their rocks off by abusing someone else. It's like prostitutes. How can someone pay someone else to have sex with them?"

"So, what you're saying that sex should only happen within a certain type of relationship?" I asked. "The two people have to be committed to each other in some way in order for sex to happen?"

"I mean," she said, and I got the impression she hadn't really thought this through. "Well, I guess I don't know."

"Here's what I believe," I said. "If someone wants to enjoy sex, they have a few options. They can find a partner, and stay with that partner, and do all the things they want to with them. Another option is to find a group of people who like to do things, and work within that group of people. Or they can pay someone to give them what they want or need in that way. None of those options seem so bad to me. It works for medical providers, for grocery stores, for churches, and most other things."

"Churches aren't like that," she said. "They want to help people."

"As long as the people follow the rules the church sets out," I added. "When someone in the church comes up with an idea that isn't within their rule set, though, it usually ends badly for the person with the new idea."

"I don't know about that," she said.

"What happened to Jesus?" I asked her, knowing that she went to a church, and using my background in theology that partnered with my historical training.

"Well," she hummed. "That was different. He set out to do that."

"Okay," I said. "How about Martin Luther when he nailed his proclamation to the door of the church? Pretty sure they weren't too happy about that."

"I mean," she began. "Religion is always changing."

"Because people question it," I said. "Let's look at something different. The Revolutionary War was all about finding the freedom for the Colonies from King George. That was definitely outside the norm of the time, but it turned out pretty good for us, didn't it?"

"I see that, but..."

"But, what?" I asked. "Humans are always finding things that work better for them. Whether it's a belief system, a political system, or a sexual revolution. You do know that in the early 1970s, a woman couldn't have her own bank account, right?"

"You're joking," she said.

"Nope," I replied. "If you were a woman, and you didn't have a husband, the only way you could have an account at a bank was to have your father be on it with you. No husband or father, you were out of luck. Hell, even now, women aren't paid the same as men. I mean, it's better now, but it's still not equal. Eventually, hopefully, we'll get there. Same thing with sex. If a man has an issue with getting it up, they can just tell their doctor they want that little blue pill, and all is fine. If a woman goes to the doctor and wants to get birth control, they're asked if they're married, what their partner believes, and all that. Forget about getting their tubes tied. Do you know how long it took for me to find someone who didn't try to talk me out of it?"

"You got your tubes tied?"

"I sure did," I said. "I didn't want kids, and had known for a while, but it took forever to find someone who would do it. I had to answer all the questions over and over again, and then was asked if I was sure, and what if I found a guy who wanted kids? They wanted to make sure I knew it wasn't guaranteed to be reversible."

"So, what if you do find someone who wants kids?"

"We either adopt, or we stop dating," I said. "Simple as that."

"I just don't get that," she said.

"What if your husband didn't want kids?" I asked.

"But he does," she countered.

"Did you ever date a guy who didn't?" I asked.

"I don't know," she admitted.

"Okay, let me put it this way," I said. "Let's say your husband was allergic to something like cats or dogs, but you have always had pets, and couldn't see your life without having a pet. I know it's a much different thing than kids, but would you think about it before you got married? Like, you are on your first date, and he said to you that he's allergic, so he can't have them around."

"I mean, I guess I'd just go without them," she said. "Because I love my husband."

"I don't think you're getting it," I said. "Who was your first boyfriend?"

"Tobias Williams," she said, a smile crossing her lips.

"Okay," I said. "So, when you first decided you liked him, was there anything that stood out about him?"

"He was just really cute," she said.

"Now," I continued. "Let's pretend you're on your first date with Toby, and you ask him what his plans are for after school. Was it in high school?"

"Yeah," she said. "And he said he was going to be moving to Florida for college."

"Good," I said. "So, why didn't you move, too?"

"Because I didn't want to leave New Orleans," she said.

"There you go," I said. "So, you knew that moving to Florida wasn't for you, so you ended the relationship. Same thing would happen with me if a guy I was dating was determined to have kids. That's not my life plan, so it wouldn't work. No use in stringing him along if it isn't gonna go anywhere."

"I get it," she said, and had that epiphany look on her face.

"I knew you would," I said.

"But what does that have to do with this club?"

"I guess the same thing would apply," I replied. "Let's say that a guy I want to date wants to go to that club, and I don't. I wouldn't stay with him if that was his plan and not mine. It's the same as kids, or pets, or school, or any other major life choice. I work because I like it, but if a guy I was dating was angry about it, or didn't want me to work, I'd have to rethink that relationship. Even if it didn't matter whether I worked or not."

"I think I get it, now," she said. "So, some people like to do those kinds of things, and since there are so many of them, they just made a club for them all to do that stuff there."

"Sounds like it," I said, not wanting to confirm I knew more than what she thought I did.

"I guess it is kinda sad, then," she said.

"Yeah," I replied. "It's never the victim's fault for their attack. Doesn't matter where they are, what they're doing, or what they agreed to in the past. It's like saying that someone shouldn't be upset they got robbed because they gave to charities before, so how is it different."

"But sex is different," she said.

"It's just a more intimate crime," I said. "I had a friend in college who was very promiscuous. She had the reputation for sleeping with a lot of guys. One day she came to me and said she was raped. I believed her, consoled her, and we went to the clinic and security to see what we could do. Well, because she was 'loose,' as the nurse said, they wouldn't really take her case seriously. She ended up leaving school, and I lost touch with her. I still wonder what happened to her after that."

"That's awful," she said.

"It really is," I replied. "But it's super common, too. I think that whatever happened at that club, it really isn't the club's fault. It's whoever did the crime. Could they be better at keeping an eye on things? Probably. But it doesn't mean that everyone there is bad, either."

"I guess you're right," she said. "I just never thought it out."

"You're probably not the only one thinking that way," I said.

"How'd you get so smart?" she asked.

"Honestly," I said. "It's just that I've lived longer than you, which means I've seen some shit. Not gonna lie and say I know everything, but there are some things I'm pretty knowledgeable about. This just happens to be one of them."

"Thank you," she said. "For making me see that it isn't about where she was. It's about who did it to her and has nothing to do with anything else."

"Yup," I said. "There are monsters everywhere, even in places you think are safe."

The day was nearly over when we started the conversation, so I was done being around people, and wanted to head home. I also wanted to figure out what was going out into the world about the club. Initially, I'd worried about being outed as a pervert or something, but the more time I spent there, the more I realized that those people were my tribe. Except someone had infiltrated my chosen family, hurt someone I loved, and I really hoped that Lucifer would be able to figure out who it was, and they would pay for what they'd done.

Chapter Seventeen

Nick...

"Come on, baby," I said. "Let go for me."

I'd been dating Lynn for six weeks and she'd finally agreed to have sex with me. We were in my bedroom, door closed, a wedge under it to keep anyone from accidentally walking in on us, and it was late enough that my parents were asleep.

"I know you want to," I said, watching her eyes.

She'd said she wasn't sure what she liked, so I told her we could try some things and see what turned her on. I'd never had actual sex before but had watched enough porn to know what turned me on. Turned out, she really liked the same things I did, which meant she'd let me tie her to my bedframe, arms above her head, legs apart and tied to the footboard on either side. She was naked, except for the socks she'd told me to stuff in her mouth. She said when she masturbated, she tended to get loud, so she wanted to make sure she didn't wake my parents, something I could definitely appreciate.

"Come for me," I said. "Let go and come all over my hand."

I'd been using my hand to finger fuck her, my thumb on her clit, doing circles around and around. She'd been close a couple of times, *but never fully fell over that edge. Maybe I needed to try something different.*

"You want me to fuck you?" I asked and she nodded, her eyes wide, but her smile was clearly there in them.

Both of us were virgins, at least within the confines of never having actually had penetrative intercourse with another person. Pulling my hand away from her, I opened the foil packet and pulled out the condom, slipping it on me. I'd been hard since she'd said yes, so just that little bit made me wonder how long I'd last. I climbed up on to the bed, settling myself between her thighs, and pressed myself against her opening. Her hips rose up to meet me as I slid inside, and it was everything I'd hoped it would be.

"You like that?" I asked, and again she nodded.

I began to move, slowly at first, then speeding up as her breaths became labored. I'd slid my hand between us, running my thumb over that bundle of nerves at the apex of her sex, circling it round and round as I watched her eyes flutter shut. Oh yeah, that's what I wanted to see. Between her lifting her hips and me sliding in and out, I knew I wasn't gonna last very long, so I slowed myself down just enough to pull that edge back while still giving her what she wanted. When she finally came, I felt her pulsating around my cock, and I couldn't hold off any longer, losing my load inside the rubber with each stroke, barely holding myself up above her on the bed I'd tied her to.

I bolted up in bed, cock hard, brow sweaty, and wanting to fuck damn near anything I could get my hands on. I hadn't had a wet dream, or anything close to it, since I left college. There had always been plenty of girls wanting to hook up with a star athlete, and I was very willing to oblige them in their requests.

The memory of my first time in that situation, though, was a shock. Nothing had been as good as that, even the ones I'd fucked after in the same way. It was like that first time was something I had to live up to, and everything paled in comparison. Either way, I figured I'd get in the shower, take care of my cock, and then get on with my day. After the shower, though, I was definitely gonna have to find some coffee. It was too fucking early for this shit.

"DUDE," JP said. "You look like hell."

"Thanks," I said, my shades covering my eyes from the blinding sun.

We were heading to the stadium for our last game, having won the first two, and then it was back on the bus to head south. I wished we were going to my home city, but we weren't going quite that far. Just to Sacramento, who were playing well this season. Hopefully, we'd continue with our winning streak when we got there and handle the next weekend series in Houston with at least three of the four games on top.

I thought about asking Maggie to come up and see me, but I didn't want to put myself out there in any way that would connect me to the club, and all the shit that was coming out about it. I'd seen some news reports and social media posts about the rape, so the truth was out there, but at least I hadn't been mentioned. What with the actual article about me coming out about the same time, I had to wonder whether I would be connected with it. Timing could make people want to do that, but as far as I knew, no one had actually recognized me at the club, aside from the bouncer and the guy at the door.

Whatever was gonna happen, I was gonna have to deal with it. I just hoped that my name wouldn't be leaked as someone who was there that night, or that I was involved with the rape, because I most definitely wasn't. Nothing else had been said in what I'd seen that actually named names. It was more of a secret whisper of several famous people having been there, and if they named names without any charges, they wouldn't be in business for long. I was happy they were keeping that mentality.

As we pulled into the parking area in the stadium, I wanted to ignore the rest of the world and focus on the game. I was really connecting with the rest of the team, and we were working together like a well-oiled machine since I'd come over. Maybe this was the turning point, the moment when I actually became a member of the team fully. If it was, and it felt that way, I was willing to dive headlong into it and not look back.

My contract would keep me with the team for the rest of the current season and the next, so I might as well get used to the team and how they played. The winning streak we'd been on hadn't hurt that in any way, and if we kept it up, we just might make a run for the championship. Of course, that started with today's game, and we had to get in there and play it, because it wasn't gonna be handed to us, that's for sure.

"Let's go," I said as we finished the top of the first inning with a double play.

"Oh yeah," JP said, as he passed me on the way to the dugout.

He would be up first for the team, while I was hitting in the five spot after Lowe. I sat on the bench, along with several of the other players, waiting to either get myself ready to hit or head back out onto the field to play defense, it all depended on what the others in front of me did at the plate.

The game went quickly, both pitchers hitting their marks, causing most players to get out, or if they did get on, be left stranded. I'd gotten out the first two at bats I had, and as I stood in the box in the seventh inning, we were holding onto a one to nothing lead, and looking to add on, so we had a bit of breathing room. My goal for this at bat was to hit the ball somewhere they weren't, so I could get on, and move along with the guys behind me.

They'd brought in Kors again to start the inning, and he'd gotten Lowe to ground out to their shortstop. I felt fairly certain I could tell what would be coming, but didn't want to rely on it, so I watched for any sign as to what he'd throw. Nothing stood out to me, so I simply waited, my bat bobbing over my shoulder. His rock was even, the leg kick high, and he let it fly, releasing it high, and I had to duck to keep from being hit in the head.

"Ball," the ump called, and I stepped out of the box and looked at him.

Hopefully he'd make the warning to both teams to not throw at each other, but that was apparently not gonna happen. Instead of arguing, I stepped back into the box, digging my back foot into the line at the back, then tapping the plate before getting ready to swing. Again, easy rock and leg kick, but this time, the ball was low and sliding in, just above my belt, and I took the swing, catching it on the label and shoving it down the right field line and into the stands. It got out so fast I wasn't sure it was actually gonna make it over the fence.

Dropping the bat off to the side, I jogged down the line toward first, giving our coach there a slap on the hand before rounding and going toward second. As I made my way from second to third, their shortstop said something under his breath. I couldn't hear it because the fans were booing too loud, and it honestly didn't matter. High five to the third base coach as I rounded it and headed home, stepping on the base and pointing to the sky.

Dad would have loved to watch me play the last few years, but he ended up with cancer right after I was drafted. The minor league games were too far for him and Mom to travel to, so he had to settle for watching what he could online. By the time I got to the majors, he was way too frail to have him at the field. It sucked that he only saw me play in high school and college, never in the big leagues that he drove me so hard to make happen.

JP came up to me as I was sitting on the bench after my home run.

"What's up?" he asked. "You should be on cloud nine right now, hitting that homer."

"Sorry," I said, not able to hide the sadness from my voice. "Just wishing Dad was here to see it is all."

"Ah, man," he said, sitting next to me. "I'm sorry. It's probably because I brought it up earlier, huh?"

"Nah," I said. "Just thinking about life and how shit-tastic it seems to be right now."

"Well," he said. "At least it looks like we might take this one. Break out the brooms, baby."

"That'd be nice," I said.

Just then, we heard another crack of the bat, and launched ourselves up onto the steps to see Crawford's ball fly over the left field fence, and into our bullpen.

"Yeah," I said, moving down the line to greet him as he came through the gauntlet after he'd cleared the bases.

I looked at the scoreboard and saw we were actually up by four now, so I had totally missed the fact that Jones had gotten on after me, and that Crawford had brought him around. With the larger lead, we were sitting pretty good to take the whole series, but we couldn't slack off. This team had been known to blow up at times, and they'd been kept down enough the series that it just might be in them to come back and win this thing.

Chapter Eighteen

Charlotte...

"Hey," Lucifer said as I walked up to him and another man, one who had on the vest from one of the local motorcycle clubs. "Give me a minute and I'll come find you."

"Okay," I said, turning away from the men.

I didn't get a look at the guy's face but was pretty sure he wasn't wearing a mask as the rules of the club dictated. I was also much earlier than the usual time folks started showing up, so there were very few people actually in the house at the time. That was likely why this guy was here, because he could talk to Lucifer without a million people around.

He was decently tall, probably right around six feet, and had hair on the longer side, touching the collar of his vest. I didn't like longer hair on guys, so he did nothing to my insides, which said a lot for how I was feeling. Lucifer was someone I could definitely see myself with, but he was of the 'no touch' variety, so it hadn't happened, and likely never would.

Standing in the hallway near the front of the house, I watched as Lucifer and the other guy walked toward the front. I had been right in my assessment that he wasn't wearing a mask, but there was something about his eyes that sort of put me on edge. They were deep set above his dark beard, and they seemed hollow, like he was void of a soul or something. When he turned them on me, I felt a shiver run down my spine, and stepped back and away from him, as he passed. His eyes followed me, and I felt like prey. My heart was beating in my chest so fast I was afraid it would bust through the cage that housed it.

As they neared the door, he turned his gaze away from me, and I immediately ducked into the closest room, not wanting to be open and exposed as I'd been just moments earlier. When the door opened, I sort of hid behind it, not sure who was there.

"Charlie?" Lucifer said.

"Oh, thank God," I replied, coming out from behind the door.

"Are you okay?"

"That guy was scary," I said. "Seriously terrifying."

"Which is why I'm friends with him," he said. "He knows how to get things done and isn't afraid to do it in whatever means are necessary."

"Was that about Paris?" I asked.

"It was," he said. "But you never saw him."

"Not gonna forget that face," I said. "But there's no way I could describe him if anyone asked. I'm always of the mindset that the mask is covering their whole face, and there were no distinguishing marks or other things I remember."

"Good girl," he said, and I felt the praise all the way to my core.

Why this man wouldn't play was beyond me, but if he ever decided to come out of his space and enjoy the fruits of the house, I'd willingly give myself over for his pleasure. Especially if he praised me like he just had.

"Don't be giving me that look," he said, but there was a smile on his face.

"Do you know anything more?" I asked.

"I can't answer that," he said.

I wasn't sure if he meant he couldn't, because he didn't have the information, or that he couldn't, because it would implicate me in something I didn't want to be party to. Either way, I knew when to shut up.

"You're not dressed," he said, and while I was wearing clothes, it wasn't my normal club clothes.

"Yeah," I said. "Not doing anything tonight. I need to take some time for myself, get myself figured out right now."

"That really shook you," he said, and I nodded. "I'm sorry. Did it bring back something from your past?"

"Not for me," I said, hugging myself. "Someone I knew, and lost touch with."

"If you need me to find someone," he said, leaving the rest of the phrase empty.

"I don't think so," I said.

"Hey," he said, reaching out to me.

I went to him, and he wrapped me up, holding me to his chest. I'd never seen him interact with anyone physically in all the years I'd been in the club, so felt honored that he'd given me the opportunity.

"Everything will work out," he said, his voice resonating through his chest into my ear. "We'll figure out what happened and make it right. You know we always do."

I nodded against his chest, taking comfort in his embrace. Finally, after entirely too long, I pulled away, and he let me go.

"You good?" he asked.

"Yeah," I said. "I'm gonna head home. If you hear anything you can tell me, let me know. Otherwise, I'll see you when I see you."

"We did get another request for you," he said, almost as an aside.

"Same guy?" I asked.

"Yeah," he said.

The guy who had found Paris had asked to do a scene with me. In fact, he'd asked several times over the couple of weeks since it happened. Why he was fixated on me was a mystery, but he seemed overly persistent.

"What can you tell me about him?" I asked.

There were rules about what we could and couldn't know about any of the people who requested to hook up with us. Lucifer knew everything about everyone, though, so I trusted him to let me know if this guy was decent or not.

"He's new," he said. "So, I don't know what his likes are when it comes to this type of thing. But I can tell you that his reputation is good, and that he's new to town and the club, but not new to the life-style. His pedigree is very good, and I have no doubt he would take any and all requests as they are, and not push boundaries."

"And you know this because?" I asked.

"I had to check him out," he said. "He was one of a few new people to the club that night, and since he was the one who found Paris, I dug deep, contacted my counterparts, and vetted him thoroughly. If he's done something, it's been so covered up it didn't actually happen."

"Okay," I said, pondering the situation. "When was he asking for next?"

"I'd have to look," Lucifer said. "But I can get that information to you if you want. Or I can tell him you're on a hiatus right now, but that once you're available, we'd let him know. Right now, I've just been declining the request with a polite and generic answer."

"Let him know I'm on hold," I said. "I'm probably gonna be out for a while. I just need to get myself back together. You'd think I was the one who had been attacked."

"Suffering by proxy is a thing," he said. "It's kinda like survivor's guilt."

"Yeah," I replied.

He reached out again, and I went to him, letting him hug me, and sort of press me back together.

"Take care," he said. "And if Paris reaches out, let me know. I'll be keeping tabs on her, but she may reach out to you before she gets back to me with anything."

"Okay," I said.

I walked from the room we were standing in and out the front door. I'd told Mr. Stone to hold my car out front because I wasn't staying, and he'd done just that. I gave a small wave to him as I went down the stairs. Climbing into my car, I headed home, hoping my brain would shut off. It might have been better to play at the club, but I just couldn't get myself to even entertain the thought of it. No, tonight would definitely be a self-care night with a bath, a bottle of wine, and maybe even a chick flick to round it all out.

Chapter Nineteen

Nick...

Sacramento was hotter than normal, and we were all off our game, losing two of the three games before heading out to Houston. They were playing well, but no one liked them, especially after the cheating scandal that had happened a few years earlier. At least they'd gotten the new stadium built, and we didn't have to survive the Texas heat. I'd only played a handful of games there before, and it was a miserable experience. After the four games in Houston, which we split with the Dragons, we headed back to New Orleans and home.

With the off day on Thursday, after playing three games against the Cascades at home, I set out to find an apartment to rent for the remainder of the season. I knew I'd be in the city until at least the beginning of October, but went ahead and found a place I could stay in until November, which would cover any post-season games we might play, and give me a chance to figure out whether I wanted to relocate. I'd still go home after the season to see Mom, but it might be a good time to move to a new city, but that also depended on what happened in the next few weeks.

I'd asked a few of the guys the best neighborhoods to rent in that were close enough to the stadium, but still out of the insanity that was downtown. They'd given me a few places to look, and I'd found a couple to check out. I'd also gotten the number of a real estate agent the team used for players to help me weed out the trash places and sketchy landlords and was glad to be heading out to meet her to look at a couple of the places she found.

"Are you Nick?" a woman asked as I got out of my rental.

She was fairly tall, almost six feet, if I had to guess, and had dirty blonde hair that was styled nicely. My guess was she was pushing fifty, but I was never good at guessing ages, so would never tell her that thought, or ask her to confirm. Her dark navy skirt with matching jacket and white blouse told me she was likely the agent, so I went to her with my hand out.

"I am," I said. "Nick Hunter. Thanks for meeting me."

"Absolutely," she said, shaking my hand. "My name's Muriel Thompson. I'm always glad to help out the new players on the team find a place they can call home, even if it's only for a little while. This is a nice place, and there are a few players who have stayed here when they first came to town. Always nice to know that they've liked a place I showed them, as it's helpful to refer other folks here. It might not be exactly what you're looking for, though, so I don't want to get your hopes up too high."

"I appreciate the honesty," I said as I followed her into the building.

"Good morning," a man sitting behind a desk said as we walked in.

"Morning," she said.

"Good morning," I echoed.

"You here to show the place?" he asked the agent.

"I am," she said. "Do you have the keys?"

"Right here," he said, handing a ring with a couple of keys on it. "There's the key to the apartment, and the one to the storage unit. Apartment key fits the laundry room as well."

"Thanks," she said. "Shall we?"

I nodded and followed her over to the elevator where she pressed the up button, and we waited. It was nice that she wasn't trying to make small talk with me. We'd played a day game the day before, but I was still working on getting my body to know what time zone I was in. When the chime indicated that the elevator was there, she stepped off to the side slightly, and I figured it was to let whoever may have been coming down off before we stepped in. When the doors opened, the space was empty, so she stepped in, then turned to the panel, and hit the button for the third floor.

I'd asked to look at two-bedroom apartments, not because I needed them, but thought it might be nice to have my mom come out to spend some time near the end of the season, just to see if she thought it might be a nice place for her to have another home. Not like I couldn't afford to give her one here if she wanted to stay, and it would be nice to have her around sometimes. Not all the time, obviously, but I did like to see her regularly during the season, not just in the off season. Of course, I would never live with her for a long-term type of situation. Staying for a few days would be totally doable, but that's about it.

We walked down the hall, and she opened the door to the unit she was going to show me, pushing the door open, and stepping inside. As I walked in, I took in the space in front of me. To the left was a kitchen that looked fine, with a breakfast bar that led to a living room with plenty of space for a decent couch, and entertainment center.

"The bedrooms and bathrooms are down here," she said, turning to her right.

"Thanks," I said, following her down the short hall.

"Guest bedroom is here," she said, opening a door to a somewhat small bedroom. "Guest bathroom across the hall," she said, opening that door as well. "Master suite is in here," she said as she stepped into that room.

While it was a decent size, I knew it might not work for me. It was smaller than what I was used to, which wasn't a big deal in a rental, but it just felt like it wasn't laid out right. The bathroom was to the right of the main room, with a walk-in closet next to it. I stepped into the bathroom and knew this wouldn't work for me. It had a shower, but no tub, and it was much smaller than what I liked.

"What do you think?" she asked.

"I don't think this one will work," I said honestly. "But hopefully the next one will."

"I wanted to give you the worst one first," she said. "I was pretty sure it wouldn't fit what you wanted, but felt obligated none the less."

"I appreciate that," I said, following her back out of the apartment and out into the hall.

"You have the address for the next one?" she asked.

"I do," I said.

"Great," she said. "I'll drop the keys off and meet you there."

"Okay," I said, and we left the apartment, and she locked it up before we went down to the elevator.

She stopped at the desk while I went out the door and climbed into the rental car to get to the next place on the list. I ended up looking at five apartments, and settled on the second to last one she showed me. It was actually a three bedroom, one of which would be perfect for an office. Since I was only planning on being there for six or so months, it didn't have to be absolutely perfect, but this one was as perfect as it could be. I ended up signing the contract and would be moving in on my next off day, which wasn't for a week and a half.

I went back to my hotel and got to work ordering a couple of pieces of furniture for the apartment, including a bed and couch, as well as a television and stand. I'd thought about getting a furnished apartment since I wasn't gonna be in town long, but then decided that I wanted to have my own bed and such. Worst-case scenario, I end up putting it in storage for the off season, find a place for next year, and then see what happened. I'd be heading to free agency after that and might not end up back here again.

Once I'd had a chance to do all the things one does on their off day, I went to the website for the club I'd been to, just to see if they'd been able to get me a date with Charlie. Unfortunately, they'd let me know she was going to be out of the club for a while. I really wanted to see her, but figured I'd just have to wait it out.

Instead of licking my wounds like a pansy ass punk, I took myself out to check out the town I'd be living in for the immediate future, hoping to find something entertaining to do. Most people would assume a professional athlete wouldn't be interested in art, but they'd be wrong. While I wasn't any kind of art aficionado, I did like a good painting or sculpture, and the museum that was in the middle of the city park seemed to fit what I was looking for. I drove down toward town and found parking near the park, and enjoyed the early after-noon walk through the park to the museum.

August in New Orleans can be hot and humid, and today was no exception. I'd dressed in a tee shirt and jeans, not worrying about my tattoos showing or anyone recognizing me. It wasn't like I was that well known to begin with, what with being new in town and every-thing. Even on the bigger stage, I didn't exactly stand out as a superstar.

With my baseball hat on, and my sunglasses, I walked through the park, enjoying the outdoors until I made it to the museum. I'd looked up the hours to make sure they were open, and that I wouldn't be making the trip unnecessarily, and learned that they would be open until five, so it wasn't gonna be a rush to look through the place. It was exciting to see the wide range of exhibits they had, and that they regularly rotated their collections to allow new works to come through.

As I walked in the door, I pulled my sunglasses off, sliding them above the bill of my hat to rest on top and out of the way. There was a bit of a line, what with it being lunchtime, so I waited, looking around the lobby area. It was full of many items that seemed to draw me to them, and while I would get a good look once I was fully inside the museum proper, I simply admired them from afar, waiting my turn to pay my fee and enter the space.

"Welcome in," the girl behind the counter said. "Just you today?"

"Just me," I said, and she smiled brightly, a blush touching her cheeks.

"Any discounts?" she asked, then rattled off a bunch of options, none of which I qualified for. "That'll be twenty-five dollars," she finally said once she'd rang me through.

I paid the fee, took my ticket, which included the special exhibitions they had, and headed inside to take in my fill of art in all the forms they had to offer. The main floor had several rooms, each dedicated to a particular artist or style of art, all flowing through and into one another with ease. As I walked through, I took in the pieces that called to me, walking past the ones that didn't. It was interesting to watch the rest of the patrons in the museum gawk at some pieces that seemed mundane to me, and yet bypass those they felt were inferior.

All art was subjective, and each person had to choose what they liked and didn't, but the fact that so many people simply ignored some fantastic pieces was beyond me. Some of the pieces were ignored in favor of the ones that were more well known. I didn't have an issue with folks who wanted to only see the big-name pieces, but it was a bit frustrating to know they were missing out on so much because they passed the others by.

My mom had been the one to instill in me the love of art, and made sure I looked at each piece at the museums we'd go to. She'd dabbled in painting, but hadn't ever figured out how to get her pieces out into the world, so she mostly just painted for fun. As I got older, I tried to help her get a website up or something so she could sell them, but by that time, she'd given up any notion that she'd be able to do that sort of thing. It was sad to see her give up on her dreams, but she started to invest in my advancement, even before I tried, and with all that I was doing with the game, I didn't have a whole lot of time to put into it.

Once I started making decent money, I offered to help her get things set up, but she'd told me I should just worry about my own things. Any time I brought up how I'd love to see what she was working on, she shut me down. I knew she still painted, but she never showed me anything. Dad had been against it, saying it was too hard to take everything with us when we had to move every few years, and I think that's what killed her love of it. It pissed me off when I'd realized what had happened, but there really wasn't anything I could do. Once Dad died, I tried to get her to get back into the painting, and sharing of it all, but she simply told me she had other things to do with her time.

As I walked around the museum, I wondered whether she'd even saved anything she'd painted, and if or when she'd let me see it. It wasn't like she was old or infirm or anything like that. I just wanted to see it. I remember painting with her when I was little, side by side, each painting something she'd set up. Hers were obviously much better than the little ones I did, but she'd praised me every time, saying my use of color, or the composition, or some little thing I'd done, was masterful. She'd hang them up on the walls after framing them in cheap frames, and it always made me feel so proud that she thought I'd done so well.

By the time I hit third grade, I'd given up painting altogether, favoring playing baseball every chance I got. My dad was proud of me when I did it, and even my older brother, Lucas, thought I was pretty good. It was something I could do no matter where Dad got stationed, even overseas, and we were in Germany when I ended up going to the Little League World Series when I was twelve. Unfortunately, that didn't lead to a win, and I was sure I was a failure at baseball, and would fail at everything I loved.

Mom was my biggest cheerleader and pushed me back to playing after that hard loss. It's the reason I made it to where I was, and she would always be the most important person in my life. As I walked through the museum, I saw the pieces that I loved, and noticed which ones would call to my mom. While we had similar tastes, she preferred the more structured pieces, while I went for the wildly complicated and unmistakably different ones. She loved Monet, and I preferred Picasso. Even though our tastes were different, we could each see the beauty in what the other preferred, and that was why we were so close. Not just because we were the last two in the family.

As I walked across a hallway, I saw a head of blonde curls and felt my heart skip. *Could it be her?* I wondered. Surely my running into the goddess that had tormented my sleep for the last few weeks at a museum wouldn't be possible, but I was compelled to follow her.

When she stopped in front of the elevator, and pressed the down button, I had to know. Stepping up beside her, I took her in from the edge of my vision. Same jawline, same exquisite features, same build. It had to be her.

"Hello," I said, pressing the button to go up.

"Oh," she said, startled by my comment.

"Don't I know you from somewhere?" I asked, hoping she'd recognize me.

"I work here," she said. "You probably just saw me around."

I could tell she was trying to brush me off, and while there wasn't a crowd around us, I was sure that saying anything that implicated my extracurricular activities might push things too far.

"I'm sure I've seen you somewhere else," I said. "Do you live in town?"

"Sir," she said, turning on me, and it was unmistakable that she was my dream woman. "I don't know where you're from, but here in this town, when a woman brushes you off, the polite thing is to step away."

The fire was definitely there, and it made my cock twitch.

"Where I'm from," I said, leaning in a little closer. "People are polite."

"Welcome to New Orleans," she said. "We don't hesitate to tell things like they are."

The chime on the elevator pinged, and she turned toward it. It was heading down, so there were a few people who had to get off before we could step in. Instead of waiting for the return when it would be heading up, I went in with her.

"Excuse me," she said, glaring. "You aren't staff, so you need to wait, and use the elevator when it returns to go back up to the higher floors."

"I'm not interested in the art," I said, holding my footing. "I'm more interested in you."

That boldness had done well for me in my life, but I wasn't sure whether it would work with her. I just had to hope it was the right tactic.

Chapter Twenty

C **harlotte...**

"I'm not interested in the art," he said. "I'm more interested in you."

The brass balls this guy had was astounding. Was he thick? Or did he think the macho man act would work? Neither option was something I was interested in finding out. Since the elevator wouldn't move down until I swiped my key card, I stood there, wondering how long he'd wait before he figured out that I was not at all interested in whatever type of game he was playing. Since the door had closed, we were standing there without an audience, so I decided to just tell him what was what.

"I don't know who the fuck you think you are, but I don't play those games," I said. "Now, either get the fuck out of the elevator, or I'm calling security to have you removed."

Just then, the door opened up again, and a few people stepped in, crowding the space and pushing me closer to the guy with the attitude. He moved closer to me, nearly touching me, but not quite, as the space filled up. When the doors closed and it started to move, we were jostled a bit, and he ended up with his hand on the wall right above my head.

I had no problem with someone shooting their shot, but this guy was pushing all the wrong buttons. Did I get off on someone being dominant? Absolutely. But, I had to have it in a way that still had me in control, and this situation was not that. Besides, we were at my place of employment, and I didn't at all want to mix those two parts of my life.

As the elevator came to a stop at the second floor, his hand found its way to my waist, holding me without it looking like it was awkward, even though having his hand on me was not what I'd asked for. Normally, if I had been anywhere else, I'd have shoved him off me, and stomped on his foot to get my point across. Now, though, it felt like that might be overkill. I moved to leave the elevator, but he held me fast, his large hand gripping my hip in a way that was almost painful, but not quite.

"Do you mind?" I asked, looking down at his hand.

"Not at all," he said, not moving an inch.

I took a deep breath, let it out in a rush, then shoved him in the chest, walking out the doors just as they were closing, leaving him in there all alone to deal with whatever it was that he was having issues with, which, by my thought process was boundaries and where they should be. Much to my dismay, the doors opened up immediately, and he stepped out, and up to me. I wanted to head down to my lab, the place where I could pretend I wasn't a naughty girl, but this guy was making that all but impossible.

"Look," I said as he came up to me.

"I need to talk to you," he said before I could finish my thought. "In private."

I didn't move, so he leaned in and whispered in my ear, "I want to talk about the Lavender Lounge, Charlie."

Those few words got my attention faster than anything else would have. He knew my secret. Knew my name, and the place I played. How in the fuck did he find me?

Grabbing his hand, I turned and pulled him into a small storage room that was just off the floor, dragging him inside, and shutting the door behind him.

"Who the fuck are you?" I asked. "And how the fuck did you find me?"

"Pure chance brought me here," he said. "But I'd know that hair, those eyes, and those damn perky lips anywhere. We talked but didn't do anything else. Not that I didn't want to."

"That was you?" I asked.

"It was," he replied. "You rebuffed me so effectively, though, and I've had blue balls nearly every night since."

"There are others..."

"Not like you," he said, interrupting me. "No one in the world is like you."

I shook my head, trying to figure out how to get around this colossal fuck up. He couldn't tell anyone. Not that I really kept it much of a secret, but I certainly didn't go around advertising what I did at night.

"I'm not telling anyone," he said, as if reading my thoughts. "But I can't stop thinking about you."

"We had one conversation," I said. "And it wasn't even that."

"I know," he replied. "Which is why this is so fucked up that I want you this bad."

"Maybe it's just the novelty of it," I suggested. "The thought that I might be more than just a good fuck or something."

"That's not it," he said. "I thought about that. Believe me, I thought long and hard about that. In the end, though, it all comes back to how you carry yourself. How you cared for that girl. She was a mess, and it wasn't anything she did wrong, but you saw that and helped her. That's something remarkable."

"It's what any decent person would do," I argued.

"But no one could get her to come out," I said. "I tried, even though she didn't know me. I was hoping I could help her and find out who did this to her. I wanted revenge, and I'd only seen her for a moment. I can't imagine how that must have affected you."

"The club is dealing with it," I said. "Lucifer has his ways and knows people who handle these types of things."

"That's good," he said. "But I still want you."

"I'm not for sale," I said. "I'm currently off the menu, unavailable, and not willing to play with anyone I don't know."

Somehow, during this conversation, he'd maneuvered us so that I was in a corner, and he was blocking any exit I could even think to use. I'm sure I could have gotten away from him if I wanted, but what was weird was I felt no fear. Nothing he'd done, and nothing he said gave me any red flags, which I had a tendency to ignore, but still saw. No, this guy was something different.

The fact that he recognized me from the club wasn't so strange. I'd recognized so many people over the years that I just pretended I didn't. I'd been introduced to people as if it was the first time meeting them, only they knew me, and had fucked me in some way, shape, or form. It was always interesting to me when I met someone who thought I didn't recognize them because of how I reacted to the introduction. It wasn't something I shared, ever, so the fact that this guy walked into my place of employment, and said things that could damage my reputation, pissed me off.

What pissed me off more was the fact that it also turned me on more than I'd have liked to admit. The dichotomy of emotions running through me in that small space were something to behold, and it was all I could do to not act on the ones that had my panties getting wet.

"I'd like to see if we could do something," he said, breaking into my thoughts. "Not at the club, but perhaps dinner, or a drink. Would you be willing to meet me?"

I didn't date. It wasn't my thing. I liked a good fucking, but relationships weren't something I ever wanted to do. I'd thought Jack would be that for me, but he was very firm in that we were not, nor would we ever be, in a relationship. He would teach me all about sex, and in return, I would not push this boundary. When he'd died while I was away at college, it crushed me. That was when I decided that my heart would never belong to anyone else.

"I'm not interested," I said.

"In dinner? Drinks? Or me?" he asked.

"All of the above," I said.

It was cold, but it was the truth. I didn't want him thinking I was gonna swoon at his macho bullshit.

"Wow," he said, leaning back a bit. "I... just, wow."

"Not what you expected, is it?" I asked.

"Not at all," he said.

"Well, that's me," I said. "I don't do this kind of thing, and I really need to get back to work."

"Are you really stepping away from the club?" he asked, which surprised me.

"For a while," I said.

"Because of what happened?" he asked.

"More than just that," I said. "But that was a pressing point. Now, I really need to get back to work, so if you wouldn't mind..."

I left the rest of it unsaid, but he needed to move out of my way so I could get out of here. Him this close, with the smell of whatever cologne he had on, mixed with the sweat from the heat outside, was doing things I didn't like, especially since I was swearing off the whole sex thing for a minute. If I wasn't careful, I might just make him take me right here in the closet.

"I want to take you out," he said. "Let me do that and I'll let you go."

"Are you threatening me?"

"No," he said. "I'm propositioning you."

In the close space, which was just big enough to hold a handful of extra exhibits that would be exchanged out in the next few weeks, or ones that hadn't made it back to the storage location for the museum, it was intimate. More so than when I was naked at the club, even. I wasn't sure how I felt about it, either. I didn't do the mushy shit, because it really didn't lead to anything, and I got all my needs met outside of a traditional relationship, so it didn't matter anyway.

"Fine," I said, succumbing to his pressure. "But it's in protest, and only because I have a job to do. Pick me up here at six tonight."

The sigh from him against my temple as he leaned in ruffled me more than just wind blowing through my hair. No, there was something there, between us, that I didn't recognize, or had long forgotten.

"Thank you," he said in my ear before pressing his lips to my temple.

He stepped back from me, and shifted himself, adjusting his dick, which was obviously hard. I smiled that I had that much power over him, then brushed past him and out the door before I did something I would most assuredly regret. I held the door open, and waited for him to step out, then shut it firmly behind him.

Walking away from him felt more difficult than it should have, but I made my way to the elevator, pressing the button to take it down to my cave, my sanctuary, where I was safe and away from all the drama of the here and now. When it opened, I let the handful of people out before stepping in and pressing the button for the basement, swiping my card to gain access. I could see him watching me as the doors shut, and I couldn't help but shudder in anticipation of what might happen.

"Stop it," I told myself as I stepped out of the elevator in the basement.

"Stop what?" Gretchen asked.

"Sorry," I said. "Just mumbling to myself. Thinking about things that have no bearing on my life. You know how it goes."

"Yeah," she said. "But I'm usually the one muttering to myself under my breath. You're always so calm, cool, and collected."

"Not today, apparently," I said.

"Anything I can do to help?"

"Nah," I said. "I got myself into this mess, I'll find my way out."

"If you need anything," she said.

"It's fine," I replied. "Just something that came up that I have to do tonight. Not on the schedule, not something I planned, but it's a must. It's one of those things you look forward to as much as you dread, you know?"

"I totally get that," she said. "You want to come to dinner with Doug and me?"

"Can't," I said. "That's what the change in plans is. Dinner with a friend."

Why did I call him a friend? Were we friends? I didn't even know his name for God's sake.

"Well," she said. "If you need anything, text me, and I can call with a fake emergency. My friends and I always did that when we were in school. You know, if the date went off the rails and someone needed an out. Text the 911, and we come calling."

"That's really smart," I said. "Especially when you're young. I'm good, though, but I appreciate the thought."

"If you need me," she said.

"Thanks," I said.

We went back to work, me on my project, and her on hers. As the day wound down, and we wrapped up our projects, I watched as Gretchen continuously touched her stomach. It was an endearing thing, the way she subconsciously connected to the bundle of tissue that was growing inside her. I'd been truthful when I said I had come to terms about not having kids, but every once in a while, I thought about it. What it would be like to have a small part of me that lived outside my body, who I could watch grow and change, and become someone new.

Then I thought about the complications my sister-in-law had with her pregnancies, and how she nearly died with the last one. Of my younger sister with all the kids she'd had, and how she looked ragged and tired all the time. I enjoyed my niblings, but it was wonderful to be able to give them back to their parents when they became too much for me to handle. That wasn't something you could do if they were your own.

"What are you smiling about?" Gretchen asked as we left.

"Just thinking about kids," I said.

"Oh yeah?"

"And how nice it is to give them back to their parents when they start crying," I said with a laugh.

"Yeah," she said. "Well, I'll be learning all about that soon enough."

"And you'll do wonderful," I said. "I've seen you when you talk to kids up on the floors. You're a natural with them."

"But this one," she said, rubbing her tummy. "This little one will be my responsibility. They'll have my full attention."

"I can't wait," I said. "I can just imagine you and Doug doting on the little peanut."

"Oh, yeah," she said. "He's beyond excited."

"Have you done any of the prep work?" I asked, knowing there were a million things that needed doing before the baby even made its entrance.

"Not yet," she said. "We're still holding out, waiting until we get past that danger zone, you know?"

"I know," I said.

"But we have been talking about names," she continued. "We're just making lists right now, of what we do and don't want. It's amazing how many people tell us what we should name it, and we're like barely starting out."

"Well," I said. "Whatever you decide, it will be the perfect name. Fit for the perfect little bundle of joy."

"I just hope no one gets upset by the name we choose," she said.

"Trick is to not tell anyone until baby gets here," I said. "My sister made the mistake of telling her mother-in-law the name they'd chosen. That woman just wouldn't stop berating them, demanding that they change it. It was pretty bad. My sister ended up in the hospital during the late part of the pregnancy, and we had to all rally around and keep the monster-in-law away until after the baby was born. I don't think she's ever forgiven her, and they don't talk to her much anymore."

"That's awful," she said. "I can't imagine someone doing that."

"You'd be amazed at what some people think are appropriate things to do and say," I said. "Some people don't deserve grandkids."

"Well," she said. "My mom is ecstatic, and his is as well. They've said they're hoping for a happy and healthy baby, no matter what. I'll tell Doug that I'd like to hold off on sharing the names we choose for a while. I don't think we'd run into those kinds of issues, but you never know."

"If you need to tell someone," I said. "Feel free to tell me. I can keep the secret and tell people all sorts of odd and random names to keep them guessing."

"I'll remember that," she said.

We'd made it up to the main floor and were heading toward the front to exit. Did I want her to see who I was meeting, or did I want to keep him a secret? I wasn't sure which would be better.

"You okay?" she asked, and I looked at her.

"Yeah," I said. "Just thinking about the rest of the night."

"Need me to run interference?"

"Like I'd let the pregnant girl do that," I said. "I'll be fine. You go on ahead. I'll see you tomorrow."

"Have fun," she said and walked out the door.

I followed behind her, saying good night to the security guard as he locked up behind us, and saw my date standing at the bottom of the stairs. I watched Gretchen look at him, then back at me, and smiled at her, letting her know he was fine, and that she could go home to her husband. She pulled her phone out as she was walking toward the parking lot and then I felt mine buzz in my pocket.

Text me 911 if you need me.

I sent a response back.

I'll be fine, but thanks.

After that, I walked down the stairs and stepped up to the man who had found me outside the club and pressured me into a date.

Chapter Twenty-One

Nick...

I'd pushed her into the date in that little closet because I needed to get to know her. If she wasn't gonna be at the club, I needed to find out if she'd be willing to play outside of it. Having no way to contact her was a pain, but the fact that I stumbled into where she worked was amazing. Everything inside me was saying that I needed her. She'd said she didn't date, which was totally fine, because I didn't, either. But now that we were going to be going to dinner, I thought about changing my stance.

She walked out of the museum just after another young woman who had given me a side eye. Not that she was dressed any special way, but she looked phenomenal, and I chalked it up to her having the confidence of a woman who had absolutely no fucks to give. Something akin to being comfortable in her own skin, but more than just that. As she walked down the steps, I stood up from the bench I'd been leaning against the back of and walked toward her.

"I'm not riding in your car," she said.

"I figured we'd walk," I replied.

"Fine," she said, crossing her arms over her ample chest.

Her hair was wild around her head, blonde curls bobbing with each step. She wore a button-down shirt, which had been covered by a lab coat of sorts when I'd seen her earlier, and tight jeans. Every one of her curves was accentuated, and it was all I could do to keep myself from just diving right in. Control was something I held myself to, but around her it was hard.

"I'm new in town," I said. "Thought you could suggest a place for us to eat."

"Do you have a preference?" she asked as she started walking.

"I trust your judgment," I said.

"Good," she replied, and I fell into step beside her.

"It's a bit of a walk," she said as we went toward the edge of the park. "That's not gonna be a problem for you, is it?"

"Not at all," I replied.

We walked in amicable silence, just the sound of traffic on the road, as she guided us up and over the little creek that ran alongside the park. It was cooling down some with evening coming in, but was still warm enough to not need a jacket. I didn't mind the heat so much, but the humidity was unbearable some days. Today wasn't so bad, though, so I was comfortable.

She paused next to a cemetery on the way, looking over the fence and into the space that was filled with mausoleums and crypts and the like. I'd noticed that the city was littered with them throughout, and wondered whether she had someone she knew buried in there.

"You have family in there?" I asked.

"It's just a place that reminds me of a friend," she said.

"Are they buried here?" I asked.

"No," she said, but didn't elaborate.

She took a deep breath, let it out, then continued along the route we were walking. It didn't take long for us to come up to a handful of restaurants.

"This okay?" she asked outside a restaurant that seemed to have a Mexican theme.

"Absolutely," I replied, stepping up to the door to open it for her.

It was bright and airy inside, and there were a handful of tables outside as well. The smell was out of this world, and I looked forward to trying something that felt more like home than most of the foods I'd eaten while here.

"Two?" the hostess asked.

"Yes," I replied.

"Follow me," she said, taking two menus from the stack and leading us toward the edge of the room.

While it wasn't quite as private as I would have liked, it would serve its purpose. I pulled out the chair, allowing Charlie to sit first, then went to the other side, and sat myself.

"Can I get you anything to drink to start?" she asked once we were seated.

"I'd like a glass of white wine," she said, then answered the specific brand when the hostess asked.

"And you?" she asked, looking at me.

"I'll have the same," I said.

I wasn't exactly a wine kind of guy, but could enjoy a glass with dinner. Once the hostess left, Charlie looked at me, hands folded on the menu.

"You're not going to look?" I asked.

"I eat here often enough," she said.

"What do you recommend?"

"Depends on what you're in the mood for," she said.

"That's not something on the menu," I said, and saw a movement of her lips, like she was trying not to smile.

"Steak, chicken, fish, or pork?" she asked.

"Steak," I replied.

"Their Carne Asada is delicious," she said. "I'd suggest that. But you'll probably want to change your wine choice for that one."

"Then tell me what goes with the wine," I said.

"The Pescado Fresco," she said, not even looking at the menu. "It's seafood, so if that isn't your thing, go with something with chicken instead."

Just then, a waiter came by with our wines, setting them down in front of us.

"Are you ready?" he asked.

"Yes," I said, then held my hand out for Charlie to order first.

She ordered the same thing she suggested I get, and I told the waiter I wanted the same. He took our menus and walked away. We sat there looking at each other, and I wondered whether she would start the conversation, or if she wanted me to. After entirely too long, she finally broke the silence.

"What's your name?" she asked.

"Nick," I replied. "Nick Hunter. And yours?"

"You can stick with Charlie," she replied.

"Charlie it is," I said.

"Out with it," she said.

"I'm sorry, what?"

"Whatever it is you're thinking," she said. "You asked for this, so you get to decide what we're talking about."

I blinked, then said the first thing that came to my mind, "I want to know why you denied me at the club."

"Because I don't know you," she replied. "I don't do anything with someone until I've seen them in action. It's my rule."

"Couldn't exactly get that going," I said. "Being new and all."

"True," she agreed. "Still, it's my rule, so deal with it."

"Yes, ma'am," I said.

She glared at me, then picked up her glass, and took a sip of her wine, setting it back on the table.

"Who was your first?" I asked.

"Bit personal, isn't it?"

"Trying to get to know you," I said. "Can't rightly do that if we don't talk."

"Jack," she said, and there was just the barest hint of a quiver in her voice.

"Lynn," I replied, answering my own question for her.

"Age?"

"Sixteen," I said. "You?"

"Eighteen," she said. "He needed me to be an adult."

"Older guy, then," I said.

"You?"

"Same age," I replied. "First time for both of us."

"Nice," she said, and seemed to be warming from her frigid stance from earlier. "Jack taught me everything in the beginning."

"Lynn and I learned together," I said.

"I miss him," she said.

"I assume he's who you were thinking about by that cemetery," I said.

"Yeah," she replied, taking another sip of her wine.

The waiter came by with our food just then, setting a plate in front of each of us before walking away again.

"Dig in," she said. "I want to see if you like it."

I did as she instructed, cutting a piece of the fish off to take a bite. Flavor exploded in my mouth, and I savored it, letting the spices roll around before swallowing the bite.

"Well?"

"That is amazing," I said. "Your turn."

"I already know I like it," she said, but I pierced her with my look. "Fine."

She took her bite, enjoying the flavors as well. We continued to eat, not talking much other than what we enjoyed about the food. Once it was done, the waiter came back and asked if we wanted dessert. I looked to Charlie who ordered the Lemon Mascarpone Cheesecake for us to share.

"It's plenty big enough for us to share," she said. "Unless you wanted your own."

"I'm happy to share," I said. "What do you do at the museum?"

The question must have thrown her off, as she looked at me confused.

"Just trying to get to know you," I said.

"I don't date," she said.

"Me, either," I replied. "But that doesn't mean we can't be friends. There may be some benefits to the friendship as well."

The cheesecake arrived before she answered my question, and she insisted that I take the first bite. The tartness of the lemon mixed with the sweetness of the cake, was just the perfect after flavor for our dinner.

"I'm in preservation," she said when the dessert was nearly gone.

"That sounds interesting," I replied.

"What do you do that you could be at the museum in the middle of the day during the week?"

"I play with the Magicians," I said.

"I don't know what that means," she said.

"Baseball," I replied. "They're the major league team here in New Orleans."

"Ah," she said. "Sportsball."

"Yeah," I replied. "You don't follow the games?"

"No," she replied. "It's not something that's ever interested me."

"That's fair," I said. "Would you be interested in going to a game to watch me play?"

"I don't really understand the game," she said. "So, not sure why I would want to go."

"I guess," I said, a bit disappointed.

"I don't date," she said. "That means that I don't usually do anything that would be associated with dating or having a partner in life."

"I get it," I said.

"I don't think you do," she replied. "I live a solitary life. I work because I love my job, and I play because I love that as well. I'm not interested in a relationship with anyone outside of those two places. I understand it's an odd life to live, but it's mine, and the way I prefer it."

"I actually do get it," I replied. "I'm the same way. My teammates are more acquaintances than friends, and the few people who know me outside of that are from the club where I'm from. I don't really have relationships with anyone, so it really is something I understand."

"But..."

She left the word hanging, waiting for me to explain further.

"I felt drawn to you," I confessed. "It was weird, and definitely not something I've ever felt before. Like there was some supernatural attraction between us that I couldn't fight off. I don't believe in any of that stuff, but I honestly couldn't get you out of my mind. Believe me, I tried. I was thinking if I could just..." I stopped, because we were pretty out in the open.

"Let's go somewhere more private," she suggested.

I'd already paid the bill, and I'd left a sizable tip to have them leave us alone, but she was right. There were entirely too many people around to have this type of conversation. I followed her out of the restaurant, and we retraced our steps toward the cemetery and the park beyond.

"Spill," she said when we were away from people.

"I figured if I could just fuck you, I'd get you out of my system," I confessed. "It sounds crass, and I apologize for that, but it's what I was thinking. Still am, to some degree."

"So, why all the tries to do more?" she asked.

"I really thought I could get you out of my system," I said. "That's why I pushed at the club. Why I pushed when I saw you at the museum. I didn't think I'd find you outside of the club, so I was a bit surprised, and kind of just acted on instinct."

"Which, for the record, was a dick move," she said.

"I know," I replied. "And I'm sorry."

"What do you say to me giving you some access to me at the club?" she asked.

"What do you mean?"

"I'll contact them, set something up, have an open-door session with you, and have my own personal protector there," she said. "Will that satisfy your need?"

"It would certainly go a long way toward that," I replied.

"Good," she said. "I'll contact Lucifer and let him know what my demands are, ask him to set something up, and then contact you with respect to the session."

"That would be good," I said. "Will he just get in touch with me through the app?"

"He has your name," she said. "He knows who everyone is outside the club. He'll get in touch with you the best way he knows how, and then we can make it work through the app with preferences and the like."

"Are you going to do all the negotiating?" I asked. "Or will I get a say in what goes on?"

"Depends on what you want," she said. "There are some hard limits I have, so if your wants are outside those, they're a no-go. Within my limits, though, can be negotiated."

"Can we start the negotiations now?" I asked.

"What do you want?"

"I want you to wear that sexy red thing you were wearing when I first saw you," I said. "And I want you to arrive in that sexy Mustang that was sitting out front. The one that matched your outfit and lipstick."

"How did you know that was mine?" she asked.

"Lucky guess," I said. "Considering your lips and corset matched it perfectly, it was a best guess type situation. If I wasn't right, that wasn't a big deal. But you've confirmed it, so I want to meet you at the car, and walk you in."

"I think I can make that happen," she said, and she smiled, just a little.

Maybe I was getting to her, or maybe she was just thinking about getting this over with so she could walk away without having to look back. Either way, I was looking forward to what I might do.

Chapter Twenty-Two

Charlotte...

He'd pushed, and I'd submitted. I wasn't upset about it, though. He was actually really sexy, but so damn young. It was like he was looking for that cougar kink or something. But it was more than just that. He actually listened to me, heard what I said, and didn't try to take advantage of the small things I'd given in on. Oh, sure, he might well end up being an absolute bastard, someone I would never see again. Then again, with that chiseled look, the sharp nose, and those hands that looked strong enough to do some serious damage, he might be worth the spin.

After he'd walked me to my car, I watched him walk away. I took the long way home, winding through the city, which was horrible with all the tourists, until I was sure he hadn't followed me home. I parked in my garage, shut the door, and headed into my office. Powering up the laptop, I sent a message to Lucifer, asking him to get things set up. I gave him my limits, what I wanted, as well as the fact that I wanted him to be in the room with me when this all went down. It wasn't something he usually did, but I explained that I would feel more comfortable with him right there rather than off in another part of the house, but I wasn't sure he'd give in.

Once that was done, I headed up to shower. Getting the 'old' off me, as Gretchen liked to say, was something I preferred to do as soon as possible. That hadn't happened, though, because of this guy's demands. Nick Hunter seemed to be more than what was shown on the surface. His eyes were sharp, like he was looking under the surface rather than at just what was visible. I wasn't sure I liked him looking too close into who I was, and where I came from.

As the water ran down my body, I thought about what he might want. It wasn't so much about what he would want to do with and to me, but more about his whole life, what he wanted to do with it, and where he saw this thing going. I hadn't been interested in anyone since Jack died, at least not in any meaningful way. I'd fucked hundreds of guys, and girls, but none of them ever made me rethink my commitment to solitude.

My life worked for me. I had a job I loved that kept my savings safe, a home that was paid for, cars that I loved, and time to enjoy myself when I wanted. Why was I thinking about changing all of that? It would be one thing if it was someone I knew well, who'd I'd been with on a regular basis, but this was something else. Something I couldn't explain. A feeling more than a tangible entity I could put my finger on, and I wasn't sure I liked the way it was making me rethink my entire way of life.

Pushing forty was hard enough, what with all the changes my body was going through. Adding in a change in my mental thought process wasn't something I'd considered. I knew taking a break from the club was what was needed, and I would do just that. In my email to Lucifer, I'd told him I needed a couple of weeks to work myself back up to coming into the club. I knew he'd make sure that Nick knew, and we'd plan a good night to make it work for both of us in the best way possible.

I had to admit that I was a bit curious about what he did for a living, and once I'd gotten done with my shower, dried off, and pulled on my robe, I headed back down to my office to do some internet sleuthing. Since I knew absolutely nothing about baseball, I had to do the search engine route to find out what the name of the team was, and where I could find the players. It didn't take long for me to get to where I wanted to be, and sure enough, I was right about him being young. In fact, he was twelve years younger than me, and I had to wonder whether he knew about the age gap between us.

Instead of just focusing on his age, though, I dug deeper, looking at his bio to see that he was from California, but had grown up moving around. He played in the Little League World Series, which I thought was adorable, and had then gone to college in San Diego, which was listed as his hometown. It had his height, which was six foot one, his weight, which was 190, all of which seemed reasonable from what I had guessed.

The other stats made no sense to me, and I didn't understand the acronyms they'd put on each of the things they measured. I kept scrolling down and saw there was a place that had videos and news about him, so I clicked on a couple, watching him in action on the field. He was actually a really athletic guy, doing what I assumed to be what was expected of him. It was an interesting thing to watch this sport I had no knowledge of. I was brought up playing tennis and golf on occasion, so this was definitely outside what I was familiar with, and it intrigued me.

After I'd checked out what was on the team's website, I went to the social media links that were on the screen, just to see what he had going on where that was concerned. Most of the pictures on the sites were of him in his team uniforms, playing during a game and the like. There were a few with an older woman, who I assumed was his mother, especially since they had similar looks. She was a good head shorter than him, and the picture was older, as he didn't have facial hair in it like he had now. It was a sweet picture, with the woman looking up at her son's smiling face. My guess was it was after something important in his career, and when I clicked on the picture and read the description, it said it was after his first major league start.

Knowing that he was a family kind of guy, or at least looked that way online, made it easier for me to feel comfortable with what we were planning at the club in the next couple of weeks. I heard the chime indicating I had an email, so I switched over to that and saw that there was a response from Lucifer.

Charlie:
I have contacted the other party. The first date we have available for what you two want is in just under three weeks. He will be out of town the weekend after next, so that is the earliest available date.
Additionally, I am going to decline participation, including watching, from your scene. I am happy to find a replacement for you if you don't have someone in mind.
Regards,
Lucifer

Clinical, as usual. I didn't expect him to be willing to watch, but he was definitely my first choice. I sent a response asking if he would ask Apollo to be my watcher. While he was good for lots of things, the best thing I felt from him was safety and respect. He never allowed anyone to push another person past where they were comfortable and had a sixth sense when it came to things like that.

I'd wanted to ask about how the investigation into what had happened to Paris was going, but knowing Lucifer, he wouldn't be sharing that information. I knew he would let me know if something came up that I needed to help with, but for now I had to trust that he would make sure it was taken care of.

Yawning, I stretched, then shut my laptop down, heading up to my room to sleep. Tomorrow would be another day in the museum working on the last pieces of the collection that was due to be displayed just as September was set to begin. I loved seeing new pieces being enjoyed by the public, and the one we were working on was something that felt dear to me.

During my college years, while I pondered what I wanted to be when I grew up, I decided to take a class in art history. I'd always loved going to museums with my mom growing up, so figured I might as well learn a little more about the history of the pieces I saw. Turned out to be one of the best decisions I made in college. The professor was amazing, showing not just the masterpieces that everyone knows, but the smaller pieces that are seldom recognized for their beauty and perfection.

As I slipped my robe off and climbed between the cool sheets on my bed, I wondered what had brought Nick to the museum. He didn't seem like the cultured type, but that wasn't something that would necessarily be obvious. Being a professional athlete, though, made me think of the dumb jocks that were at both my high school and college, all of them needing tutoring and assistance just to stay at a decent GPA so they could play their sports. I'd tutored my fair share, and while they were pretty to look at, the space between the ears was not always fertile ground. Things just didn't seem to grow there, even if you planted and watered it.

Hopefully, he'd be more than the meatheads I helped to tutor in college. Thinking about it more, I wondered whether I should have Lucifer do a more thorough background check on him, just to make sure there wasn't something hiding under his pretty face. I would send another email in the morning before heading into the office asking just that. Not that he wouldn't do it anyway, but having that added information would make me feel better about it.

Chapter Twenty-Three

Nick...
    I'd gotten an email from the club before I went to bed asking for what dates I was available, and what types of things I wanted to do with Charlie. I had to go to the team website to find the calendar in order to see when I would be in town on a weekend. We were coming into September, and days off were starting to dwindle. The team was close to the top of the East division standings, but those Anglers from Indigo City were hard to pass.

It would have to be more than two weeks before we could find a date that worked for both of us, and that meant a Friday night right before Labor Day weekend. I wasn't opposed to the date, so said I was good. I sent what I wanted to do, which was basically to strip her, eat her out, fuck her mouth, then fuck her pussy. I was a pretty normal guy, I just liked to make sure my partner was able to enjoy themselves, too. I mentioned restraints, as those did tend to turn me on, and waited to see what I would get in response.

After I'd answered the questions from Lucifer, who was seriously the most dry and boring writer I'd ever seen, I took myself to the shower to get rid of the raging hard on I'd been dealing with since I first saw Charlie. Not that I hadn't taken care of that issue before the actual date, but it was still not enough. Something about her just did it for me.

If I had to guess, it would be the blonde hair, as that's what Lynn had had. All those curls that I could get my hands into and hold her where I wanted her. I couldn't wait to see if they felt as soft as they looked. She also had that high society look about her, like she grew up with money and learned how to carry herself well. She was older than me, I was sure, but that didn't bother me. I had no hang-ups about age differences when both were adults. It wasn't like I went out looking for an older woman, either.

The moment I saw her in the club, I was all in with wanting her. And honestly, I probably wouldn't be done after one time, either. I was hopeful that she'd be willing to do it again, but there was no guarantee, so I had to be ready to walk away if she was a one and done kind of woman. Although, the thought of that just devastated me.

Climbing into bed, I wondered whether she would be as good as my mind made her out to be. That was always the problem with the imagination. It never usually lived up to the hype. Like reading a book, then going to see the movie. Something was always missing, and it was usually the most important part. I pulled over my laptop to check out some film before trying to sleep. We were playing San Diego, my former team, and I knew them like I knew the back of my hand. But with the new players they'd acquired in the trade they made that sent me here, I wasn't sure I could say the same thing now. It would be good to see the guys again, though.

"Dude," Jackson said as he came out for batting practice. "Purple just doesn't look right on you."

"I know," I replied. "It's been taking some time to get used to it. Team is pretty good, though. How are things back home?"

"Have you seen our record?" he asked.

"Didn't want to say anything, but yeah," I said. "Sorry about that."

"I'm done at the end of the year," he said. "So, it's not like it matters that much to me. Still would've been nice to go out on a high note, not sitting in the basement the last month of the year."

"It definitely sucks," I said.

"At least you've got a chance to do something," he said. "You guys been playing good."

"It's been wild," I said. "Some of these teams are new to me, but it's a whole different atmosphere on this team. They're all friends, do shit after games, nothing like what I'm used to."

"We would do shit," he said.

"Yeah," I agreed. "But it's like there's this whole group of people who are family or something. Definitely feel like a bit of an outsider. Not that they don't try, though."

"Damn," he said. "Anyone you're getting close to?"

"Just JP," I said. "He's the guy I knew in college. Alej isn't bad, either. He's a decent fielder, hits well, and is pretty quiet. We work well together."

"I've seen the highlights," he said with a smile. "I'm really glad you're doing well."

"Me, too," I said. "Other than losing, how's it going?"

"Retirement is gonna suck," he said with a laugh.

"Why's that?"

"I won't have anything to do," he said.

"What about your wife and kids?"

"That's what I'm talking about," he said. "I'm not gonna know what to do with them. I'll have so damn much time I'll probably get sick of them."

"I thought that was the whole reason you were retiring," I said. "To spend more time with your family."

"I mean, it is, but..." he said, leaving the rest unsaid.

"It'll be weird," I finished for him.

"Definitely," he replied.

As we wrapped up our conversation, a few of the other players came over to say hello and ask how the transition was going. By the time I'd chatted with everyone, I was running short on time to change. I jogged back to the dugout, down the stairs, and down the tunnel. The quick change was needed, and thankfully it wasn't that hot in the stadium, what with the roof on and the air conditioner running. I never knew how weird it was to deal with this much humidity until I got here and played more than just a few games.

Bautista was pitching tonight, so we would likely see a lot of ground balls to field during the game. That always made the night go faster. Add to that, I knew these guys we were playing against very well. Knew their tendencies, their tells, and the way they liked to approach the game. It gave me a leg up on things, and they didn't have that advantage, except when it came to how they'd play me.

With the changes in the schedule, we were seeing every team at least once at home and once in their ballpark, so this would be the only time we'd see them again until the next season, especially since they weren't making the playoffs. Having talked strategy with the manager, he'd let me know to feel free to give more instructions if the need arose during the game itself.

I was hitting fifth in the lineup, which was where I'd been most of the time since I'd come over, so I felt pretty comfortable with that. The top of the lineup did well, and I was up with two on and two out in the first inning. I knew their pitcher was one to throw wild, so I waited to see what would happen. Sure enough, the guy threw well inside and plunked me on the back. Fortunately, it was a curveball and not a fastball or slider, so it wasn't that hard to take. I dropped my bat, arm guard, and shin guard at the plate and took my base, moving the guys up that ever important ninety feet.

Alej was up after me, and the first ball their pitcher threw was a fastball down the middle, and our guy didn't miss, sending it over the center field fence by a long way, and we all trotted around the bases, coming home to high five each other before heading back into the dugout. The team had this giant headpiece that I swore looked more like a showgirl mask than a Mardi Gras mask, but it worked, what with it having all the colors of the logo in it. Alej put it on as he came into the dugout, getting the congratulations he deserved for putting us up by four in the first inning.

The rest of the game, as well as the series, saw us beating up my former team in a spectacular fashion. In three games, we scored thirty-seven runs to their two and moved us well ahead in the standings for the wild card slot. We would still have to deal with the Anglers, and eventually, likely, the Dragons, but for now, our prospects looked good.

I wanted to celebrate at the club, pound some pussy, get my cock sucked, but that wasn't gonna get me where I wanted to be, which was with Charlie underneath me, her moaning my name, and begging me to continue. Three weeks was a long fucking time to wait for it, but that was what she'd demanded, so I opted to go without, at least until then, but, *fuck,* it was gonna be a long wait.

Chapter Twenty-Four

Charlotte...

I hadn't seen Nick since the dinner when he talked me into playing at the club, which actually made me feel a bit better. The fact that he'd shown up at my job was a bit off-putting, and I wasn't sure if I was happy about him knowing where I worked. I'd set up what I thought would be a good time for him, but he'd asked for several more things, which were not outside my limits, but seemed like he was trying to show off. Either that, or he wanted to get everything from me in one fell swoop. I'd declined a few things but acquiesced on others. It would likely be a decent night once it came around.

The club had reached out to me a couple of times with others who had wanted to play, but I was sticking firm on my sabbatical from there. I needed to be sure to take my time seriously, figure out what I wanted for my future, and whether I'd continue to frequent the club as much as I had in the past.

It had almost become like a second job to me, a place where I went to work instead of really enjoying the acts themselves. I'd become more of a teacher than a participant, and I wanted to draw that line in the sand, give myself time to relax and take a break, as well as the option to simply play for the sake of it.

Apollo had reached out to me directly, asking if everything was fine, and I'd assured him it was. He offered to play outside the club if I was so inclined, but I declined, thanking him for the offer, and assuring him that I just needed a break, a time to reclaim myself outside of who and what I was within the club. He, thankfully, understood, and told me to reach out if I was interested in anything, or I was in need in any way, even if it had nothing to do with sex.

The other thing that I was thinking about was Paris, or rather Rachel, and whether she had taken my words to heart. I knew she was young, and that she was just getting started in the club life and all that it entailed, so it didn't surprise me that she stepped away, either. Lucifer had assured me that his friends from the *other* club had been working hard to figure out who it was that had raped her, and I was thankful for that. They weren't a club I wanted to be involved in, but could understand their use, especially when things needed to be handled in a more private and out of the limelight manner.

Three weeks had seemed like plenty of time to work myself up to being back at the club, but when the day came, I was a ball of nerves, and Gretchen noticed.

"What's up with you?" she asked.

"Just going to something tonight," I said. "It's been on the calendar for a while, and I'm feeling a bit anxious about it."

"So, don't go," she said.

"I've already promised another party that I would be there," I said. "It is something I agreed to and am just working myself back into that mindset."

"I'm sure they'd understand," she said. "If they don't, well they can kick rocks."

I laughed at her words, and said, "Only you could make a statement like that and not sound like an idiot."

"What?"

"Kick rocks," I said. "It's adorable, but definitely not what most people would say."

"I know," she said. "But, if I'm gonna be raising a tiny human, I need to be sure that my words are ones they can use. Kids pick up anything you say."

"Which is just another reason I should not be raising kids," I said. "My mouth tends to get away from me if I'm not careful."

"I've never noticed," she said.

"Because I can act like a grown up occasionally, if the situation calls for it," I said. "Speaking of which," I continued. "How are things going with you? Sick? Uncomfortable? Anything?"

"Sick, yeah," she said. "And the number of things that stink all of a sudden are ridiculous. Like, who would think that peaches would make me gag?"

"Well, that would be the end of it for me," I said. "I do love me some good peach cobbler. I'll make sure I don't bring them with me for lunch."

"Doug is very sad that he can't have peaches right now," she said with a little laugh. "He'll get over it, but it's still sad."

"When you're over it, let me know," I said. "I'll bake him up something absolutely delicious, full of all the peaches he can stand."

"He would love you for that," she said.

We were eating at one of the tables in the café, both of us having brought our own lunches. There really wasn't a place for employees to have their lunch breaks, so this was where we usually ended up.

"You sure you don't want to come to dinner with us?" she asked.

"No, I'm good," I said.

"Because I could totally talk Doug into going out," she said. "It would be an excuse to get out of whatever you have for tonight."

"While I appreciate it," I said. "This is definitely something I need to do. Besides, I've been planning for weeks, and it would be a shame to let it go without at least getting it done."

"You make it sound like you're gonna be cleaning your gutters or something," she said, packing up the rest of her lunch.

"Not quite that exciting," I said.

"Sounds terrible," she replied as she stood up, pressing a hand to her back.

"Are you sure you're okay?"

"Yeah," she said. "It's just the way the baby is sitting kind of messes with my back sometimes. Doc said it was normal, so I'm not worried."

"Okay," I said, wondering. "But, if you feel like you need help with something here, let me know. I can totally jump in and help if I need to."

"Thanks," she said.

We walked back into the museum proper and headed to the elevators to go back to our workstations to finish out the day. While I was unsure about exactly what to expect when I got to the club, I was also sort of looking forward to it. Nick had been good about staying off my case about the things I turned down, hadn't pushed more than asking about alternatives, and had accepted the 'no' answers he was given.

I was in that strange state of anticipation and dread, except it wasn't really dread, more like a little bit of fear. But fear wasn't really the emotion, either. It was one of those fear of the unknown, even though I knew what was actually going to happen. I had only seen him the two times, once at the club right after the rape, and again at the museum and dinner after. I knew he was tall and strong, and that I was able to do some research on him online helped, but it was still not completely a known commodity.

During the weeks leading up to it, he had asked several questions about safe words and actions, about what I wanted to get out of it, and several other things that most negotiations would take into consideration. Every one of my requests was acknowledged and agreed to. He was definitely catering to my wants and needs above his own, which spoke volumes about him.

Some guys would push back, demand that what they wanted was more important than what I was willing to give up, but he was completely different. He'd asked for things, asked for alternatives, and taken every response I gave as it was meant, with my limits in mind. It was a heady thing to be in so much control, and I was relishing that power. I just hoped it would live up to the anticipation.

The afternoon seemed to drag on, with Gretchen and I conversing about the weekend plans she had and what I hoped seemed like a logical plan for myself. They were anticipating an ultrasound in the next week or so to get some measurements, and to finally be able to see the impending arrival, and I couldn't be happier for her. While my path didn't include children, my siblings' kids, and my friends' kids, were the lights of my life, and I doted on them as any aunt would, spoiling them in every way possible, within the limits of their parent's rules. Gretchen and Doug's little one would be no different.

By the time I headed home, I was more than looking forward to letting go, and planned to prepare myself for what we had discussed. I had a light dinner, making sure I wasn't going to be hungry during our session, but also making sure I wasn't so full that it would cause any indigestion issues, either. Nothing fucked up a sex scene more than someone having to leave for bodily functions that were not intended to be part of the scene.

After dinner, I took a hot shower, brushed my teeth, dressed in the corset and dress I'd worn the night we first met, and did my hair and makeup, including the red lipstick that matched my car. It was my favorite outfit, and I looked forward to meeting him at my car when he'd said to arrive, which was much later than I normally would have gone to the club. My guess was he wanted the late start time to allow for him to go back to wherever it was he was staying, and get himself into something for the evening, what with them having a game that night.

I could admit that I had checked to see what their schedule was to help me know that was what was likely happening. I had even watched a couple of the games that week, so I sort of knew what it was he actually did for his job. He'd invited me to attend a game, but

I'd declined the offer, not wanting to blend my real life with my club life in any way. It would be different if we'd met at the museum randomly, and not at the club, but we hadn't.

The weirdest thing to me, though, was that I was considering this more of a date than just a time to unwind and let myself go without consequences or emotions. It was an odd feeling to be nervous about it, almost like this was something new. But it wasn't – at least where this type of thing was concerned. It just felt different because it was with a new partner.

I wanted to convince myself of this more than anything, but it somehow didn't work. Instead of feeling comforted by the fact that I'd done this a million times before, I was as nervous as I'd been twenty years earlier, getting myself dressed to go meet Jack in the park. All the emotions had been building, and with me having stepped back from the club, and sex in general, it was all flooding in on me and a little overwhelming. Instead of fighting it, though, I used it to hype myself up. I turned on my television, flipping until I found the game, and sat to watch him in his element. Maybe that would help me get settled in, and ready for the night.

Chapter Twenty-Five

Nick...

The bat reverberated in my hands, the vibrations going clear up to my shoulders, as I continued with my follow-through, extending the bat all the way around my swing as I watched the ball climb. As the bat came down on its natural trajectory, I continued watching as the ball flew toward the left field fence. Once I was sure it was going to stay fair, I dropped my bat and started toward first base. Before my foot hit the bag, the whole crowd had surged to their feet, and I gave a high five to the first base coach before making the turn to take me the rest of the way around the bases.

As I trotted home, the team was surrounding the plate, all cheering and jumping up and down, allowing the umpire the barest of space to confirm that I did, in fact, touch home plate before the true celebration commenced. There were pats on my helmet, slaps on the back, and an entire case of sunflower seeds was dumped on my head, something they did here that we didn't do back in San Diego.

I knew, having hit the walk off home run, that I would likely be required to speak to the local reporter for the station that played the games, and I wasn't that upset about it. I'd done after-game interviews plenty of times, but this would be my first with the new team. Of course, it was the first really big thing I'd done on the field so far, so it made sense that they talked to others along the way.

"Nick," Angie, the reporter said, giving me the wave indicating I should join her. "You good to interview?"

"Sure thing," I said.

"Thanks," she replied, then pulled the mic up and waited for her cue.

I watched the camera, and when the red light on top went on, I knew we were live.

"Thanks, guys," Angie said. "I'm here with the hero of the night, Nick Hunter. First of all, welcome to the team."

"Thanks," I said.

"Now, walk me through that last at bat," she said.

"I knew we needed to get some base runners on if we were gonna take this one without going into bonus baseball," I said. "So, I just was looking for something to connect. Fortunately, he left that fastball up in my zone, and I couldn't do anything but swing."

"Your swing was perfect," she said. "Almost textbook. You've done pretty well since coming over, too. How has the shift been for you?"

"It's always interesting to go to a different team," I said. "While this is my first trade, I've moved through the system, and it's mostly the same. You meet new people, learn new strategies, and try to find your place. I'm happy this team seems to be working toward what all players want, which is a championship. I'll be glad to be a part of what gets us there for the first time."

"Spoken like a true native of the city," she said. "Thanks for the chat. Back to you in the booth."

The light on the camera turned off and she dropped the microphone.

"Thanks for chatting," she said.

"No problem," I replied, then headed down the steps and into the dugout.

The only people left in the dugout were the team's guys who cleaned up after the game, grabbing gear that'd been left behind, making sure everything was moved to the clubhouse before the venue cleaning crew came in. We made a mess in the dugout every single time, but it was the way of the game. The walk down the tunnel wasn't long, and when I walked into the clubhouse, everyone cheered. It was a bit disorienting, but I smiled and went along with it, taking my congratulations from the teammates and coaches on my way to my locker.

"My man," JP said as I came over to him. "That was amazing. We're gonna go out and celebrate. Come with us."

"Sorry," I said, pulling my jersey over my head. "I already got plans for the night."

"Then cancel them," he said. "Or, better yet, bring her with you."

"Not gonna happen," I replied as I grabbed my shower kit to head to the showers.

"It's your first big hit with the team," he practically begged as he followed me. "You gotta come."

"It took a lot to get this plan in place," I said. "I'm not going to cancel. That's not who I am. I can go out tomorrow, or any other night. Tonight's booked."

"Damn," he said, clearly upset.

"We can do it tomorrow night," I said. "I'll even hit another home run to make it special."

"I'm gonna hold you to it," he said, piercing me with his gaze.

I laughed, and he joined me, then walked back to the clubhouse, likely to tell whoever it was that was planning on going out, that I wasn't gonna go with them. I showered, toweled off, then went back to my locker to get dressed. Once I was done, I headed out to the garage to grab the rental. I really needed to get my shit shipped out, or at least a car.

Honestly, maybe I should just buy one to have while I was here.

Would definitely be cheaper than renting, even if I did turn it in any time we headed out of town. Maybe that was something I could do tomorrow. Tonight, though, my entire focus would be on Charlie. Making her scream my name over and over again. At least that was what I was hoping for.

I'd taken long enough that there weren't any reporters outside the clubhouse, and the walk to my car was pretty uneventful. There were some of my teammates who gave me a bit of a hard time on the way, but nothing I wasn't prepared for. Climbing into my car, I pulled out of the stadium, and onto the surface streets, merging into traffic as I listened to my GPS route me the fastest way to my destination. While it wasn't far, with traffic, both vehicle and pedestrian, it would take a bit to get me there.

I was glad we hadn't had to go into extra innings. I'd have had plenty of time, but I wanted to be early, get a drink at the club, and be prepared for when she arrived. Helping her out of her car, that gorgeous red Mustang, was part of the plan, part of the act. There was just something about it, and I couldn't resist asking for that to be included.

Pulling up in front of the house, I was glad to see that she hadn't arrived. I'd been insistent on her not arriving early, and she had heeded that demand. I'd definitely have to reward her for that.

"Good evening, Saturn," the man said as he opened my car door.

"Good evening," I replied, letting him open it as I stepped out.

I'd left it running, and headed up the stairs of the club to meet with Mr. Stone and check in. It was fine for me to be early since I had a time slot for playing, which was something that Lucifer had indicated in our communications.

"Welcome back," Mr. Stone said. "You're early."

"I am," I said. "Lucifer had indicated that it would be fine since I had a time slot scheduled for a room and scene."

"That you do," he said looking at his screen. "Please feel free to go to the bar and partake of the offerings there until your time slot comes up. Will you need a reminder?"

"There's a clock in there," I said. "I'll keep a watch and will be back out here to meet my date about ten minutes early."

"That will be fine," he said and gave me a nod.

Nodding back, I stepped up to the door and opened it, letting the sounds and smells surround me as I entered the building. As the first time I came to the club, there were plenty of things that were obviously sexual in both sounds and smells, and I was sure I would run into similar things to see that would likely tantalize my senses as well. The rooms to either side of the entry were open, and one had something going on, the office where I had headed to watch that first night.

A woman was sitting on the desk, her black latex outfit forming along her curves. Below her on the floor, on his hands and knees, was a rather large man, his stomach nearly touching the floor beneath him, completely naked except for the mask on his face. I couldn't see whether he had anything on or in him from the angle he was at, but I stepped up to the doorway to watch.

"Why, hello," the woman said, her eyes taking me in from the top of my head all the way down to my shoes. "Care to watch?"

"From here is fine," I said.

I wasn't much of one to be dominated, at least not in the way this man was, but watching someone work was always entertaining. The woman wore heels that were very high and sharply pointed at the base of the stiletto. Her mask looked like a cat, with the ears pointing up from the eyebrow level, all covered in fur as black as her outfit. She held a short whip in her right hand, coiled and ready to snap at the least provocation.

The man at her feet had pink stripes across his back, likely the result of doing something that displeased her. His hair was very short, not shaved, but closely cropped, and I could see the straps to a ball gag across his cheeks and fastened at the back of his head. Not something I enjoyed, either wearing or having my sub wear, but this wasn't my scene, so I wasn't going to share my preferences.

"Turn your ass to our guest," the woman said, snapping her whip against his back.

He scurried on his hands and knees, shifting so that I could see he did, in fact, have something in him. There was an anal hook in his ass, the hook going up the crack to his back where a strap was attached and went up along his back to attach to the gag at the back of his head. I was sure it was uncomfortable, but could also understand the pleasure that it must be giving. Below his ass, I could see a cage was clamped around his cock and balls, keeping them tightly within the metal that surrounded them. It looked pretty uncomfortable, his cock unable to become erect, even though it looked like it was straining within the confines she'd put it in.

Like his back, his ass was striped with the same pink lines indicative of the whip she held in her hand. It was a nice crisscross pattern, which showed her expertise with the weapon.

"Would you like a turn?" she asked, and I wasn't sure whether she meant with the whip, or on the floor.

"I appreciate your work," I said. "But I already have something lined up."

"If you change your mind," she said, not needing to finish the sentence because we both knew what it would be.

I nodded and watched, as she let the whip unfurl then let it fly, snapping against the man's ass again, the stinging report echoing through the room. Her laughter followed me as I stepped out and continued up the hall. My goal was to get to the bar, which I had seen in the main living room area the first night I was here.

Once again, the area was covered with naked and nearly naked bodies in sexual acts of all sorts, the sounds and smells wafting around the open space. As I walked past the couch and toward the bar, Tiffany was walking away, and she reached a hand out, pressing it against my chest before the rest of her body followed, her hand sliding up and over my shoulder.

"You're back," she said. "Wanna play?"

"I've already got a commitment," I replied.

She pouted, her bottom lip sticking so far out it was almost comical.

"I want you to spread your seed in me," she said. "Don't you wanna do that? I'd make the best mommy."

Batting her eyelashes, she pushed up on her toes, sliding her tits across my chest as she did it. I hadn't touched her, hadn't moved my hands from my side, but as she came close to kissing me, I put them on her hips, shoving her down to the floor and setting her away from me.

"Like I told you last time," I said, making sure my voice was firm. "I am not at all interested in anything like that. If you're looking for that, you're going to have to find another partner."

She gave a kind of harrumph noise, her hands going to her hips, the pouting lip back in place. I kind of shook my head a bit and moved to go past her.

"Why doesn't anyone want to give me a baby?" she whined.

"Maybe because you're so fucking desperate," a man from behind me said.

Turning to look over my shoulder, I saw that he was sitting on the couch, a blonde woman sitting on him, her back to him, riding him in the reverse-cowgirl pose, not even stopping due to the interruption of the room. She was in the zone, one hand on the arm of the couch, clutching it for dear life. The other hand delved to the front of her pussy, furiously fingering her clit in a desperate need to push her over the top. The guy had his hand on a chain that was between clamps on her nipples, tugging so hard that they were extended from her body at an alarming distance, and I was sure they would pop off at any moment.

"Oh, oh, oh," she began, and I could see she was going to fall, so I stood and watched.

The man pulled further on the chain, and she leaned forward enough that he had access to her ass, where he shoved his hand down, likely sliding a finger into it to push her that much further. The guttural sound she let out as she climaxed was a heady thing, and I looked forward to getting a sound similar to that out of Charlie once we got there.

197

The entire room was watching, and she just kept going, orgasming over and over again, the man working furiously behind her to keep her right there. Finally, after quite a while, she sort of collapsed on top of him and he let go of the chain, sliding that arm around her middle, pulling her up and against his body, kissing her neck as he spoke softly in her ear.

It was obvious they were a couple, or at least two who were committed to being together on a regular basis. She was completely spent, exhausted, and wrung out. The rest of the room resumed their play as he pulled her off himself and slid her next to him on the couch. He got up, pulled up his pants, and scooped her up to go somewhere, likely the bathroom to clean them both up.

Moving across the room, I stepped up to the bar they had set up next to the back wall. I wasn't much of a drinker, preferring to keep my senses clear, especially when I played, but I had a bit of a case of the nerves, anticipation setting me a bit on edge, and a shot of alcohol would take that off, smooth me out, and calm me down just enough.

"Can I get a whiskey sour?" I asked at the bar, and the man behind it nodded and started making my drink.

I slipped another hundred out of my pocket and set it on the top of the bar as he made my drink. When he handed it to me, he slipped the bill down, and into a drawer behind the bar. I took a sip, wanting to make sure it wasn't too strong, and was pleased with the bite of the lemon juice overpowering the bite of the whiskey. I tipped the glass up to him with a smile, then turned, and surveyed the room.

There was about half an hour before Charlie was scheduled to arrive, and I wanted to enjoy a little entertainment before I headed out to get her. From where I stood I could see the sectional that was the main piece of furniture in the room, with the coffee table in front of it, a woman tied to each leg, blindfolded, and being fucked in both her mouth and pussy. Over the back of the couch on the left was a woman, face almost all the way down into the seat cushions, with a man behind her, cock deep in her ass, the sound of his impact singing over the moans.

Next to her was a man sitting on the cushion at the end on that side, a woman standing on the cushions over him, her back to me, pussy on his mouth, him shoving a dildo in and out of her ass as he ate her out. His other arm was wrapped around her legs, holding her upright. She was holding her tits, pulling on them, and moaning loudly, shifting her body as he did his work. On the floor in front of them was a woman who looked entirely too young to be there, sucking the man's cock. She wore one of those school uniforms, the ones with the plaid skirt and crisp, white shirt. The skirt barely covered her ass, and the top was unbuttoned, her tits hanging out.

The couple who had entertained the room earlier was back, him sitting on the couch where he'd been before, her on the floor in front of him, sucking his cock. His eyes were closed, and it was as if he was just letting her do it, not that he was enjoying it at all. He must have sensed me looking at him, as he opened his eyes, and looked across the room at me.

"She likes to do it," he said. "Doesn't do much for me, but it makes her happy."

His smile was genuine, and I could tell he simply let her do what made her feel good. She'd put on a little robe of some sort, so she was mostly covered, but it was short enough that her ass hung out the bottom of it. I could see her pussy with the angle she was at, and it was weeping, so whatever she was doing was turning her on. She pulled off him and looked over her shoulder at me with a smile, then tipped her ass up a bit more, reached back, and pulled her cheeks apart, exposing both her pussy and asshole to me before sliding her hand down and shoving her fingers inside her lips, the digits disappearing inside her with ease.

"You can fuck me if you want," she said, pressing her ass out toward me.

"Thanks for the offer," I said, tipping my glass to her. "I already have plans. I'm enjoying the show you're putting on, though."

"I like to have people watch," she said, then turned back to her man, pulling his cock into her mouth again.

"Can I fuck your woman?" another man asked.

He had a look about him that kind of sent alarm bells going in my head, and the guy must have had the same thoughts.

"No," he said.

Just that one word said everything anyone would need to know. It was firm, but polite, and brooked absolutely no argument.

"Fine," the guy said, backing away with his hands up in surrender.

I watched him walk away, and meet up with a couple other guys, all of them having the look of someone who came from money and expected everyone to be impressed with that fact. Like, their family was wealthy, so they could do whatever the fuck they wanted. I made a mental note to mention it to Lucifer if I saw him.

As if my thoughts brought him to life, he stepped out of the kitchen and into the living room area, looking at what was going on, and spotted me. I gave him a kind of head nod thing, hopefully indicating that I'd like to talk to him, and it worked. He nodded back, then turned his head toward the room I'd met with him in, my last time in the club. Pushing off the bar, I walked around the table and couch, past the three boys who thought they were men, and through the kitchen toward the back room.

"What's up?" he asked as soon as I was in the room with the door closed.

"You see that guy?" I asked. "The one who wanted to fuck that girl, and her guy told him no?"

"I did," he said.

"Something about him ain't right," I said. "The three of them are giving off serious creep vibes, like they think they can buy whatever they want, and no one can turn them down."

"I've been watching them," he said. "They're on the short list for the attack a few weeks ago."

"Wouldn't surprise me," I said. "Do you know who they are?"

"Yeah," he said, and I believed him.

"Good," I said. I caught sight of the clock on the wall and said, "Shit. I gotta go get Charlie."

"I knew the time was coming up, so was surprised you were still in there," he said. "I got these guys. You go enjoy your night."

"Thanks," I said.

"No problem," he replied, and I walked out the door, heading to the front of the house to meet my date.

Chapter Twenty-Six

Charlotte...

I pulled up outside the club in my car and saw Nick standing at the top of the steps. I had to admit that a little thrill went through me as I watched him come down at a slow, methodical pace. It was like he was stretching this whole thing out, and that made me even more excited. It had been years since I'd looked forward to coming to the club the way I had tonight, and that made me a little sad.

When I'd first been brought here, of course by Jack, it was an all-new experience. We'd done plenty of things together, but coming to a place where there were other like-minded people was something new. It took a bit to get me comfortable being together in front of others, but he'd worked up to it slowly, and by the time he'd died, I was a full-fledged member in my own right, and had made many connections myself.

It was the place I went when I was lost after his death. Some would have called me reckless or said that I was simply trying to avoid the pain that was caused when I lost him. They were right in that I wanted to avoid the pain, but I also wanted to be somewhere we had been together, doing something we both loved. And I'd always felt safe inside this house, so this is where I had escaped to.

Now, though, I had that same exhilaration coursing through me that I had the very first time. The anticipation of the unknown, the realization that something new and exciting was waiting just inside that front door, and while I knew what actual acts were planned, I didn't know how it would all work out. It was what had been missing for me, and the reason I had stepped away initially.

"Charlie," he said as he opened my door.

"Good evening," I replied, sliding my feet out the door, and taking his hand to help me stand.

"I've paid for your parking," he said with a smile. "Everything is set up for us. I'm looking forward to the evening we've planned out."

"As am I," I replied, and it was true.

He took my hand and tucked it into his elbow, his other hand atop it to hold it in place as we walked toward the house. Climbing the stairs after so many weeks was comforting somehow, and knowing that everything had been arranged, and that I didn't have to think or make decisions, just helped me to relax that much more.

"Charlie," Mr. Stone said.

"Good evening," I returned.

Nick took his hand from mine to open the door, and the life that spilled out the portal as we went through was a boost to my nerves, both heightening my senses and calming me, all at once. None of it was new to me, the sounds and smells and even the sights, but it was as if I was seeing them all in a whole new way, turning back the pages of time to when I first walked into the building.

The door to the left, the one that led to the office, was open, and I saw Medusa sitting on the desk, her subject on his hands and knees on the floor in front of her. She saw me looking, and struck him with her whip, a smile caressing her lips at the slight grunt he let out. To the right, the door to the bedroom at the front of the house was closed. It had been reserved for us, and we had given instructions on what was to be available in the room when we began.

While I'd asked for an open-door session, I was second guessing that decision now. When Nick opened the door, Apollo stood from the chair he was sitting in, smiling down at me, his white teeth bright between his dark lips. Most would find him intimidating, and be terrified of both his size and strength, but to me, he was just a man who loved to cherish the women he worked with.

"I'd like to close the door," I said when we were both in the room.

"If you're sure," Apollo said, then looked to Nick.

"I'm sure," I replied, turning and looking at my partner for the evening as well.

"As the lady wishes," he said, moving to close the door, shutting out the rest of the house.

The rooms weren't soundproof, but the house was old enough, and had been refurbished well, so that it was as close to that as possible. We could still hear people as they went up and down the hall, and if someone was loud enough, we'd hear them no matter how far away they were. But for me, it felt better to have that barrier between what we were about to do, and those who weren't part of that plan.

I'd stayed where I was, giving the preference to Nick, and what he wished to do moving forward. My dark dress would be easy to remove, simply an unzipping of the zipper at my back, then letting it slide from my arms. I wasn't going to do the job, though. It was Nick who was in charge now, and he would be the one to direct things moving forward.

His pewter looking mask hid most of his face, but his eyes were there, dark in the holes they looked through. The beard was neatly trimmed, and his suit was a deep blue that was nearly black. The difference from this night as to what I could remember from that of a few weeks ago, was that his tie was red, so nearly matched to my corset, rather than the bright blue he'd worn then. I was sure he'd done it on purpose and had to agree that it was a well thought out plan.

"Thank you," he said as his hand came to rest on my shoulder.

"You're welcome," I replied, bowing my head just enough to show reverence.

Stepping behind me, his hand slid across my shoulder blades, the other one sliding up my arm to rest where the first had vacated. My hair had been left down, per his request, and he would need to move it aside to get to the zipper. Waiting for that to happen was equal parts intoxicating and infuriating. When his right hand slid over, sliding my hair from behind my head and up and over my shoulder, I shivered, anticipating his first touch. A light kiss caressed the spot where shoulder met neck, and it was so brief, so gentle, I wasn't sure it was real.

"You smell divine," he whispered against my skin, causing goose flesh to rise under his breath. "I can't wait to taste you."

Another press of his lips to that spot as his hand found the pull, sliding the zipper open, exposing my back to him at such a slow pace it was nearly indescribable. As it reached the end of the fastener, his knuckles touched the space just between my panties and corset, warm and firm, and I relaxed just that little bit more, giving up control to the man at my back.

Gently, he slid my dress from my shoulders, sliding them down my arms so that the fabric pooled at my feet. I didn't move to step out of it, instead waiting for him to instruct me on what he'd like me to do next. Even though I had never been with him, I trusted him. Moreso, I trusted that Lucifer and Apollo would protect me should the need arise, though I was somehow confident in the fact that it likely wouldn't.

I turned my head slightly toward the camera in the room, giving a slight smile to it knowing that Lucifer would be watching me, watching us, and he would likely relive these moments on his own later. Likewise, Apollo had been given the freedom to watch and play with himself during our session that night, and if I knew him well, which I did, he was already hard, cock in hand, imagining it was him touching me.

The warmth from my back had moved away, telling me that Nick was likely looking me over from behind, and I felt just a bit naughty and shifted my hips, raising my ass just that much more into the air, giving him a clear view of it. I was met with the intake of breath from both men, and smiled at the knowledge that I had that power of them with just the shift of my body. It was one thing to let someone be in charge of you, telling you what to do, but it was quite another to know that, though they were the ones who thought they were in control, you held everything in your hands, and could crush their desires with a simple word or action. You could just as easily send them to sensational heights with another, and that was what I'd just done.

His hand at the small of my back with just the slightest bit of pressure, told me he wanted me moving, so I stepped carefully out of my dress, making sure my heels didn't get caught on the fabric enough to make me trip. He steered me over to the massive bed, with its four posts at the corners, thick blankets and sheets on the mattress, and hooks, harnesses, and cuffs set all along the sides and up at the tops of the canopy.

We'd negotiated a list of things he'd wanted to do, but the order hadn't been set. He'd said he wanted to have the freedom to choose what happened when, based on my reactions to each thing as it came along. He did say that he wanted to restrain me, which was completely fine, but hadn't said exactly how or in which position. I'd given my limits, and that I would not be gagged or bound in a way that was unnatural for me, which he'd willingly accepted.

There was to be oral, both him on me and the reverse, as well as penetration, both in my pussy and ass, if we decided to get that far. He wasn't sure exactly how he'd feel, but did want those options. He also wanted to use some toys if it felt right, and I'd agreed, so those had been brought in and set up on the table next to the bed. Looking at everything that was set out, that thrill rose up my spine again, and my pussy started to ache for attention.

Standing at the foot of the bed, he put a hand on my hip, and turned me to face him. It was somewhat hard to read him, what with the mask on, but the tilt of his lips told me he was enjoying himself so far, so that was a good thing. Stepping into my space, he backed me up to the footboard, the mattress just at my ass height. He slid a hand down my arm, taking my wrist and raising it above my head. Working the cuff around it, he let it hang there, not pulled tight by any stretch of the imagination, mirroring the action on the other side.

I had plenty of movement, my arms not stretched at all. I wondered whether he would leave them loose or pull on the restraints to make them taught. Either option would be fine for me, so it was really what he preferred. His hands slid down my sides, hooking his thumbs on my thong and sliding it down my legs as he kneeled in front of me. Pressure against my ankle told me to lift each foot as he removed the panties from my body, setting them aside.

As he peered up at me from the floor, I saw the smile had widened, and it made me return the look. He was enjoying every moment of this, and the feeling was coming off him in waves that gave me the same feelings. I was aroused, excited, and feeling very powerful, even in my restrained state.

Reaching to the side, he tugged on one of the restraints at the base of the bed, pulling it over and sliding my foot out to meet it, where he secured it around my ankle. Doing the same on the other side, he effectively opened me up to him.

"I'm going to lick you now," he said, his voice deep and low. "I want you to relax, enjoy my ministrations, and then come all over my face. Will you do that for me?"

"Yes, Sir," I said, sliding into that submissive place in my mind. "It would be my pleasure."

Pressing up some, he knelt before me, a hand on each hip, he leaned in, sliding his nose up the inside of my thigh, drawing another shiver from me. As he came to the apex of my legs, his nose dove through my curls, almost as if he were trying to memorize my scent.

"Mm," he hummed.

The sound vibrated against my pelvis, and I shifted my hips forward, begging with my motion for him to make good on the promise he'd said. He pressed his lips to my body in the middle of my pubic hair, a gentle touch before sliding himself down. I watched with rapt attention as he peered up at me, then stuck his tongue out, swiping it against the top of my sex. I sucked in a breath, the touch setting me on the path I knew he was driving me toward.

"So sensitive," he said, and I heard a chair slide a bit.

We both looked over, and Apollo had pulled the chair he'd been sitting on, further into the room, giving himself a better view.

"Sorry," he said, and I smiled.

"I'm glad you're going to enjoy this," Nick said.

Apollo wasn't usually a watcher. He much preferred to participate, so the fact that he was willing to be my security, knowing he was only going to be able to watch, was something I was very happy about. Nick giving him the permission to enjoy himself was even nicer.

With his hands on my hips, he shifted me a bit more, putting my pussy more in front and giving himself better access to it. Again, he leaned in, and this time his tongue swiped from my entrance all the way up to my clit, pulling the bundle of nerves into his mouth. My eyes slid shut, my whole countenance settling in to enjoy his playing with me.

His teeth gripped me, biting down just enough to give me the pain and pleasure mix, and I could feel that buildup of pressure from within me. I knew he was pushing to see if he could make me orgasm without penetration, something he'd indicated he wanted to do. I'd been honest in telling him that it wasn't usually something I could manage, but was willing to let him try.

Gripping my hips, he tilted me even more, pressing his mouth firmly against my body, his tongue going to town, sliding up and down my slit at a pace that was unimaginably fast, his front teeth still pressing against the nerves at the front of me. Relaxing as much as I could, I let myself go, let his mouth against my body build that pressure, but I was stuck. I wouldn't, or couldn't, fall over that ledge, and it was frustrating, but not something I hadn't experienced before.

After far too long, he pulled a hand from my hip, sliding it between my legs, and thrust three fingers up into my cunt in a rapid motion that nearly lifted me off my feet. I exploded, feeling the waves roll through me over and over again, barely able to stay on my feet. He didn't let up when I started, but kept punishing my pussy with his hand, his teeth wrapped around the bundle of nerves at the apex of my sex, biting firmly to keep me at that impossible height as stars exploded inside me, bursting out and into the ether to evaporate on the wind.

He stood abruptly, shoving his fingers into my mouth, fucking it with them as I tasted myself on him. After a few strokes with his fingers, he pulled them out, wrapped his arms around me, and pressed his lips to mine, his tongue finding entrance with ease as he continued his onslaught of my senses. The taste of my pussy mixed with the minty flavor of his toothpaste or mouthwash was a blend I enjoyed, sucking his tongue with fervor, wanting to get every last drop of it back into myself.

When he pulled back, I opened my eyes, and his held a sort of wonder I hadn't seen in entirely too long. It was as if he were saying that he'd never experienced something so wonderful, and that he was glad he'd shared it with me. Unspoken words traveled between us, and we somehow just knew what the other was thinking.

"Wow," he whispered, his breath against my mouth.

"Yeah," I replied, my breath coming in quick bursts.

"I kinda want to skip everything else and just fuck you," he said. "But then again, I don't want to miss anything along the way."

"I'm at your mercy," I replied, and meant it.

It wasn't just that he had me tied to the bed, but more that he had just rocked my world so spectacularly that I was in his debt, a willing participant to whatever he deemed necessary to get him to a place where he was happy.

I could hear Apollo breathing heavily in the background, but pushed the sound away, preferring to think that it was just the two of us in this space, sharing this moment, communing together in a way that was almost metaphysical.

"I want you alone," he whispered against my ear, as if I'd said my thoughts aloud.

"Apollo," I said, my voice much more solid than I felt.

"Charlie," he said, and I could hear the edge in his voice, the question without actually asking it. He wanted to know if I needed his help, which had been his entire purpose for being in the room with us.

"I'd like to be alone with my partner now," I said, and I heard him stand.

"Charlie," he said again, and I could see him over Nick's shoulder, the question clearly there in his eyes.

"It's my decision," I said. "I'm fine, I promise."

He waited, just a beat, and Nick stayed where he was, arms wrapped around me, head bowed to my shoulder, lips touching my neck, but not in a distracting way. Apollo nodded, looked between us again, then gave another nod before walking over to the door and opening it. I closed my eyes and listened for the click as he shut it behind him, and then we were alone.

Chapter Twenty-Seven

Nick...

    The click of the door, and we were alone. Finally. I didn't mind an audience, but did prefer to keep myself clothed unless I was with just my partner for the time. Not that it mattered that much, but I was somewhat shy in certain aspects of my life, and me fucking someone was one of those things. I had fucked in front of an entire audience before, and it was an amazing thing, but most of the time, just the two of us was what I'd preferred.

I'd agreed to having Apollo in the room simply to assuage Charlie's fears. I didn't feel it my place to demand privacy, especially when I was the one who had pushed so hard for this. Now that he was gone, though, I felt just that little bit of an edge leave me. I was sure she sensed it, as she turned her lips and pressed them to my ear, the only place she could reach.

"We're alone," she whispered, and I took in a deep breath, taking the smells of lavender and springtime with it.

"Are you sure you're okay with this?" I asked, pulling back so I could look into her eyes.

"I am," she said, a smile pulling at the edge of her lips.

Running my hands up her back, I slid one up and unhooked the cuff on her left arm, allowing her to bring it down, and she promptly put it on my shoulder. I did the same with the other arm, and it also came to my shoulder. With her heels, she was only about half a foot shorter than me, so she didn't have to look up too much to see my eyes. I wanted to pull my mask off, but knew the rules of the house. I also wanted hers off, to take away that little bit of anonymity it allowed. I wanted us to be with each other, truly in the moment, without those barriers between us.

"What are you thinking?" she asked, and I guess I must have been telegraphing my thoughts, because I replied, "That I want to lose the masks."

Her tongue darted out, licking her lips that were still perfectly set, no smudging or smearing from the kissing we'd done, and I wondered whether it was a permanent thing. She darted her eyes over my shoulder to the corner of the room, a place I imagined a camera was hidden, then back to me.

"We can do that," she said. "I just need to let Lucy know before we do."

"How do we let him know?" I asked.

Again, her eyes darted to the corner.

"Do you want me to untie you?"

"No," she said.

She reached up behind her head and pulled the straps from her mask, loosening it so that it pulled away from her face. The metallic lace came away, and she let it down slowly, never taking her eyes off the camera. Holding it out in her hands, she then shifted slightly, setting it on the bed behind her.

"Your turn," she said.

Like hers, mine was a metallic structure, and it fell from my face easily after she'd untied it. Holding it up so that the camera could see it, she then turned and set it on the bed next to hers.

"Now what?" I asked.

"Give it about a minute," she said, then smiled. "Okay. We're all alone, now."

Her eyes were bright when she turned them back to me, like this was something she hadn't done before, and I wasn't sure whether that was a good thing or not. The fact that she trusted me was something I was very thankful for, and I rewarded her with a kiss on her neck. Her hands had come around mine and she pulled me against her, tilting her head to give me easier access to the spot I was working. The way her body fit against me was as if we were made to be together, and that gave me a moment of pause, ultimately deciding that it was just something my brain was thinking, not something I needed to worry about.

Pulling back from her, I looked at her face, the smile on her lips telling me she was enjoying the night so far. Moving back half a step, I slid her hands from around my neck to the front of me, pressing them against my chest before sliding them down, lower and lower, until she was at my belt.

"Undress me," I said, my voice soft in the hush of the room.

"As you wish, Sir," she said.

She swiftly unbuckled my belt, sliding the button at the top of my slacks from the slot it was secured through. The zipper followed, slowly lowering until it reached the bottom. Her hands slid inside the waistband of my pants, around to my back, as she shoved them off me, the fabric easily sliding down my legs. I was wearing boxer briefs, and my cock was straining against the soft material.

"May I?" she asked, not yet touching me after my pants were gone.

"Please do," I replied, and her hand slid along the waistband of the shorts, pressing them down my legs to land on top of my slacks.

She didn't touch me, at least not right away, but kept her head down, rolling her eyes up to look at me through her lashes. Licking her lips, she reached out, then paused, waiting for me to give her permission. God, she was such a good girl. Giving a nod, she let her hand slide from the tip down the length to the base, then back again, giving a little twist as she reached the tip again, the precum lubricating her hand as she took another slide down.

"I would like to take you into my mouth," she said, a question without actually being one.

"Should I unhook you?"

"If you want," she said. "But I can kneel as it is."

I offered my hand, and she took it, using it to keep her balance as she got to her knees in front of me. It had to be an awkward thing, her ankles tied to the bedposts as they were, but she managed to keep herself upright, then let her hand land on my thigh, the other remaining on my cock. Another swipe of her tongue along her lips and I was plunging between them, her taking me all the way to the back of her throat, the feel of her swallowing around the head of it making me even harder.

Letting off, she leaned in again, a slow and steady rhythm as she worked me with her mouth, the tongue sliding along the bottom of my dick, then swirling around the head as she came off. I put a hand onto the end of the bed, giving myself something to hold on to as she worked me in and out, over and over again.

"That feels so good," I said, keeping a tight rein on my control. "You're such a good girl, so good at sucking my cock."

"Mm," she hummed against me, the vibration nearly causing me to lose my control.

I pulled back and out of her mouth, a pop sound as she released me. She looked stricken, like I'd taken away her favorite toy, but I knew I wouldn't last too long if she kept going, and I wanted the night to continue for as long as possible.

"Up you go," I said, holding a hand out.

She took my hand and I helped her stand. I toed my shoes off, pulling my pants and boxers off at the same time, then knelt and unhooked her ankles from the cuffs around them. When I stood, her hands went to my chest, fingers working the tie from my neck. She quickly finished that task and went to work, unbuttoning my shirt. I let my jacket slip from my shoulders, and fall to the floor with my pants, and by the time she got to the last button, I let that fall as well, but she'd held onto the tie.

Once I was naked, she looked me up and down, her eyes like a caress along my skin. Again, her pink tongue slid out, swiping along her very red lips, as if she could taste my body without actually touching it. Her hand was still on my chest, resting there as if she was keeping me still. My tie was over her shoulder, the color matching her lips and the corset she wore. While I wanted to see her tits, the fact that she was all trussed up inside the fabric and boning of the top made me also want to wait.

Taking my tie from her shoulder, I turned her around to face the bed, then pressed a hand between her shoulder blades, bending her over the foot of the bed. She went willingly, her hands keeping her from simply falling flat on her face. Sliding my hand along her back, up to her shoulder, and down her arm, I pulled it behind her body to the base of her spine, then did the same with the other arm, pressing her hands together in a sort of prayer-like fashion before wrapping my tie around her wrists to secure her where she was.

Nudging her feet a bit, she opened for me so I could see her beautiful pussy, the pink folds inviting me into them, and all I wanted to do was bury myself balls deep. But I needed to make this last, needed to enjoy as much of her as I could, so I knelt behind her and licked her from her clit to her asshole, tasting her flavor along the way.

"Mm," she hummed, her hips flexing of their own accord.

"I want you to hold out as long as possible," I said. "I want to get you right to the edge, and when you're there, I want you to let me know. I don't want you to fall off that cliff until I'm ready for you to, okay?"

"Yes, Sir," she said, and her cunt wept for my attention.

"That's a good girl," I replied, then licked her again from front to back.

I was slow at first, just using my tongue to get her warmed up. Then I added a finger, dipping it into her warm core, feeling around to find that rough patch just inside, working it once I discovered it. I

215

thought about adding a toy to the mix, but wanted to keep it just the two of us, so kept up with the finger, sliding it in and out of her.

Keeping my fingers in her pussy, I pressed my thumb to her clit, working the bundle of nerves over and over, feeling her clenching my fingers inside. She was getting close, so I backed off a bit, slowing my pace, reducing the pressure on her clit. She gave a bit of a whine, so I smacked her ass with my free hand, and she yelped, pressing her hips further into the end of the bed. I wanted to edge her, keep her so close without falling over, and she was right there.

"So close," she murmured, her breath coming in quick pants. "So very close."

"Do you want to come?"

"Please," she begged, her cunt gripping my fingers as I slid them in and out, paying special attention to the patch that had the most nerves inside her.

"Call my name when you come," I said.

I swiped my finger from my free hand through the mess I was making in her pussy and shoved one finger into her ass, the lubrication sufficient for me to find no resistance.

"Oh God," she cried. "Oh, God, Nick."

Her pussy spasmed against my fingers, her ass pulling the other inside, as she came over and over again. I didn't let up, continuing my onslaught of punishment on her pussy and ass as she clenched and shook with the orgasm as it rolled through her. Finally, spent, she relaxed, her legs nearly buckling, but holding her up just enough.

I pulled my hands free, thrilled with the additional spasm her body gave at the removal, and stood behind her.

"You good here?" I asked.

"Mmhmm," she hummed, her eyes closed, a smile playing on her lips.

Stepping back from her, I walked to the bathroom that was attached to the bedroom we were in, washing my hands thoroughly to ensure there would be no cross contamination. I wanted her to remember this night with only memories, and not an infection of any kind. When I came back, she hadn't moved, and my God was she beautiful.

"Would you like a shower?" I asked, and she shook her head, just enough for me to see the motion. "Then let's get you untied and up on the bed. I'm not done with you, yet."

"Mm."

The sound was both an agreement, and a testament to the state she was in. She was in that post-orgasm haze, and completely at my mercy, and it was a heady thing to have so much control over such a beautiful and amazing woman. I untied her hands, and she wiggled her fingers just to get the blood flowing again. The tie hadn't been tight, but it was likely just a matter of mind rather than physical.

She pushed herself up on the bed and stood, and I wrapped my arms around her waist, my front to her back, my cock resting up against her ass. She shimmied her ass just enough to make me notice, and I pressed into her harder.

"You want me to fuck that ass?" I asked.

"Please, Sir," she replied, her voice holding the emotions that were more than just physical, and it gave me pause.

"I'm going to fuck your pussy first," I said. "But not until you come a couple more times."

Her head was against my shoulder and she rolled it on her neck to look up at me and smiled.

"I'd like that very much," she said, her eyes hooded with desire.

Chapter Twenty-Eight

Charlotte...

He walked me to the edge of the bed, then helped me up. It was high, but not so much that it needed steps. Those types of beds were in the upper bedrooms. The bedding was soft, the comforter a riot of color, and I scooted myself up to the top, shoving the blankets toward the foot in order to get onto the sheets that were much easier to clean. He grabbed the edge of the top and pulled it toward the foot, moving it well out of our way for whatever it was he had planned.

So far, he had already outdone my expectations. That I was comfortable enough to let Apollo go and have Lucifer turn the camera off said a lot about him. Normally, I stuck to my rules, no questions, no argument, but tonight felt different. He felt safe, and he'd proven himself to be so. I had my safe words, my safe signal, and felt confident he would respect that.

I'd gotten a glimpse of the tattoo on his forearm at the museum, but this was the first time I could see the whole of it, as well as the other ones that were further up on his shoulder, likely always covered by his shirts. He turned to the nightstand next to the bed, fishing out a couple of condoms from the bowl on top, and I shivered thinking what he might do to me next. There were letters down the back of his arm, USMC and MNBL. I was sure the first was for the Marine Corps, but didn't know what the other one was. The thing that threw me was he was a baseball player, so it didn't make sense that the first tattoo meant that.

"You good?" he asked, and I turned to look at him.

"Yeah," I replied.

"It's my granddad, dad, uncle, and brother," he said.

"Were you in?"

"No," he said. "My dad would have kicked my ass if I'd gone in. Did try, but he shut that shit down."

"I wondered," I said.

"Lost my brother when I was a junior in high school," he said. "That's when I tried to get in. Dad found the paperwork and shut it down before I even got started. He was right, though. Mom wouldn't have survived if I'd done it."

"I'm sorry," I said. "I shouldn't have…"

"Totally fine," he said, cutting me off. "It's good to remember that there are real people behind the numbers. It's why I did the tattoo, to always remember."

"I never knew anyone who was in any kind of service like that," I said. "It really wasn't a thing in my…"

He waited, giving me time to finish my thought, but I wasn't sure how to finish it.

"Come on," I said, reaching out to him. "Let's not think about such serious subjects when you're standing there naked and you haven't fucked me yet."

He laughed. Full-on, no-holds-barred amusement falling right out of him.

"Who could say no to a request like that?" he asked.

"Hopefully not you," I replied as he climbed up onto the bed beside me.

He'd lost some of his firmness, so I slid my hand down and

grabbed hold, stroking it along its length, slowly from base to tip and back again. Watching his face, he closed his eyes, simply enjoying the feel of it all. The way he was, on his knees next to me, one hand holding the foil packet with so much promise, just revved my engine. He opened his eyes, though they stayed hooded, and looked at me. Something shifted in that moment, and I couldn't tell you what it was, but it was as if we fell into step, into rhythm, into a kind of communication that didn't require words, and it was amazing.

"I'm going to fuck you now," he growled, his voice so low if I hadn't been paying attention, I might have missed it. "I'm going to make you come all over my cock. You're going to scream my name, and everyone in the whole fucking house is going to hear you. Are you ready for that?"

I shivered. I couldn't help it. The way he said it, the positively possessiveness of his words, just flipped my switch. I nodded, licking my lips, and let my legs fall open for him.

"I'm gonna need you to tell me," he said, and the little curve of his lips told me he was serious, yet amused.

"Yes, Sir," I said. "I am very ready for you to fuck me so hard I come all over your cock. I will call out your name and it will ricochet from the rafters. Hell, they might hear it all the way down the block."

"That's my good girl," he said, and God, did that just do it for me.

He moved and settled himself between my legs, then handed the condom to me. Sitting up, I took the foil packet and tore it open, sliding the slippery disk from the pouch. I stroked his cock, sliding up and down it to get it as hard as possible, then pinched the tip of the condom before rolling it down the length of him. I could feel his eyes on me as I did the task, their dark stare pressing on my hands as if he were touching them directly. Once he was covered, I tipped my head up and looked at him.

"Lay back," he said, and I did as he told me. "Good girl. Now, get those fingers on your pussy and start stroking that clit. I want you all primed up before I shove inside you."

"Yes, Sir," I said, immediately following his instructions, my finger finding that nub of nerves at the apex of my sex and stroking it with fervor.

"Oh yeah," he said, watching me intently. "You're such a good girl. You should definitely be rewarded."

Leaning over me, he pressed one hand by my side, the other holding him at my entrance. Sliding along the slit, he moved it up and down, gathering the natural lubricant my body was making as I played with myself. All at once, he found purchase and shoved into me hard, all the way to the base, and my God, did that shoot a fire through me. He held himself against me, pinning my fingers between our bodies, his eyes dark as they looked into mine.

"I didn't hear you," he said, and I blinked, unsure what he was getting at. "You forgot to call my name," he added.

"Which name should I use?" I asked, smiling up at him as he pressed against me.

"Nick," he said. "I don't want you to call anything but my real name when you come."

"You sure?" I asked, knowing that privacy was the rule of the club. It's why we used nicknames and code names instead of our real ones. It was why I hadn't given him my real name.

"I am *not* going to be called some random ridiculous name when you're coming so hard you see stars," he said. "I want everyone in the fucking world to know it's me that's fucking you, that's driving you over the edge, that's shooting you into the stratosphere."

"Then fuck me," I said, shifting my hips against his.

Shifting, he hooked his free arm under my leg, lifting it up over his shoulder, angling himself to hit me deeper.

"Keep those fingers moving," he said, then started to move, in and out slowly.

If anything, I was good at following directions, and I started stroking my clit, faster and faster with his increased speed. It didn't take long for our bodies to start to ring through the room, the slap of skin on skin as he pumped into me, harder and harder with each stroke. It was music to my ears, and I loved that we were both without our masks, our true selves sharing this moment of ecstasy. I could feel the energy exchange between us, flowing on the ethers, bouncing off our bodies as we rocked the bed with our motion.

"I'm close," I said as the build up inside me rose.

"I'm listening," he said, continuing to pound me into the mattress.

Concentrating on my fingers, the feel of him sliding in and out of me, and watching his face as his smile grew with each breath I panted out, I fell. Headfirst, hard as can be, and exploded into a million pieces. Sparks flitted around my eyes, blood rushed through my ears, and I gasped with every breath. It was a full body experience, where everything slowed down and sped up all at the same time, and I couldn't grasp anything for more than a bare moment before it flew away. I felt him shudder, stutter, then slam into me full force, a few short strokes, then he collapsed on top of me, and I was bathed in his scent, his body, his everything, and it was the most wonderful place I could imagine being.

Chapter Twenty-Nine

Nick...

"My God, woman," I whispered in her ear. "The things you do to me. The things you bring out of me. I've never felt that before."

She ran her arms up and down my back, her leg having been returned to its rightful place as soon as I'd finished. I didn't want to move, didn't want to let her go.

"Only thing that would be better would be to not have had that barrier," she said, then sucked in a breath.

I don't think she meant to say it out loud, but she had, and I had to agree. But that wasn't something I did. No, I kept myself covered at all times. Except I had let her suck my cock without a condom, and that wasn't something I did. This time with her, with just the two of us, felt like something more than just sex, though. Not that the sex wasn't fucking amazing, but it was something else, something I didn't have a name for.

Pressing the mattress, I pushed up off her. She looked at me, questioningly, and I wasn't sure what she was asking. Nothing would be better than staying right where I was, buried deep inside her, looking at her well-fucked countenance. But I needed to pull out, get that condom taken care of, before an accident occurred.

"Don't move," I said, giving her a quick kiss.

Pressing the bottom of the condom to the base of my dick, I slid out of her, feeling the aftershocks quiver inside her, watching her shudder on the bed.

"You did good," I said, and she looked again like she wasn't sure what I was talking about. "You called my name. Loud, clear, and very good. I'm sure everyone heard you."

Her eyes went wide for a moment, then she smiled. Yeah, she was definitely my new favorite toy, and I planned to play with her as much as she'd let me. Strange as it seemed, I didn't want to be with anyone else again, and that wasn't normal for me. Instead of thinking more about it, though, I simply got off the bed, walked to the bathroom, and pulled the condom off, setting it on the towel that was on the counter. I washed myself up, then got a washcloth warm and wet, just like she was, and took it with me to take care of her again.

She was still, eyes closed, breathing slowed to a normal pace, arms resting at her sides, her legs like a butterfly open to either side, exposing her sex to me, and I reached over and wiped along it, gathering the fluids we'd created from her. When she shuddered again, I knew she was in that afterglow space, and simply did what needed to be done, cleaning her up so she wouldn't have to deal with anything after she left. Honestly, I wished we were anywhere but at the club. If we were in my hotel room, or wherever it was that she lived, she wouldn't have to move.

Once I had cleaned her up enough, I went back to the bathroom, and dropped the cloth into the sink. Going back to the bed, I climbed up next to her, shifting her a little, then laid down next to her, pulling her against me. She came willingly, cuddling into my side as if she were built to be there, letting out a soft sigh. I held her close, her corset a bit scratchy against my body, but not wanting to do more than just hold her.

We stayed like that for a while, her breathing softly against my chest, me with my nose in her hair, taking in everything I could from her while she was here. I didn't know how long we lay there, but it wasn't nearly long enough, and a knock fell on the door, rousing us from our rest.

"Charlie?" I heard, and it was Apollo.

"Yeah," she mumbled, shifting at my side.

"You're about to lose your time," he said. "You have about fifteen minutes until someone else has the room. You guys good?"

"We're good," I said. "Thanks for the heads up."

"No problem," he said, then pulled the door shut, leaving us alone once again.

"I don't want to get up," she said.

"Wish we didn't have to," I replied. "But that's the way these kinds of things go."

Pushing her up to a sitting position, I shifted myself, getting upright as well. I went to move off the bed, but her hand on my thigh stopped me. I turned to look at her, and there was something in her face. I placed my hand on her cheek, and leaned in, kissing her softly on her lips, watching her eyes close as she melted into me.

As much as I wanted it to last forever, I pulled away after a moment, resting my forehead on hers, looking into her eyes, trying to tell her without saying anything, that this was different, this was special, and I was completely all in where she was concerned. What-ever she saw in my eyes, made her smile, and I saw a similar senti-ment in hers reflected back at me.

"Let me help you," I said, sliding to the floor and turning to help her down.

We moved over to where her clothes were, just panties and her dress, but I helped to put them on her, sliding the panties up and over her very nice and shapely ass. Then sliding the dress up and over her hips, holding the opening as she slid her arms into the sleeves before pulling it up and over her shoulders. With my hands on her shoulders, I turned her back to me so I could zip it up. Once she was done, she walked to my pile and began to disassemble the mess they'd become, finding my boxers first and helping me into them.

Neither of us spoke as we dressed each other. Whether it was to not break the spell we'd found in that room, or because we weren't sure what to say, it didn't really matter. I enjoyed the quiet, punctuated occasionally with moans and cries from outside the room. By the time we were dressed, including our masks, I knew that we would be recreating at least part of what we'd done. Whether it would be at the club, or somewhere else, I didn't know.

"Ready?" she asked when she'd finished tying my tie.

"Just gotta grab the condom," I said, and she gave me a face. "Last thing I need is someone stealing it and using it to cause me more havoc than I care to endure."

"Never thought of that," she said.

"Probably because you wouldn't do it," I replied.

"True," she said.

I grabbed the used condom, tying it off at the end so nothing escaped, and shoved it into my jacket pocket. I'd take care of it when I got back to my hotel. Coming back into the room, she was still standing where I'd left her, a glazed look on her face.

"Ready?" I asked, and she turned to me, her smile growing.

"Wanna go somewhere else?" she asked, and I was surprised.

"I'll go wherever you want," I said. "Where did you have in mind?"

"Follow me," she said, then slid her hand into mine and pulled me behind her toward the door.

She swung it open, and Apollo was standing just outside, a young woman next to him, her body covered completely in latex, tight against her body, leaving nothing to the imagination.

"Hey," Charlie said to Apollo.

"Sounded good," he said.

"It was," she said, her smile wide.

He looked over her head at me and gave me a nod, whether it was approval or appreciation, I couldn't say.

"Come on," Charlie said to me, then tugged on my hand.

We walked to the front door, and I opened it once we got there, holding it wide for her to precede me outside.

"Charlie," Mr. Stone said as we stepped out. "Saturn. Did you enjoy your evening?"

"We did, thank you," Charlie said.

"Yes," I replied. "It was quite enjoyable."

"That's good to hear," he said. "Did you need me to get your car, Saturn?"

I looked at Charlie and she nodded.

"If you wouldn't mind?" I said.

He turned and pulled my key from the container that held them, handing it to the man who was standing at the side. He took the key, jogged down the steps of the house, and headed to wherever it was they kept the cars for guests.

"When will you be back for your car?" he asked her.

"I'm not sure," she replied. "I'll take my key now, though, if it's fine to keep it here."

"It will be safe here," he said, pulling her key out of the same box he'd pulled mine from, handing it to her.

We'd barely finished the conversation when my car pulled up in front of the building, the man who had driven it over, climbing out of the driver's seat, and leaving the door open for me. I walked down the stairs, Charlie's hand in the crook of my arm, and opened the passenger door for her to slide in. Once she was settled, I shut the door, walking around to get in myself.

With the doors shut, we were alone for the first time that night. I shifted the car into gear and pulled away from the curb, waiting for her to tell me where we were going. It took a moment, but then she spoke.

"Head toward the Quarter," she said. "I know a place."

"I'm not sure how to get there from here," I said. "I'm new in town, and really haven't done much exploring."

"You found the Lavender Lounge easily," she said, and I looked over to her with a smile. "Fine," she said, then told me which way to go, directing me when to turn.

It was crowded, like unbearably so, and I wasn't sure whether it was going to be a good idea to leave the car in the area, but I trusted her to know. We ended up parking in the lot for the casino in the Quarter, as she said it had better security than most of the other places. Once we were parked, we climbed out, me helping her out of the passenger side, and then headed out toward the street.

Joining the crowd, we wandered through the area, her leading the way, and me walking beside her, holding her hand. The amount of people that were out and on the street at this early hour was insane, but I guess the city gave New York a run for their money when it came to a city that never sleeps.

We ended up down by the river, walking along the banks until we got to a set of stairs that sort of just went down to the water. There was a paddle boat to one side that was all lit up with lights like a Christmas tree. The water was dark and looked deep, and I didn't want to go too far down, not wanting to get into it at all.

She tugged my hand, and I followed her down, but she stopped a few steps up from the water, sitting on the cement. Instead of sitting beside her, I sat on the step above, right behind her, a leg on either side of her body, my arms coming around her to hold her against my chest as we watched the waves lap against the steps.

It was quiet, even though we were so close to the action, and I enjoyed the calm after the walk we'd taken. As much as I loved the game of baseball, it was the crowds that I didn't like. Not that I was against fans, or them in the stands, but the onslaught of people coming up to you, expecting you to do whatever they wanted, thinking they had a right to you because you were somewhat of a public figure.

"What'cha thinking?" she asked, tipping her head back to look at me.

"Just how quiet it is," I replied. "I like the quiet."

"Then you're in the wrong town," she replied.

"It's been actually fine," I said, pressing my lips to her forehead. "Daytime is when I'm available to walk around, and that seems to be the best time to come into this area."

"Good to know," she replied. "I'm usually in my cave during the day, only coming out after the museum is closed."

"You telling me you're a vampire?" I asked in jest.

"Don't joke about such things," she said. "There are stories of them all throughout the city. You can find things you shouldn't if you look in the wrong places."

I was a bit taken aback. She didn't seem to be the type of person who believed such nonsense, but the way she said it indicated she truly did believe in those things. Not wanting to ruin the night, I let her have this belief, and went back to holding her and watching the water.

We sat for quite a while, just watching the water, until she shifted forward and turned toward me. Her movement was smooth, feline in nature, and she was straddling my lap before I even registered it. My arms naturally went around her waist, and her lips crashed onto mine. While it was unexpected, it wasn't undesired, and I returned the kiss, opening myself to her exploration, her hands going into my hair and holding me to her. When we came apart, she was gasping for air, her chest rising and falling, her eyes brightly reflecting the lights from behind me.

"Fuck me," she said, and I blinked. "Right here, right now, nothing between us. Just fuck me."

"I don't want..."

"I've had my tubes tied," she interrupted. "I won't get pregnant, I'm clean, I don't want kids, and you wouldn't have to worry about anything."

She shifted her hips, rubbing herself on me, and it was making me hard again.

"How do you know..."

"I trust you," she said. "I've never done this before. Never wanted to even risk it, but I trust you, believe you, and want this. Will you be my first?"

The sincerity in her voice was clear, and I wanted very much to say yes, but I was hesitant. I always, *always*, wore a condom. The fact that I didn't when she was giving me a blowjob was a fluke, and not something I did. She could see the hesitancy in my face, even though the light was behind me, because she sat back a bit.

"You're not ready," she said, and it was as if a weight had been lifted. "That's okay. I understand."

She was dejected and hurt, and I knew it was my fault, so I pulled her to me, back onto my lap, and held her for a moment.

"I want to," I confessed. "I really do. I've just always had a rule, and I've never broken it. Fuck," I muttered, angry at myself. "I never do anything without a condom. That I let you suck my dick without one is a big step outside my comfort zone."

"I didn't know," she said, her hand on my cheek. "I wouldn't have if—"

"No," I said, my finger to her lips. "I wanted it. I would have stopped you if I didn't. I just...I'm not quite ready to jump all the way into this. I mean, I am, but I'm not, if that makes sense."

"It does," she said. "I've never wanted to be in an actual relationship before. Well, early on I did, but he died, and I just never wanted anyone else. This feels different, though. Does it feel that way to you?"

"I thought it was just me," I said.

"Definitely not just you," she said, and her smile was wide. "We'll wait, but know that it's something I'm interested in, and am good with waiting."

"How do you feel about exclusivity?" I asked, surprising even myself with the question.

"I don't know," she answered, and I appreciated her honesty.

"Completely fine," I said. "But will you think about it?"

"I had pretty much taken a step back from the club," she said. "Had told them to decline all requests, which was a hard thing to do.

Going back, though, but not actually doing anything with anyone but you, was a strange experience. I've never done that before."

"You usually do more scenes?"

"I do," she said. "But they're always negotiated and worked out well in advance. I do a lot of mentoring to the newer members, those who want to take on the submissive role, but aren't sure how to do it. Or those who want to learn to be more dominant without pushing too hard or being cruel."

"That's a good thing to do," I said. "I can respect that."

"I needed the break, though," she said. "It was time for me to take a step back and reevaluate my life, my future, and where I saw things going. Sure, I could be a club girl my whole life, but I've got a career, something I love just as much as the sex, and let me tell you, I fucking love sex."

"Never would have guessed that," I said with a laugh.

"Yeah, well, that's me," she said with a shrug.

She shivered then, and I could tell it was from the chill in the air. It was getting late, and we both probably had places to be the next day, so I helped her to stand, then stood myself, taking my jacket off, and wrapping it around her shoulders. She tucked herself into my side as we climbed the steps and made our way back to the garage where my car was parked.

The city had quieted some, but there were still several people out and about, and we had to make our way through them to get to the casino and my car. She stayed tucked into my side, her arm wrapped around my middle with mine around her, holding her to me. To anyone else, we must have looked like a couple who were on their way home after an evening out on the town. While that was true in a sense, it didn't capture the two of us entirely.

Were we a couple? I didn't know the answer to that question. But the fact that she was willing to think about it, to not shut me down immediately, said something, and I was willing to wait and see where this went.

Chapter Thirty

Charlotte...

I'd given him my phone number, he'd given me his, and he'd said he was going to be out of town starting Sunday evening for a week. It was pushing into September, so the days were getting shorter, the nights longer, and he had talked about possibly going back to San Diego once the season was over. I wasn't sure how I felt about that, but hadn't wanted to push anything either. He'd asked about exclusivity, whether I was interested, and I'd been hesitant. Now, though, the next day, I wasn't sure how I felt about him talking about leaving, either.

It was weird that I was having so many feelings about him after just one time together. Never had I had this much of a reaction to anyone since Jack, and it was making me question whether I should just step back completely, both from the club and him. Thing was, I really liked him. He was good to talk to, fucking amazing in bed, and just seemed like an all-around nice guy. So, why was I having second thoughts?

Instead of dealing with the issues like an adult, I shoved them to the back of my mind and decided to bury myself in work. I'd been given the task of finding a new exhibit, so I spent the rest of the weekend doing research in my office. It was something I'd asked to do, a position I wanted to move into, and since they knew I could do the work, they let me loose.

Emails were sent, meetings were scheduled, and inquiries were communicated clearly. I was interested in having a specific artist as a featured exhibit, and nothing was going to deter that dream. This particular artist was what catapulted me into my love of art and was someone I wanted to showcase. They weren't one of the major artists who everyone knew, so it had initially been a hard sell. But my persistence, and my determination, had finally won out, and I was about as close as I could be to getting something set up.

Between my new work, and the regular duties I had at the museum, the week flew by, and when I got a text from Nick the next Monday, I was a bit thrown off. He'd asked if I wanted to have lunch sometime this week, but I was too busy to leave the museum, so I offered dinner, which he had to turn down because of his work schedule. It seemed we were destined to not be able to work this relationship type thing out, so I sort of just put him out of my mind.

Ignoring the problem wouldn't solve it, but I had bigger things to think about, and so I just figured we'd sort of fade apart. Not that I didn't think about him every time I showered, every time I climbed into bed, every time I looked at my box of toys. No, he was constantly on my mind, at the edge of my thoughts, sitting there waiting to be brought back in.

Finally, when I couldn't ignore the temptation any longer, I sent a text to him asking to meet me after his game one Friday night. I'd checked the team's schedule and knew they were at the end of the season, so he would likely be heading back to the West Coast once it was over, and this might be the last chance I'd have to be with him. His response was swift, almost immediate, and he agreed, asking me where I wanted to meet.

Offering my home seemed a bit too forward. Besides, if he was just going to vanish, I didn't want that memory to taint my sacred space. I loved my home, would never leave if I could help it, and sharing it with someone else just wasn't something I wanted to do. Instead, I offered to pay for a hotel room, so long as it wasn't one of those cheap hotels that never changed the sheets. I told him I would be willing to pay for an entire weekend with him. To my delight, he agreed, and told me to pick the place and tell him where to show up.

Now, in addition to the research I was doing for the upcoming exhibit, I had to find a place that I could rent for the weekend. I wanted some anonymity, but also wanted to be in a place where there were people. It was a contradiction, but actually made sense in my mind. I found a home I could rent for the weekend on the outskirts of town, booked it, and sent the information to Nick. When he didn't respond right away, I was a bit confused, as well as hurt. Then, I looked at the time and realized it was because he was playing. I would get an answer when he'd finished his work.

One of the other things I wanted to do before he actually left was go to a game and watch him play. It wasn't something I would normally do, going to a sporting event, but it intrigued me. To watch him in his natural habitat, doing the job he loved, would be a way to see a different part of him. I wanted that, wanted to know if the exclusivity he asked about was something I might consider. I sent another text asking about going with him to the game on Saturday night. We could meet after the game Friday at the house, fuck our absolute brains out any which way we wanted, then sleep until it was time for him to go to the game. I could go with him, or meet him there, and watch him work. Then, when he was done, we could go back to the house and fuck again until we both were spent before he had to leave the next day to do it again. It seemed like a logical plan, but I would have to wait to see what he thought.

Going to sleep took some work, and it didn't come until the wee hours of the morning, giving me only a few hours. I was so exhausted I forgot my phone when I went to work, so had to wait until I got home to see if I had gotten a response from Nick. It felt like I was in school all over again, waiting on word from Jack that he would play with me. I didn't like that feeling, and began to have second thoughts about a relationship with Nick.

Add to that, Gretchen had been out of work for a couple of days with some scares with her baby. It had been insane with the added work from my conquest for the exhibit, and my missing Gretchen at her position within our regular area of work. Finally, I found a house to rent. It was in an area that was decent for the city, but not right in the middle, so was still quiet enough. I sent the address to Nick, told him I would be there already, and would be waiting for him when he was done with the game. I'd asked him to text me when he was heading out so I could be ready for him.

I'd packed a bag for the weekend with several different outfits, as well as nearly my full box of toys. I wanted to give him options, plenty of things he could do with, and to me, and was excited to see what he would choose. When I walked into the museum, I knew something was wrong.

"What's going on?" I asked Kendra, our front desk person.

She just shook her head, a tear trickling down her cheek. My first thought was that someone died, and I honestly wasn't sure who it might be. We had a handful of staff that were older than me, but not to the point that they might die unexpectedly. Then I wondered whether some of the volunteers who would come in and help direct folks around might have passed. Plenty of them were far past retirement, and that was my guess as to what had happened. It was sad, but they were all at the age where it was definitely a possibility.

"Charlotte," Frank said, and I turned to him.

When I saw his face, I knew something had happened with Gretchen. My best guess was that she lost the baby, but I couldn't know for sure until I asked the question, or he told me the answer.

"Gretchen is going to be out for an indeterminate amount of time," he said.

"She lost the baby?" I asked, already knowing the answer.

"She did," he said, and I could tell he was holding back emotions. "It was pretty terrible from what Doug said, and I told him she could take as much time as she needed. That being said, I'm going to have to ask you to step in a bit and take over some of her projects and tasks."

"Absolutely," I replied. "Is anyone setting something up to help them with anything? Meals or care packages or anything like that?"

"Nothing's been set up," he said. "I know that everyone would love to help, we just don't know what to do."

"I'll reach out to Doug and see how we can support them," I said.

"I'd appreciate that," he said. "Don't work yourself too thin, though. If you get overwhelmed or need help, let me know."

"No problem," I said. "I'm sure I'll be fine, but will let you know if I need anything."

"We have volunteers here who can jump into some things," he said.

"We may want to reach out to one of the other museums in the area to see if they can spare someone to help me finish up this incoming exhibit," I said. "The one Gretchen and I were working on. The one I've been trying to get set up is going to be fine, but this one is set to be revealed to the public in the next couple of weeks, and there is still a bit of work to do."

"I'll reach out to my counterparts," he said. "I'm sure they'd be willing to send someone in to help out."

"Thanks," I said.

Walking to the elevator, I pulled out my phone and shot a text off to Doug, asking how we could support them. I knew it wasn't likely I would get a response right away, and I felt bad that I was planning an epic weekend while my friend was losing her child, but there was nothing I could do to change her situation, so I vowed to make sure I was there for her when everything was over. As soon as I stepped off the elevator, my phone started ringing.

"Hello?" I asked as I answered, having not looked at it beforehand.

"Charlotte," Gretchen said, and then broke down sobbing.

"Hey," I said. "It's okay. Everything will work out. I don't know how or when, but I promise you, we'll figure this out."

"I miss her so much," she sobbed, and it took a minute for me to realize that she was talking about her baby. "She was absolutely perfect, and now she's gone, and it's all my fault."

"Oh, no, baby," I said. "You did nothing wrong. You did the best you could, but sometimes it just doesn't work. I wish I could fix this for you."

"I'm sorry," she said, then there was a muffled voice before Doug took the phone. "Hello?"

"Doug," I said. "It's Charlotte, from the museum. She called me."

"I'm sorry," he said. "I just went to the bathroom. I didn't think she'd call."

"It's totally fine," I said. "Tell me how I can help. What can I do?"

"I don't know," he said, and I could hear the strain in his voice. "We're still at the hospital. They're going to keep her overnight. I'll call you later and give you an update, but the doctors are coming in."

"Okay," I replied. "If I don't answer, it's because I'm busy working or something. We love you guys and are here to help however you need us."

"Thanks," he said, then the line went dead.

I took a deep breath, let it out slowly, and thought about what she had said. She'd said the baby was perfect, but I wasn't sure what that meant. She was only a few months along, like three or so, so I wasn't sure what she meant that she was perfect. Maybe they'd shown her some diagrams of what the baby might look like. Never having wanted kids, I didn't know if the embryo would look like a bean or a baby at that stage, and didn't really want to get sucked down a rabbit hole of finding out. I had work to do, and a weekend to look forward to, and I really wanted to see about getting to a game before it was all over.

Chapter Thirty-One

Nick...

"Big plans?" JP asked as I grabbed my gear to head out to the car.

"Yeah," I replied.

"Figured," he said. "You never hang out with us. Why's that?"

"Still learning the city and the team," I said. "Besides, it's only been like a month or so. And I hang out when we're out of town."

"Closing in on two months, dude," he said. "Would be nice if you did something here in the city with us."

"Maybe this week," I suggested. "I just have something planned for the weekend."

"You seem to have a lot of plans for someone who's still learning the city," he said.

"I found something I liked," I said. "No need to explore, at least not right now. Besides, I'm boring."

"Nah," he said with a laugh. "You're mysterious, and the guys don't know you. That just makes you all the more interesting. You're like the forbidden fruit or some shit."

"They're gonna be so bummed when they get the truth," I said, laughing at myself. "See you tomorrow."

I climbed into my car, started it up, and plugged in the address Charlie had sent me into my GPS. I was still new to the city, and having someone tell me how to get somewhere was important, especially on this particular night. We hadn't discussed particulars about what we wanted, but the way she'd responded the last time we were together, I was really looking forward to the time we would get to spend uninterrupted.

Getting out of the Quarter with the traffic from the game, as well as the regular Friday night crowds, was rough, but once I was through most of it, the drive to the house she'd rented was quick. It was in a neighborhood, or neighboring town, I still wasn't sure how they all worked here, and down some side streets. Pulling up in front of the unassuming single-story home, I parked in the driveway next to her Mustang. I was glad she brought that car, as it helped to confirm I was at the right address.

Putting the car in park, I opened the door and popped the trunk, walking around to pull my bag out. It was a regular wheeled carry-on bag, but it had a few new toys I'd purchased the day before that I was looking forward to trying out. Shutting the trunk, I took myself up the walkway to the front door, knocking when I got there.

"Hey," she said after she opened the door a crack and peeking out.

Opening it further, she stepped back, letting me inside the home she'd rented. The lights were low, so I hadn't noticed what she'd been wearing, but she closed the door behind me, and I turned to look at her. That same red corset, black stockings pinned to the bottom of it, and bright red panties that were lace and clearly needing to be removed.

"You look ready," I said with a smile, standing my bag up on its base.

"I need this," she said, and I detected something in her voice.

"You sure?"

"More than anything," she said, pressing a hand to my chest. "I need you to make me not think for a while. Be in charge, take me out of my head, and let me forget the rest of the world."

The way she was begging told me that something had happened. I didn't know what, or whether it was to her specifically, or to someone close to her. Either way, she needed to let go, to be released from the here and now, and taken to a place that would be full of all the pleasure she could handle. My goal was to do that for her. I wanted her to forget everything except the moment we were sharing, and that started at that moment.

"Hands behind you," I said, and she obeyed, moving her hands behind her back. "Grab your elbows," I added, and I assume she did as she was told, but couldn't be sure since it was behind her back.

Pulling my suitcase to the couch, I opened it, pulling out a length of rope I'd brought with me. It was bamboo, so soft to the touch, and I returned to her, walking around and standing behind her. Pulling the end out, I took it and slid it between one hand, and her arm where she was holding it. Keeping the bundle together, I wrapped the rope around her arms all along the connection, from one wrist to the other, then back again. It wasn't so tight as to cut off her circulation, but it definitely didn't leave any room for movement from them.

"Good girl," I whispered in her ear, her body shivering just a bit with the breath that floated over it.

With my hand on her back, I guided her through the dimly lit living room and down a hall toward what I assumed were bedrooms. She must have gotten to the house early, because each room had a small light turned on, and the master bedroom had candles set up on the nightstands, well away from anything that might catch fire. They weren't lit, just there, with a lighter next to them for easy use.

"You want to have some wax play?" I asked, and she nodded, muttering, "Yes, Sir," quietly.

"Did you get the right kind of candles?"

"Yes, Sir," she said, and I could hear a hint of excitement in her voice, which was a nice change from the tone she'd had just a few minutes earlier.

Walking her closer to the bed, I pulled the blankets down so that only the bottom sheet was there, then I went into the bathroom and took the plastic shower curtain down from its hooks to place beneath her. No need for us to ruin a good set of sheets, or for her to have to pay damages if we could avoid it. Plastic wasn't ideal, but it would work in a pinch.

When I came back into the room, she hadn't moved, still standing next to the bed, her arms bound behind her. The panties I'd seen were actually a thong, so her ass was visible, and I was tempted to give her a good smack before getting things started. I didn't, though, wanting to ease into things with her. The emotion I heard in her voice earlier told me she was in a fragile state, even if she was letting go right now. Her mind was likely clouded with whatever had upset her, and my goal wasn't to beat it out of her, but to give her so much pleasure she forgot, even if it was only for a little while.

Placing the shower curtain onto the bed, I made sure it covered plenty of space so we could enjoy the time without worry. Once it was set, I slid one of the pillows underneath it right next to the edge of the bed, the other into a place that I figured her head would end up, then pressed her back, holding her bound arms so she didn't fall flat on her face. I had to move the pillow for her head a bit, but she was patient as I got it into the right place.

Her head was turned to the side, her eyes open, but hooded, and her breathing was slow and steady. Everything about her told me she was ready to enjoy whatever I had planned. I lit the candles, double checking them to make sure they wouldn't be too hot for her. Nothing said sexy like burned skin. Next to the candles was an ice bucket, full of ice cubes, and that made me smile. She'd thought of both temperature extremes, and I had to assume she was a willing participant in both options but would ask before I began. While the candles were warming up, the wax melting enough that I could use it to drip on her, I went to work getting her into a place to be ready to take the enjoyment I was going to give her.

Running my hands up her back, I slid them over her shoulders, giving them a good massaging. The way she was bound would put pressure on them, and I knew they would need help in getting comfortable again once I was finished. Next, I slid my hands down her arms, squeezing them to make sure the muscles weren't too tight. Nothing fucked up a good time more than cramps in the wrong places.

By the time I got to her hips, she'd sunk into the bed, her breathing was even slower, and her eyes were closed. She was definitely letting everything else go, and I couldn't have been happier. I hooked my thumbs into the straps of her thong, sliding it down and over the stockings. She'd done the right thing by putting them on after she'd hooked the stockings to her corset, which told me she was definitely experienced in this sort of thing.

Gentle pressure at her ankle, and she lifted her foot just enough for me to slip the panties off before doing the same with the other foot. She was completely bare where it mattered most, and I used the moment to nudge her feet a bit further apart. Not so far as to make it uncomfortable, but so that I could have access to her pussy and ass, both of which I intended to use as much as possible.

"You're already so wet for me," I said, sliding my fingers along her pussy lips. "You did nothing to get you there, did you?"

"No, Sir," she said, and I smiled.

"Good girl," I said, sliding up and down her slit, her aroma filtering up to me, a scent I would love to smell all the time. "Shall we start with hot or cold?" I asked.

"Cold, please," she said, and I was happy to give her what she wanted.

Taking an ice cube from the bucket, I set it on the top of her ass, right where the crack ends at the base of her spine. She sucked in a quick breath, then shivered, but relaxed back into the rhythm she was in before. Ever so slowly, I slid the cube back and forth along the tops of her globes, getting it to melt just a little bit. Then, I slid it down the crack, along it to her asshole, where I pressed it against her back entrance. I didn't want to shove it in, just get that cooling sensation going for her.

When I felt she had handled that well enough, I dropped the cube onto the shower curtain at her hip and picked up another one from the bucket. Instead of warming it a bit on her back, though, this time I stuck it right on her clit, pressing the cold against the bundle of nerves at the apex of her sex, knowing that the sensation would cause a great reaction. She did not disappoint at all, and sucked in again, this time, though, she pressed back against my hand, working to get more connection with the ice I had against her.

"So eager," I murmured, my other hand on her back to hold her in place. "You want me to slide this up your pussy?"

"Please, Sir," she practically begged.

I didn't want to disappoint her, so did as she desired, sliding the cube up her slit until it came into contact with the opening of her cunt, sticking the corner of the cube slightly into the space. She sighed out in pleasure, her body sinking further into the mattress. Oh yeah, she was loving this attention, and seemed to be getting out of her head.

I took my leg and pressed it against the cube, holding it in place, while I took my hands to work the ties loose on her arms. I wanted to take her corset off, get a chance to see those tits she'd had bursting at the edge of it, since that hadn't happened the last time we'd been together. I also wanted to use the wax on the more sensitive spots on her, if she was game. Not her pussy, but around her tits might be nice.

When her arms were free, I massaged the striped flesh of them, working the blood flow back into them. I placed them on either side of her body, her eyes still closed as she let me work her in whatever way I wanted. I found the ends of the ties for the corset and began to undo the knot, loosening the fabric and, after unhooking her stockings, splayed it away from her body, shifting her arms so the cloth could be beneath her. I reached around and in front of her legs to unhook those connections to her stockings as well.

"We should probably take this completely off," I suggested. "Don't want to stain it with the wax, now, do we?"

She shifted herself and I pulled the fabric from underneath her, setting it off to the side at the foot of the bed. The way she was tied into it left beautiful marks along her back, and I ran my hands up along the ridges, pressing into the spaces they left behind.

"Are you ready for some hot?" I asked.

"Yes," she said, barely a hush of air coming from her mouth.

I picked up the candle and tilted it just enough so that I could feel the temperature of the wax that had built up inside the glass. It was warm, but not terribly hot, but I didn't want to burn her, so let just the slightest amount drip onto her shoulder. She sucked in a breath, then relaxed as the wax hardened on her skin. Another drop on the other shoulder elicited the same reaction, a quick intake of air and then relaxation as it cooled enough to get hard.

Wanting her to get to that high we all reached for, I stepped back and set the candle down, the ice cube falling to the floor at my feet. I bent and picked it up, setting it next to the melted one that was on the curtain atop the bed. I slid my jacket off, tossing it onto a chair that was in the corner of the room. My shirt followed as I toed my shoes off. My belt came undone, and I wondered whether I should hold on to it for a little spanking but decided to let it go for now. We had all weekend, and there would be plenty of time for that type of punishment.

Instead, I let my pants fall to the floor, stepping out of them after sliding my feet back to pull my socks off. My boxers went down as well, and I was now more naked than she was, what with her still wearing her stockings and heels. She'd set a box of condoms on the nightstand, nestled between the candles and ice bucket, so I pulled the box open and took one out, tearing the package open, and rolling it down my length.

Leaning over her, my chest to her back, I asked, "Would you like me to fuck you?"

"Yes," she said, another whisper of breath. "Please fuck me."

"As the lady wishes," I replied, then stood up behind her.

Taking another cube, I set it at her entrance, sliding it up and down her slit, cooling the heated core of her down, then pressing it against her asshole. It was big enough that it wouldn't accidentally go in, but even if it did, it was just water, so nothing harmful would come of it. Lining myself up at her entrance, I slid inside easily, her cunt sucking me into her like it was meant to be there.

The chill of the cube against my pelvic bone was an interesting sensation, and I had to admit I liked the feeling. I reached over and picked up the candle again, being careful to only drip it on places that were not so sensitive as to be damaged by the heat. I started at the top of her spine, far enough down that her hair that wasn't swept to the side was still safe from the wax, and dripped it, bringing the candle in a line down her back along her vertebra.

Her one hand went up to pull her hair further out of the way, though she didn't need to worry about that. As I got closer to her ass, she shifted her body, tilting her ass up enough that it was making it hard to stay inside her. The hand that wasn't holding the candle pressed against her, and I took one foot to sort of kick her legs further apart. I let a good amount of wax pool at the curve of her back, that dip near her waist that was a hollow, then tipped the candle back up and set it on the bedside table.

She was absolutely beautiful, and had chosen a deep burgundy candle, and the color against the white of the sheets and the paleness of her back was like a piece of art. If I'd had the talent, I'd have taken time to paint it, the vibrant colors against her skin in the flickering candlelight of the room. Even the small lamp that was on did nothing to deter from the beauty I saw before me. All I wanted to do was give her pleasure, and I started to move to do just that.

Chapter Thirty-Two

Charlotte...

He'd been slow and steady, soft spoken, checking on me each step of the way, and pushing all the right buttons with every touch. The way he pressed into me, the ice at my ass, and the wax sliding along my spine, it was as if I were in heaven. All the senses were heightened, and I waited anxiously to see how he would play with me.

When he began to move, the ice slid away, down to where he was entering me, and I wasn't sure whether it was a good sensation or not, but he quickly picked it up, dropping it next to me on the shower curtain. He'd been so thoughtful about putting that down, and about making sure my clothing was out of the way so it didn't get ruined. Everything he'd done had been for me. Not that he wasn't going to get pleasure out of it, but he was being exceptionally attentive to my wants and desires, and with where I was mentally, it was the perfect escape.

The rhythm he had going, sliding in and out of me, slow and slower still, was setting me off, pushing me ever so slowly to the edge of the cliff I wanted to jump off. I knew, just from the last time we'd been together, that he'd get me there eventually, edging me along until I couldn't help but fall.

His hands were at my hips, holding me steady as he pumped in and out of me. After a bit, he moved his hands up, sliding them through the wax that was hardening on my back, moving the liquid around and around, as if he were painting me with it. It was both erotic and relaxing, a combination I hadn't quite experienced before, but decided that I did, in fact, like it. Lines and circles, shifting up and down my back, as the wax cooled along my skin, and I just let him work me.

"You are a fucking work of art," he growled in my ear, and I hadn't even felt him move to bend over me. "I want to keep you absolutely perfect as you are right now, but want to also continue to play with you, and see what other remarkable works we can create."

His chest was pressed against my back, and I imagined any hair he had on his body would be stuck to the wax. I wondered whether it would hurt when he pulled away from me but didn't have much time to ponder that because he slammed into me hard, harder than he had before. I felt his hands slide under my body, his hands wrapping around my breasts, holding me where I was as he pounded into me repeatedly.

Just as I was about to tip over, he stopped, holding himself inside me, holding my body against himself, and just breathing heavily into my ear. The ragged breaths fluttering my hair, rushing along my cheek. He hadn't come, that much I knew, but I wasn't sure why he stopped.

"Stay put," he said, pulling away from me and sliding out.

I did as he requested, my eyes staying closed, not wanting to know what he was going to do next. The anticipation was almost as erotic as the acts had been, and the thrill of not knowing was just that much more. I heard him move around the room, then heard the sound of material, and guessed he was pulling a tie or his belt from the clothing he'd set aside.

Again, the heat of the wax dripped along my back, and I startled as it hit me, but didn't move much. Then, I felt his belt, the leather texture distinct in nature, as he slid it around on my ass. He wasn't hitting me, just running it up and down each cheek, as if he were testing the waters.

"I want to pink your ass up," he said. "Would you like me to spank you?"

I opened my eyes and looked down my body, the dark wax running along my side where he'd painted me. The eager look on his face was clear, he wanted to do this. I didn't mind spanking, but preferred a hand to a belt.

"Please only use your hand," I said.

There was a moment of disappointment in his face, but then he set it aside, stepped off to one side, and swatted me. It was a quick report that sounded in the room, and I could hear the gasp that escaped my lungs. The sting was sharp, but he was already massaging the cheek he'd hit, and it was more a surprise than a pain, as it always had been.

"You look so pretty in pink," he said, then smacked the other cheek, again rubbing it with his hand immediately. "You blossom so well."

He bent down and kissed each side, then slid between them, and ran his tongue up my slit from clit to asshole, causing me to shiver and moan in pleasure. I heard the ice clink in the holder it was in, then felt the chill against my cheeks, the feeling of relief rushing over me. Then it was pressed against my opening, his hot tongue on my clit, and I wondered how he was managing to do all the things until he sucked me into his mouth, his teeth setting against my sensitive flesh with just enough force to be painful, but not so much as to make it actually hurt. He had found that fine line between pressure pain and actual pain, and he sat right on the edge of it, and oh, did he do it well.

When his finger plunged inside me, my body convulsed, holding him inside me as the orgasm rolled through me, wave after wave pulsing along my veins, riding my nerves, exploding into the atmosphere until I was nothing but stardust.

Somehow, I ended up on his lap, his arms wrapped around my body as I came back to myself, a slow rocking motion holding me together as I remembered how to exist. His lips were pressed against my temple, murmuring softly that everything would be fine, and that we would go again when I was ready. Finally, I found my voice, mumbling something about the wax or ice or something, but he just kept shushing me until I just sat there, letting him care for me in that moment. It was a beautiful thing, something I wasn't sure had happened before, but something I definitely needed.

"You good?" he asked once we'd been still for a time.

I nodded, unsure why he was asking, but then he ran a thumb across my cheek and I realized that there were tears staining them. Quickly, I tried to brush them away, unsure what had caused them, and upset that he'd seen them.

"No," he said, his voice firm but soft. "You're safe. I've got you. Nothing's going to hurt you here. I promise."

I had no idea what his words were caused by, but I must have either said or done something that told him I was afraid. I couldn't for the life of me figure out why I was afraid, though. Finally, after a bit more time. I pushed a bit away from him, sitting up more, and looked into his face. The concern there was both delightful and terrifying, because I had no idea what had brought it out.

"What happened?" I asked.

"I don't know," he said. "One minute you were flying high, the next you were sobbing. It kind of freaked me out, to be honest."

"What was I saying?"

"Nothing," he said. "You were just sobbing. I was really worried. You weren't acting like this was normal, and I didn't know what I had done that set it off. I just wanted to make sure you were safe."

My hand was over my mouth, and I was trying to figure out what had caused my reaction. I'd never cried during or after sex, so what had made this happen?

"I don't know what to say," I finally said. "I've never had that happen before."

"Are you okay now?"

"Yeah," I said. "Just embarrassed."

"No need for that," he said with a smile. "We should get cleaned up. You're a mess."

I laughed at that and nodded. I could feel the wax cracking along my back and knew it was likely to leave a big mess on the floor, but I could clean up when he was gone the next night for his game.

"Let's go," he said, sort of pushing me up and off his lap.

He got up after me, then took my hand and walked me from the room to the other bathroom in the house. Since he'd effectively made the master bath unusable for a shower, it made sense that we were heading to the other one. I did hope to get some shower sex, though, so hopefully he was up for it once we got all soapy.

The little night light was on in the bathroom, and he didn't bother turning anything else on. When he started the water in the tub, I could already feel myself beginning to relax. There was something soothing about the sound of running water. I couldn't explain it, just knew that the sound helped to calm my soul.

"How hot do you want it?" he asked.

"Warm enough to get the wax off, but not so hot to burn my skin," I said.

I wasn't one of those women who liked to have scalding showers. I mostly liked the lukewarm kind. Enough to help relax the muscles, but if they were too hot, I tended to rush. And this was not something I wanted to rush.

"Here we go," he said, pulling the plunger up to get the water running out of the showerhead. "Let's get you undressed while it warms up."

I'd completely forgotten that I had anything on until he mentioned it. He knelt at my feet, pressing a hand to my calf, inviting me to raise my leg so he could take my shoe off. I used his shoulders to balance myself and did as he requested, lifting the foot so he could take off my shoe. He repeated the action for the other leg, then raised up a bit to roll the stockings down. It was almost more erotic than what we'd already done, the way he was undressing me. So much care and compassion with his movements.

When my stockings were off, stuffed into my shoes, he pressed his lips just above my pubic bone, as if in reverence to me in some way, and I sighed, letting my eyes close and take in everything he was offering. He stood, wrapping his arms around my waist, pressing his body against mine, and I was struck with how strong he was. The muscles rippled under his skin as he moved, his arms like bars against my back, while his chest was like a brick wall at my front. Everything about him said he had the power to do what he wanted.

"Ready to get in?" he asked, and that just proved to me how in tune with me he was.

"Yes," I said, and he pulled the curtain back enough to help me into the tub.

I stepped forward, giving him room to come in behind me. The spray of the water was the absolute perfect temperature, warm enough that it would take care of the wax on my back, but not so hot that it would scald me. I let the water run down my body, stepping under it enough that it went down my back more than my front. He reached past me, taking the handle of the showerhead and pulling it free from its holder, bringing it around behind me to work on my back. Although my hair wasn't long, it was past my shoulders, so I pulled it to the front enough that it wouldn't get into the wax, just as I'd done when he started letting it drip on me.

I watched the red run off me and down the drain, knowing that I would have to boil a few pots of water to run down there and get rid of the residue so it didn't clog the drain, but it would be worth it, and something I could do tomorrow. Tonight was all about being connected to Nick, his body on mine, hands working their magic along my skin as he was now, and ending with more orgasms than I had been given in entirely too long. This was going to be a good night.

Chapter Thirty-Three

Nick...

Her body was warm, the water doing what it needed to loosen the wax enough to come off her skin. I worried about what it would do to the drain, but not so much as to stop what I was doing. She was absolutely beautiful, and if I could get away with it, I'd spend the rest of my life showing her exactly how beautiful she was.

Standing in the shower with her, I cleaned up our earlier escapades, getting everything off that I'd put on. It was weird that she'd cried after her last orgasm, but she said it was nothing, and I had to believe her. Sex should be good, but if it made you cry, something was wrong. She may not tell me now, or ever, but I swore that I would make sure to never cry again, except to cry out in ecstasy. That was something I could get behind.

She turned to me, having already cleaned her back, and took the wand from my hand, shifting to place it back into the cradle I'd pulled it from. Her hands were on my chest, and she looked up at me, bright blue eyes hooded, a soft smile on her lips. She was a good head shorter than me, now that her shoes were off, and I wondered whether she felt intimidated by my size. Nothing seemed to indicate that, though, which made me happy. I didn't want to scare her, just please her.

"Will you fuck me in here?" she asked.

"I didn't bring a condom," I said.

"I know," she said. "I've had my tubes tied, have never had sex without a condom, and really want to with you. If you're not comfortable, I am fine with that, too."

As much as I wanted to do what she asked, I just couldn't get my head around it. Like her, I'd never had sex without a condom, even just for a blow job, until she did the other day. But I wanted to and told her as much.

"I want to," I said. "I just need to get my head wrapped around it. It's not that I don't trust you, because I do. Completely. I just need to figure out what I need in order to get myself over whatever is blocking me from saying yes."

"It's okay," she replied, her hand still on my chest. "When you're ready."

Her hand slid down from my chest to my abs, and lower still, until she reached my cock, holding it in her hand and stroking it from base to tip, slow and steady. I tipped her head back, wetting her hair as she continued to work on me. Once her hair was wet, I picked up the shampoo and squeezed a generous portion into my hand. While her hair wasn't long, it was pretty thick. Working the suds into the curls, I massaged her head with my fingertips. Her stroking had stopped as she let me minister to her. It definitely wasn't her regular shampoo, because the lilac smell wasn't there, but it was a fresh smell, like the beach in San Diego, salty and clean.

When I was done with my massage, I tipped her head back again, rinsing the soap out with the waterfall from the showerhead. She grabbed the liquid soap that was on the shelf in the wall, poured some into her hands, then worked it into a lather. Her hands again went to my chest, rubbing the suds around as she moved lower again on my body.

With the soap on her hands, they slid much easier over my cock. I knew she was experienced, considering where I'd met her, but she had this down to a science. Her twist at the tip, pulling just enough to stretch the skin, was a master move, and I appreciated her putting those skills to use.

I pressed my hand against the wall behind her, letting her stroke me until I couldn't take it anymore and stilled her hand. Turning her away from me, I put a hand in between her shoulder blades, and pressed her forward, her ass presenting itself to me nicely. Without further thought, I pressed against her entrance and slid in, the soap adding enough lubrication to make it not hurt either of us. Once I was fully inside, I wrapped an arm around her waist, the other still pressed against the wall. Slowly at first, I began moving, pulling out to the tip, then pressing in, over and over, riding that edge where I knew I would fall, but holding out until I got her to fall before me.

Slow and steady, in and out, over and over, the movement becoming a rhythm, our bodies dancing to a beat that matched our hearts. With the water falling over her back, my hand wrapped around her waist, her hands against the wall to keep me from thrusting her head into it, we danced, and oh, by all the gods of the universe, I let myself just go, just feel and experience this time with her.

She pulled one hand from the wall, dipping it in front of her, slicking her fingers along her clit, working it to find her pleasure, and I felt the light flicks against the base of my balls as they hit her hand. The pleasure she was giving herself was tightening around me, and I had to hold on, keep the rhythm steady, until she found her release.

After riding that edge for too long, she finally moaned, a long and low sound, coming from somewhere deep inside her, flowing out of her mouth while her body pulsed around mine. She spasmed, her hand losing its pace, and returning to the wall to hold herself where she was. I kept my pace even, stroking inside her even as she squeezed around my cock, pulling me in whenever I pulled out. It was sexy as fuck, and I didn't want it to end, but my body betrayed me, releasing my orgasm inside her. I thought about pulling out, but she wouldn't let me go, so I stayed there, filling her pussy with my come.

I was effectively holding her up, my feet against either side of the tub, my arm around her middle, the other against the wall of the shower, her going nearly limp in my arms.

"That was..." She paused, catching her breath.

"Incredible?" I asked.

"More than that," she said. "So much more."

I let my cock slide out of her, the water washing away the remnants of our love, and I stalled, that word sitting there, not said, but there nonetheless. It was heavy, but not so much that I couldn't bear it. I just didn't want to put it on her shoulders, either.

"You okay?" she asked, turning to look at me.

"Yeah," I said, my voice low. "Just thinking."

"I'm sorry," she said, trying to turn away from me, but I stopped her, my arm around her waist, pulling her to me as I said, "Nothing to be sorry about."

"I pushed," she said.

"I know," I replied. "But you requested it. I wasn't sure whether I wanted to, but I'm glad I did. I don't ever want to be with you with anything between us again."

She looked up at me, her eyes wide, and said, "You mean that, don't you?"

"Absolutely," I said. "And I'd be fine with never being with anyone but you again, too."

The confession fell out of my mouth before my brain had time to filter it, and I wasn't at all upset about that. It took a minute for it to register with her, I think, but once it did, she smiled, and it was as if she were sunshine after a rain delay, holding a promise of so many things I couldn't imagine my life without.

"Exclusivity," she said.

"If you want," I replied.

There, in the shower of a house she'd rented, we both confessed our desires, admitted that we belonged together, and that we should spend the rest of our days, at least until we grew tired of each other, in an embrace of passion.

And I couldn't be happier.

Epilogue

Six months later...

Charlotte...

"Hello?" I said, answering my phone at lunch.

"Charlie?"

The voice was familiar, but I couldn't quite place it.

"It's Rachel," she said, and I knew the name, but was still a bit confused. "Paris?"

"Oh," I said, remembering the life I had before the one I'd started with Nick. "How are you?"

"Umm," she said, and I could hear noises in the background that sounded like she was in some sort of business or something. "I need your help."

"Sure thing," I said, knowing I would do whatever she needed. "What do you need?"

"Can you come to the UMC hospital?"

"Are you okay?" I asked, concern lacing my voice.

"I just need your help," she said, and I heard the faint sounds of a baby in the background.

"Absolutely," I said. "What's going on?"

I'd gotten up and was walking to the elevator to head down and let them know I was going to be leaving.

"I had a baby," she said. "But I don't want it. It's a reminder of that night."

"Are you giving it up?" I asked, instantly thinking about Gretchen.

"I want to," she said. "But there's all these people asking all these questions, and I just don't know what to do."

She started crying then, so I said, "I'll be there in a few minutes. Would you mind if I brought a friend with me? She may be interested in adopting, if that's the way you want to go."

"Okay," she said, a sob breaking the word apart.

"I'll be there soon," I said. "Don't sign anything until I get there, okay?"

"Okay," she said. "But they keep telling me I need to make a decision."

"I want you to be strong right now," I said. "I want you to look the next person that says that to you in the eye and tell them that you have family coming to help you work everything out, and if they don't stop asking, that when I get there, all hell is going to break loose."

"Thank you," she said.

"Everything will be alright," I said, almost more for myself than her.

"Please come soon," she said.

"Just a few minutes," I replied. "I promise."

She disconnected the call just as the elevator arrived. I hopped on, swiped my card, and headed to the lower level where I found Gretchen working over one of the newest pieces we'd received.

"I need you," I said, and she looked up.

"What's up?" she asked.

After they'd lost their daughter, she was a mess. When she came back to the museum, we all sort of tiptoed around her, not wanting to upset her. She, of course, told us to knock that shit off, she wasn't gonna break, and that it was weird the way we were all treating her. I'd been the first to start in with the jokes that we used to do, and after that, everyone else sort of settled, and things went back to normal.

"I might have the answer to many issues," I said. "But I don't want to get any hopes up. Would you go with me on blind faith?"

"For you, of course," she said.

She pulled her gloves off, dropped them into the bin, then went to the employee locker room where we both grabbed our stuff. I sent a text to Frank to let him know we were leaving in an emergency, but nothing that he had to worry about. I told him I'd fill him in when I had more answers, but for now, asked that he just not tell anyone else what was going on. He'd been kind to reply that whatever it was, he would deal with any blowback.

"This is weird, right?" Gretchen asked as we climbed into my car.

"I'm thinking it's a blessing in disguise," I replied.

It didn't take long for us to get from the parking lot for the museum to the parking lot of the hospital, and Gretchen was silent as we parked.

"I promise, this is a good thing," I said.

"I trust you," she replied. "It's just..."

"I know," I replied. "And if I could have done this differently, I would have. Trust me."

She nodded, climbing out of the car. The walk to the hospital seemed miles long, but we went in and I went up to the desk to ask where Rachel was. They gave me the information for the obstetrics area but told me that she would have to approve us entering. I assured her that she'd called me and asked me to come.

Pressing the button for the elevator, Gretchen was silent next to me. I worried that this wouldn't work but had to have faith in bigger powers than I had within me, that this was some kind of divine intervention. When we stepped out onto the right floor, Gretchen held back. I grabbed her hand, gave it a squeeze, then sort of pulled her out. There was a box next to the door with a buzzer, and I pressed it and waited for a response.

"Who are you here to see?" the voice asked.

"Rachel," I said. "I'm sorry, I don't have her last name. But my name is Charlie, and she called and asked me to come."

"I'll see if I can find someone," the voice said.

We waited in the little lobby until the voice came back.

"Please push the door," she said, then there was a click, a buzz, and we were able to push the door open.

There was a nurse's station right through the doors, and the woman sitting there looked up at us.

"She's in room twelve," she said, pointing down the hallway.

I headed in that direction, but Gretchen didn't move.

"Hey," I said. "You okay?"

"I shouldn't be here," she said.

"Nonsense," I replied. "Trust me. This is going to work out. I promise."

She took a shuddering breath, her hand on her heart, and then nodded. I wasn't sure if she was going to cry or freeze or what, but I had a plan. A plan to help two people I cared deeply for. Finally, she moved, taking the hand I'd offered her, and we walked down the hall.

There was a baby crying from inside the room, and I wasn't sure Gretchen was going to be able to hold up, but I walked in, pulling her with me. That's when I heard another crying in the room. Sure, the baby was crying, but there was a soft sobbing coming from behind the curtain. I shoved it over and took in the picture. The room was dark, the shade pulled most of the way down, and the only light on was the one that was aimed at the ceiling. Rachel was on the bed, the baby in the glass bassinet next to her, and she was just a mess.

"Charlie," she cried and reached out to me.

I went to her, letting go of Gretchen and taking the young girl into my arms.

"Shh," I shushed. "It's all gonna work out. Everything will be fine, I promise."

Somehow, in those few seconds, the baby stopped crying. I turned, and saw that Gretchen had the infant in her arms, holding it against her chest, humming softly while rocking back and forth. When I turned back to Rachel, she had a look of awe on her face, like no one had even been able to stop the cries.

"How did she do that?" she whispered.

"She's wanted to be a mother forever," I said. "She just kind of has a way about her that calms everyone."

"I think she's hungry," Gretchen said. "Do you have anything to feed the baby?"

"I don't know," Rachel said, as a sob broke through again. "They keep telling me to feed her, but I don't want to."

"Let me call the nurse," I said, pressing the button on the device attached to the edge of Rachel's bed.

"Boy or girl?" Gretchen asked, looking to Rachel for an answer.

"Girl," she said. "I think. I don't remember. It's all been a rush."

"Don't worry," Gretchen said, coming over to the other side of the bed. "Do you want to feed her with a bottle? Or would you rather I do it?"

Like with everything Gretchen did, she was kind, caring, and always thinking of someone else. Even now, when I could see that she desperately wanted to do everything for this child, she was offering the choice to the person who held the power, even if she didn't want it.

"You," Rachel said.

"That's just fine," Gretchen said just as a nurse came into the room.

"Oh," she said, as she wasn't the one at the desk from earlier. "I didn't realize you had company."

"I think the baby is hungry," Gretchen said. "Our friend is going to go with formula feeding, so would you mind getting a bottle for us?"

Her simple words made Rachel relax, a palpable thing that settled in the room.

"Of course," the nurse said. "But we try to get them to try breast-feeding first."

"Fed is best," Gretchen said. "And Rachel isn't interested in that. It will be more convenient for her if we get a bottle. Please."

"Be right back," the nurse said, turning and leaving the room.

"How did you get her to listen to you like that?" Rachel asked.

"It's all about perception," Gretchen replied. "Tell them what you want and expect them to follow through. If they don't, just look at them until they figure out what they need to do. It takes time to get good at it, but I've had years working with idiots who don't understand that I really do know what I'm talking about."

"Present company excluded," I said.

"Oh, of course," she replied. "You're way more badass than I am, trust me."

"Here we go," the nurse said. "It's just two ounces. We don't want to over feed her."

"Thank you," Gretchen said, taking the bottle from the nurse's hands when she tried to hand it to Rachel. "That'll be all for now."

I don't think the nurse was used to being summarily dismissed in such a fashion, but she took the news like a pro, and left the room.

"You're sure?" Gretchen asked, holding the bottle out to Rachel.

"I don't want to," Rachel said.

"Completely fine," she replied. "If you change your mind, just let me know."

Gretchen sat on one of the chairs that were in the room, and settled the baby in her arms, tipping the bottle up to her mouth. She took to it greedily, and Gretchen had to pull it out a few times, just to keep her from drowning in the milk. Once she was quiet, I turned to Rachel to ask the question I was dreading an answer to.

"Does the father know?"

"I don't know which one of them it was," she said.

"Which one?"

"There were four," she said, looking at her hands clasped in her lap. "I didn't think they finished in me, but obviously one of them did. I don't know what to do."

When she turned her face up to me, her eyes were filled with tears, and all I wanted to do was make everything okay for her. I pulled her to me, sitting on the edge of the bed, and held her as she cried silently on my shoulder.

"Who knows?" I asked once she'd settled.

"Just the hospital, and you guys," she said. "Not even my mom knows. I don't know what to do. What do I do?"

"Do you want to keep the baby?" I asked. She shook her head, an emphatic denial of that completely.

"Would you be open to adoption?" Gretchen asked, the baby up on her shoulder, the empty bottle on the stand next to the bed. "Open or closed?"

"I can't keep the baby," she said. "But I don't want her to be in the system."

"I would love to offer my home," Gretchen said. "I know you don't know me, but you know my friend and coworker. I'm happy to get to know you, sit with you until you feel comfortable. My husband and I have completed all the work to get on a list for adoption, but if you're willing, we can go the private route."

"You don't even know me," Rachel said. "Why would you do this for me?"

"Because you need someone to love your baby," Gretchen said. "And my husband and I need a baby to love. I am happy to keep you in our lives, in her life, as much or little as you want. I'd even be willing to let you come live with us if you wanted. I don't know what your home life is like, but the fact that you're completely unprepared for this baby tells me it isn't exactly the perfect life. Not that any home is."

"Yeah," Rachel said. "My mom is gonna freak out about this. We can't afford a baby, or the hospital bills or anything else that's gonna come from it. I'm afraid she won't let me give her up, though."

"How old are you?" Gretchen asked.

"Twenty-one," Rachel said. "I'll be twenty-two in a few weeks."

"That makes you the one who gets to decide what happens with your body and your baby," Gretchen said. "I know you aren't sure what to do right now, but I promise to be there to help you in any way I can. Starting right now, you and I are a team. I've got your back, and I won't abandon you."

The tears started running down Rachel's face, and she didn't even try to hide them. It was like a wash of relief came over her, unburdening her from everything that she'd been through, making my rash decision to bring Gretchen with me the absolute right one.

"Here are the rest of the forms," my attorney said. "I know it's complicated, Rachel, and you will probably have a bunch of questions. I'm hopeful that my explanations so far have been easy for you to understand."

"They have," she said.

We were sitting at my kitchen table, Gretchen and Doug on one side, with little baby Elizabeth Rose in Doug's arms. Rachel was at the head of the table, my attorney sitting next to her, patiently walking through every piece of paper that he'd brought to make the private adoption legal.

They'd chosen an open adoption, and Rachel had moved in with Gretchen and Doug. Her mom was beyond pissed that she was moving out, but she kept the baby a secret from her, not wanting her to try to get any connection with her. It all made sense when I went to help her move, along with a few of the guys I knew from outside the club. She was a nightmare, and we were thankful we were able to get everything she absolutely needed in one trip.

That was another thing that had been taken care of. We'd taken a DNA sample from the baby and given it to Lucifer so he could hand it off to the club he worked with on those things that simply couldn't be shared in public. Turned out that the baby's sperm donor was some rich businessman's son who had come to the club a few times and had shown his ass. He was removed from the allowed guests.

Somehow, he disappeared after that, which I wasn't exactly sad about.

Rachel never knew, because it would just be one more reminder of the terrible night she'd experienced. Now, she was living with a couple who were treating her like the adult she was, helping her get through college, and setting her up to be an amazing "aunt" to little Elizabeth. The doctor had called it a cryptic pregnancy, one that Rachel didn't even know existed until she went into labor. Thankfully, she hadn't done anything that caused any problems for the baby, and she was absolutely perfect in every way.

Nick was set to be back in town the upcoming weekend, and we were going to celebrate his new contract. He'd found a house he loved and had brought his mom out for some time with him. I'd met her, and she was absolutely amazing. Her love of art was just remarkable, and I'd encouraged her to try her hand at painting again. Nick had told me she gave it up, and that she even let me see anything was a miracle, but she was truly an artist. One that I hoped would continue her gift and one day have her pieces hanging in my museum.

We'd spent the entirety of the winter together in my house, at least until he got his own. It was amazing the number of places you could have sex. Places I hadn't even thought of. Thankfully, he was very creative, and we were well on our way to trying things out in every room of both houses. He'd even snuck me into the locker room at the stadium where we fucked in the showers. It was all great until someone walked in on us. That was the one and only time it happened.

The club was in our past, though. Even though it was what brought us together, we were no longer a part of that life. We were exclusive, a couple, and had no reason to share what we did with anyone else. Not that I didn't miss some of my friends from there, but I'd given Lucifer permission to give my contact information to a select few people on the grounds that they meet me in a public place to discuss future friendships.

I'd also met several of the teammates, who were all very nice, even if they did tease Nick with the fact that he was falling for a cougar. I mean, twelve years is a decent age difference, and if the ages were reversed, no one would bat an eye. Somehow, though, being the older one in the relationship caused him no issues. He only wanted me, and I was more than happy with him.

Note from Author:

Caught in a Pickle, book 2 of the New Orleans Magicians Baseball Team, will be coming soon.

In the meantime, check out the first book in the Seattle Cascades Baseball Team series, Extra Innings, where you'll meet a whole new team of sexy baseball players and the women they love.

Here's the universal link for Extra Innings:

https://books2read.com/ExtraInnings-Cascades

About the Author

Born and raised in the Pacific Northwest, CM Kane was fed a steady diet of sports, particularly baseball. Having this love of the game instilled in her at an early age, she found that nothing was better than getting lost in the game. Storytelling was another gift that was encouraged in her youth, and she's taking to the written word to explore a new aspect to the game she loves.

Website:
    https://www.authorcmkane.com

TikTok:
    https://www.tiktok.com/@authorcmkane

facebook.com/AuthorCMKane

x.com/AuthorCMKane

instagram.com/authorcmkane

amazon.com/author/cmkane

Also by C.M. Kane

Seattle Cascades

Made in the USA
Monee, IL
02 November 2023